Copyright 2022 Melanie Jacobson

All rights reserved

No part of this book may be reproduced in any form or by any means without express written permission of the author, except for quotations used in an official book review.

For the Zoom crew,
Who got me through this one

1
ANNEKE

There he was, sliding into my DMs again: the hottest man I'd never met.

It super bugged me when people let their phones take over their lives, but for a month now, I'd been in training for World's Biggest Hypocrite. Every buzz sent a tingle down my spine, because it might be him. Ledge-Case. The nerdy music guy on Noteworthy, the social media network for hardcore music nerds.

Buzz. Was that LedgeCase arguing about Social Distortion? No. Just Miles, making sure I would be at the opening.

Buzz. Was that LedgeCase backing me up in a debate with Punk_-God87 about the Dead Kennedys? No. Just my agent, trying to talk me into an Alpine ski bunny shoot.

Buzz. Was that …

Anyway, you get it. All day, every day. It didn't help that sometimes it *was* LedgeCase, another dopamine hit keeping me connected to my phone.

Buzzzzzz, buzzzzzz, buzzzzzz. A ringing phone was definitely *not* LedgeCase, my internet boyfriend who did not yet know he was my internet boyfriend.

I glanced at the screen and frowned when I saw Miles's name. "Hey," I said, answering it. "What's wrong?" He was in New Orleans, two hours ahead of me in LA, and that meant it was almost midnight for him.

"Hey, Anneke."

"What's wrong?" I demanded again.

"Nothing."

I didn't believe him. We'd been friends for five years, and I knew when something was getting to him. "Then why are you calling my actual phone like it's the nineties?"

"Because I'm bucking the Gen Z stereotypes and bringing back talking on the phone."

"Nope. Bye." Miles hated being on the phone as much as I did.

"Fine, maybe I'm calling because …"

"Miles, if you ask me one more time if I'm coming to your club opening, I swear on my ancient *oma* that I will come into town just to burn it down. And I love my grandma too much to make that threat lightly."

His sigh held a layer of exhaustion I hadn't heard in a few years. I straightened and leaned forward, listening harder. "What's up? Everything okay with Ellie?" That was the one thing I could imagine truly bumming him out.

"She's great. Hanging in there with all the pre-opening craziness like a champ. It's the club. Opening night sales are …"

A pit formed in my stomach. This was all Miles had thought about for two years until Ellie came along a few months ago. And even then, he'd met her when she was helping him find the perfect property for the jazz club he'd dreamed of opening in New Orleans.

"How can I help? I can call some contacts and pump up the guest list. Or I could—"

"I don't want to put too many out-of-town VIPs on the list," he said. "We need locals to come and fall in love with this place, but so far, ticket sales are low. The club opens in two weeks. I thought we'd be sold out by now."

"You know what you need to do, Miles."

He gave a short laugh. "Yeah. Ellie said the same thing. Don't worry. I'm absolutely going to sell out and use my name."

"I'm FaceTiming you." I ended the call and switched to FaceTime. He answered, his handsome, familiar face filling the screen. "How is it selling out to tell the people of New Orleans that one of their hometown heroes is coming back to open a club? You should have put your name on it from the very beginning."

He shrugged, a movement I could sense more than see on the screen. "I don't see how it's any different from slapping my name on bottles of barbecue sauce or sneakers."

"Do you care about barbecue sauce or sneakers the way you do about showcasing new talent?"

"No."

"Then it's definitely not the same. This is a good move."

His expression wavered between resignation and hope. "Yeah?"

"Yeah. Stop being a tortured artist and start being a savvy one. Put the word out that it's you and that you're bringing a whole slew of famous friends in for the grand opening."

"About that …"

Now the expression on his face was almost pained. I gasped. "Are you *uninviting* me?"

"What? No. Why would you even think that?"

"I can't imagine what else could put that look on your face."

"Asking for a favor I don't want. A big one. That's what's putting this look on my face."

"You look like JoJo when she eats lemons," I said, glancing at my roommate's Maltipoo. She begged for one every time I sliced them for my water. "I don't know why she still eats them. And I don't know why you act like this every time you ask for a favor. I owe you approximately eight hundred million."

He laughed. "All right. I know you're coming, but how would you feel about hosting an exclusive VIP after-party for some of the more connected locals?"

I tapped the side of the phone with my thumb and pretended to consider it. "Depends. Is this a heels gig?"

"Yeah." A smile tugged at the corner of his mouth. "I know that means paying a premium on the return favor."

"Definitely. I want some passes to give out to a person of my choosing."

The smile flattened. "If that person's name rhymes with Shemerick Schmide …"

I rolled my eyes. "It's definitely not Erick."

"I don't know why you're always trying to convince that guy you're worth his time, because he's not even worth two seconds of yours. Also, his music sucks."

"No, it doesn't." My on-again, off-again situation with Erick put him at the bottom of Miles's list of favorite people, somewhere below the *Rolling Stone* critic who had panned his debut album as "forgettable fluff." Erick might be the only person lower on Miles's list than that critic, but to be fair, Miles had been stuck patching me up emotionally a few times after Erick's and my epic fights.

"Fine, his music is irritatingly good," Miles conceded. "I wish it sucked, because he sucks so much."

"I agree. I haven't talked to him in three months."

His eyebrow went up. "For real? Good job, kid," he said when I nodded.

"I'm thinking someone more local. A guy who owns a record store. Seems like the kind of person who could spread the word pretty well about the Turnaround."

"Which store?"

"Ledge Records."

"You know the owner? I've met him a couple times. Cool guy."

Inside of me, every tiny nerve-ending fluttered and then strained toward Miles. Miles who had information I desperately wanted. Miles who would tease me mercilessly if I told him how I "knew" the owner. Ugh.

"So you don't care if I give him a couple of passes?" *Also, could you tell me about him? Are my online detective skills on point? Can you confirm that his name is Jonah, and he is the literal cutest beanie-wearing hipster that ever owned a record store? And that he says the smartest and funniest things online as LedgeCase?*

"No, that's a great idea," Miles said. "I can't believe I didn't think of that. He's the kind of guy whose opinion matters to other people who care about music and not just the scene."

I grinned. Part of the reason Miles and I got along so well was that we'd both hated everything about "the scene," the swirl of industry insiders and hangers-on who moved from one party and hotspot to the next in LA, so predictable and plastic and yet so essential for both of us in our careers. "Great. I'll drop him some passes. I have a shoot on Thursday, then I'm free. I'll fly in whenever you need me."

"If you come Monday, that should be plenty of time. I want to introduce you to Ellie, but I'm going to be crazy busy between now and opening night. I feel okay about neglecting you for a few days but not forever."

"You can neglect me forever. I don't care. But I get dibs on your home gym first, and by myself, because you make stupid noises."

"I do not."

"You absolutely do." I grunted and pulled a few gargoyle faces.

"That's not what I look like."

"It a hundred percent is."

"You're the worst."

"Love you, dummy. By the way, have you said that to Ellie yet? Told her you love her?"

"Not yet. Soon." There was a smile in his voice. He was so gone on that girl. I couldn't wait to meet her. I usually had to wait a while before I met any of Miles's girlfriends, mostly because he rarely had girlfriends that lasted long enough for him to want to introduce me to them. But Ellie was special. I'd known it the second he'd texted to tell me that she'd accused him of "unilateral decision-making." A word nerd after my own heart.

We ended the call, and my phone buzzed again with a notification from Noteworthy. My heart gave a dorky, answering buzz, and I fumbled it open.

You have a new message from LedgeCase.

I'd been roaming the virtual halls of Noteworthy for two years, getting in arguments over whether Uncle Tupelo or Gillian Welch was the greatest alt-country album of all time, professing my love for The Ramones, passionately defending my interpretations of Hold Steady lyrics.

Could I have hung out with most of these artists in real life any time I wanted to with a single call to my manager? Well, the living ones, anyway?

Yeah.

But that old saying about how you should never meet your heroes? Truest. Thing. Ever. Any artist who wanted to hang out with Anneke the

Dutch Supermodel was not my thing. I was much happier in the anonymous online crowds of fans as AnnieBird.

And my favorite anonymous hang was LedgeCase.

Except I'd figured out who he was by accident. When Miles had set the opening date for the Turnaround, I'd gone online to do some New Orleans research. It was weird that I hadn't made it out there on my own, but I'd never been booked for a photoshoot there. I liked researching every new city I visited, looking for specific things when I went, places that gave me the true vibe of a city. Local delis. Gardening shops. Libraries. And ... record stores.

Which was how I'd figured out that LedgeCase owned Ledge Records in New Orleans. I hadn't put it together at first, but when I put the store on my itinerary, I poked around on its website to see if the store had a Thelonious Monk album I'd been hunting for. It didn't, but it showed a feed from the store's social media accounts, including a Twitter feed where the account manager used the phrase "That'll salt your lemon."

It wasn't something I heard often ... except when LedgeCase used the same phrase sometimes. How likely was it that a music nerd named LedgeCase and the social media manager for a record store called Ledge Records weren't connected?

No chance. It didn't take much digging before I found a couple of pictures from events with a guy named Jonah Collier tagged in the photos and identified as the store owner. Jonah who didn't have any personal accounts that I could find. Jonah who didn't wear a wedding ring. Jonah who was slightly gangly, like his skinniness was natural and not the kind I had to earn with ruthless carb counting and gym sessions. Jonah who wore a beanie with "Ledge" on the front, and a different concert T-shirt in each photo, but the worn-out kind, the kind that had been broken in by someone devoted to the band on it.

Was it a huge coincidence that the guy I'd been chatting with online for weeks lived in the city where my best friend had moved? The city where I'd be spending a lot more time in the future?

Or was it fate?

I flopped back on the sofa and stared at the ceiling. I could feel my face stretching into a cheesy smile and I didn't care. My no-nonsense Dutch mother would scoff at the idea of fate. But my father, the California hippie who'd swept her off her feet in Amsterdam, would toast the idea with a glass of the wine they'd been growing for the past fifteen years at their Napa winery.

I held up an imaginary glass to toast my dad. It couldn't be an accident that I'd found the secret identity of my internet crush without even trying.

"Thank you, fate!"

JoJo cocked her head at me.

"It's a thing," I promised her. "Now let's see what Jonah has to say."

2
JONAH

AnnieBird: Does it hurt to be so wrong?
LedgeCase: It would if I were wrong. I'm not.
AnnieBird: No way is The Who the greatest band of all time.
LedgeCase: It's not The Beatles. Can you hear how hard I'm rolling my eyes across the internet?
AnnieBird: No, because the sound of victory is drowning out all other sounds. Just because something is popular doesn't make it bad. I AM RIGHT.

I snorted, and Bailey looked up from the pile of T-shirts she was tagging as we wrapped up for the day in the office.

"What?" she asked, shooting the plastic tagger with extra force.

"This chick I argue with on Noteworthy all the time. She's painfully wrong. Again."

Bailey tagged another Ledge Records T-shirt. "Is there anyone you don't argue with about music?"

"Dad."

"Anyone not dead?"

That won another snort. Not too many people could handle our morbid sense of humor, but it worked for us.

"You're not answering," she said. "That's because there is literally not one person on earth you don't argue with about music."

"They're not arguments."

"Your word, not mine."

I glanced at my screen where the message window with AnnieBird was still open. "I meant debate."

The office door opened, and I knew it would be my mom without looking. An hour after closing, she was the only one who'd have the keys to let herself into the store.

She poked her head around the door. "Y'all need to come get supper. I've got to be to work in a half hour, but I can eat with you if we go now. I made corn chowder with shrimp."

Bailey slammed down the tagging gun and hopped up. "I'm in."

"Jonah?"

Normally, I'd say no, tell her I would eat later. I had so much to do with balancing the books, but I needed a break. We'd be just as close to going in the red when I came back after dinner.

"Coming."

I followed them out of the store, locking it behind me, then around the corner to the house we shared, the one I'd grown up in. Our neighborhood, the Seventh Ward, was becoming popular with younger house hunters looking for affordable property in a community that had character, but we'd been born and raised here. It wasn't "quaint" to me. It was just home.

Bailey scooped the mail from our box on the way into the house and sorted it while I dished up bowls of soup for everyone. "Bill, bill, bill, ad, ad, bill," she muttered, tossing them each into their pile.

I tried not to think about how many "bills" had been in that sentence.

"Ooh, invitation." She paused to open it. "Jonah, I think you'll want this. It's for the new club opening in the Bywater. The Turnaround, it's called." She paused for a minute, skimming the words as I set her bowl in front of her. "Says it'll be a jazz club focused on local acts, new talent, and 'reinvention.' That sounds interesting."

"I can't afford tickets," I said.

She held up two. "They're included."

I snatched them from her hand. "Then I'm in." It had been a couple of months since I'd seen live music other than the local neighborhood bands.

And while it was true that a neighborhood band in New Orleans was in a different league than anywhere else, except possibly Nashville, it would be nice to hear some new acts.

"The card says that the Turnaround owner recognizes you're a tastemaker, and he'd be delighted to have your company."

"Miles Crowe," I said, finally putting it together. "He was that guy who was on that show forever ago."

"Oh, yeah. *Starstruck*." Her expression grew confused. "Why would you go to his club? That's not your thing."

"His music isn't, but I've met him a few times in the store. He's cool. Good taste in music even if I don't like his stuff. This is a good lineup." I took the invitation and read through the list of acts. "Really good. Want to come?" It was strange to think that Bailey was old enough for clubs like this now, because she was so much younger than me—seven years—but she was twenty-two, a senior at the University of New Orleans, and more than legal to go to the show.

"Nah, I need to study."

"But it's not until next week," I said.

"I *always* need to study. Don't you remember what your last semester of college was like?"

Barely. I'd aged a decade in the three years since our dad had died and I'd taken over the record store. My dad had always been able to supplement the store's income with his music skills, but I didn't want to go that route. Not after one too many betrayals.

"Bring Mom," Bailey suggested.

Mom snorted. "Heck no. I don't have to do my time in the clubs anymore." She said it the way only the long-suffering wife of a musician could. "I loved seeing your daddy on stage, but that's not my scene. You need to find a date, honey. Try an app."

That made Bailey laugh. "Or invite the next indie chick who walks into the store and slobbers over you."

I scowled at her while Mom reached over to squish my cheeks. "Leave him alone, Bailey. He can't help it that I made him so cute. Now y'all quit cutting up so I can eat my soup and get to work."

She'd been working as a blackjack dealer at the nicest casino in the city. Which ... okay, I didn't know how "nice" any casino could be with their crappy carpets and general air of desperation. But hers was as close to nice as casinos ever got, I guess. It definitely made her a comfortable living. Not fancy-house-in-the-Garden-District comfortable. But making-the-mortgage-and-buying-fresh-shrimp comfortable.

Still, I hated it. Bailey always said Mom was a "babe," and every kid probably thinks their mom is beautiful, but Bailey was right. Men hit on her all the time. Marina Collier had aged well, and in her early fifties, she still turned heads, especially some of the high rollers who came through the casino. She thought it was funny, but even though she'd quit telling us the stories of some of their more outrageous efforts to entice her into being their "lady" while in New Orleans—offers of cars, expensive French Quarter townhome leases, and furs to name a few—I knew they still tried.

Honestly, they'd have better luck if they offered her an endless supply of soft pajamas and cocoa mugs because that was more her speed any time of year. And if one of them ever discovered her addiction to baby animal TikToks, we'd lose her forever.

"So who are you going to bring?" Mom asked. "One of your boho beauties?" It was her term for Bailey's "indie chicks."

"Stop, y'all." But I had no hope either of them would lay off.

"You haven't dated since ..." Bailey changed direction mid-sentence when she saw my face. "In forever. He has opportunities, Mom." It was a tattling tone. "At least once a week, some poor girl comes in and tries to get his attention. Cute girls too."

"Take one of them to this thing," Mom ordered.

"If I take one of the customers at the store, will both of you leave me alone?"

Bailey's jaw dropped a tiny bit, and she exchanged a quick glance with Mom. "You're caving pretty easily," Bailey said.

"Take it or leave it, only offer," I said.

"Yes," they said at the same time.

"Deal. But you have to drop it right now."

They both looked like I'd starved them of oxygen, but they didn't say anything else.

"I better go," Mom said, carrying her bowl to the sink. "My shift starts soon."

"Who are you going to take?" Bailey asked after she left.

"Don't know yet." I did know. Big Al. I hadn't promised it would be a girl. And Big Al would love something like this.

AnnieBird would too. I wished she was local. She'd dig this lineup. But since I had no idea where my Noteworthy sparring partner lived—or even if she might be a dude as old and hairy as Big Al, living in a basement somewhere—Big Al would do. At least with him, I'd know he was into the music. With half the girls who came in the store, I didn't think it was my vibe they liked as much as the fact that I bathed, not always the strong suit of scruffy dudes on the music scene.

But I'd flex on AnnieBird about it as payback for her insisting The Beatles were the greatest band of all time. Yeah, right. It was a cardinal rule that you couldn't take that position on the music boards—even if she was maybe, sort of not wrong—and pure stubbornness for her to double down on it, and I'd tell her so as soon as I finished scarfing down my soup.

If only getting along with real life girls was half as fun as arguing with AnnieBird, I might not be looking forward so much to a date with Big Al.

3
ANNEKE

I didn't know what I expected to find when I landed in New Orleans four days before Miles's big club opening, but it certainly wasn't my best friend wearing a haunted look when he opened the front door of his gorgeous French Quarter house.

"You look like hell," I said. Dark circles ringed his eyes, his cheekbones looked painfully sharp, his mussed hair looked like it had never been handled by the most exclusive stylists in LA. "The opening not going well?"

He drew me into a long hug then dragged in my single suitcase and shut the door. "Ellie and I broke up."

"What? No. *No*. She's perfect for you."

He shrugged.

"Let me make you some coffee." I glanced at my watch. I'd caught an evening flight out of LAX. "Ugh. It's too late for coffee. I'll make you some tea, and you tell me what happened."

He led me to the kitchen without any argument and detailed the broad strokes of their breakup. I'd known about their biggest prior obstacle: a meme. Miles had hired Ellie to find him a property for the Turnaround before he'd realized she was the poor girl he'd turned into a viral meme a dozen years ago. Even *I'd* posted that "so not my thing" meme. I'd used it recently in a debate with LedgeCase about whether Fuel was the most underrated rock band of the nineties. (No. Correct answer: The Wallflowers. Jakob Dylan couldn't help how big his dad's shadow was.)

It had been hard for Ellie to get past, and I understood. She'd been fourteen when Miles was on *Starstruck*—the biggest thing on TV when we were kids—and when the finalists did hometown performances, Ellie had been in Miles's audience having a fangirl meltdown, snot-cry and all. It had gone viral when "viral" was new. Then an interview he did about it the next week about his reaction to her—"She's so not my thing"—turned into gifs and memes that wouldn't die. She'd wanted nothing to do with him when he came back to town. Miles hadn't even recognized her until he'd already fallen hard for her.

"I mean, we talked the meme thing out weeks ago, and I got it," he said. "I really did. But with the club opening, the media's coming around, and I don't want Ellie to have to relive all of that. People don't know that was her, and she doesn't want them to. I tried to deflect attention from her by downplaying our relationship in an interview with the local news, because they'd be most likely to make the connection. I was trying to protect her, but it hurt her so much."

"Oh, Miles. That's hard." My poor, dumb, well-meaning friend. "I know your heart. This whole thing sounds like a big miscommunication. Talk to her. You guys are too good together to not fix it."

"I've tried. She's not even taking my calls. Texts either." He hunched over his tea, looking miserable, and I sat on my side of the table, watching him and feeling helpless.

I slumped. "Sorry. I changed my mind. I don't like her if she makes you feel this bad."

We sat in silence, commiserating. Usually, it was Miles consoling me after another fight with Erick. It was nice to be able to do it for him, except I'd rather he was perfectly happy and never needed any consoling, ever. "I don't like it when you're sad."

He rested his head on the table. "If you need me to put on a happy face, I will, but I don't want to."

"No," I said, leaning over to pat his head. "I don't need you to do that. But let's get some sleep, and in the morning, you can tell me how I can help you get ready for the opening."

"It involves wearing grubby clothes and doing lots of grunt work."

"Perfect. Can't wait to see the place."

He led me to a guest room, and I gasped when he opened the door. "Did you do this for me?"

He rolled his eyes but gave me a small, pleased smile. Miles's personal style was contemporary but in the way that would feel at home on my parents' winery ... soft, neutral colors and edges on traditional silhouettes, all well-suited for Napa. But I'd inherited my mother's taste for interiors, and Dutch design was more minimalist but with bright colors and touches of whimsy, and combinations of things that didn't seem like they would go together.

"I found a local designer and told him to make it Dutch. You like it?"

"Love it." It was mostly white with rustic furniture, but there were pops of color and whimsy—a bright blue pillow, a sculpture of twigs—that made me smile.

"You have your own bathroom," Miles said. "Towels and stuff are in there. And I have breakfast stuff in the fridge. I'm heading over to the club after we eat."

"I want to come," I said. "I'll be up." I was used to having to sync with new time zones. The two-hour difference would be nothing.

He paused at the door. "I'm glad you're here."

I knew he meant it, but he looked so sad. I was going to have to fix this Ellie situation, but for now, I smiled and said only, "Me too. See you in the morning."

Except, instead of going to bed like I should, I logged into Noteworthy to send LedgeCase a DM.

AnnieBird: Exploring a new city tomorrow. What do you do to figure out their music scene?

The typing dots appeared almost immediately, and I wondered if he ever waited around, hoping to get messages from me like I sometimes did from him.

LedgeCase: Find a record store. They always know what's going on locally. And they'll have flyers up from local bands and stuff.

I collapsed onto the exceedingly comfortable bed Miles had bought for me and tapped out a quick, *Good tip.*

Maybe that was exactly what I would do tomorrow after Miles didn't need me anymore: go explore Ledge Records and see if my internet boyfriend was as cute in real life as he was in the store's social media posts.

———

Turned out Miles kept me too busy at the club for any ... "stalking" was such a strong word. Any *investigating.*

Even if there hadn't been a million things to attend to, like rearranging the club's merchandise display in between taking selfies with members of the staff as they figured out who I was, I still wouldn't have wanted to leave Miles. He was more distracted than I'd ever seen him, slipping into broodiness if left with too much time between tasks.

Man, I might have to rethink my position on Ellie if she could leave him hanging in this much pain. "Still not answering her phone?"

He shook his head.

"She will. Let's check the liquor inventories again." It was busy work, and we both knew it, but he needed it, and we both knew that too.

I finagled the RSVP sheet from Jordan, Miles's partner and club manager, and spotted Jonah's name and a plus one on it. Jonah Collier.

I had his last name and therefore more, uh, investigating power, but I tried not to be any creepier than I already had been and resisted the urge to google him. Barely. Most guys felt like they knew everything about me after a few mouse clicks, because so much space had been devoted to the boring details of my life in photos and interviews. All of that was the barest scratch of the surface. I wanted to get to know Jonah in real life, not just Internet Jonah.

But the RSVP *did* send my nerves into overdrive. I poured the energy into Miles, and spent all day, every day with him for the next few days, trying to keep his head in the game on the opening, doing anything I could to distract him from Ellie. When she finally called him Thursday night, I thought maybe there was a light at the end of his very dark tunnel, but he came back into the kitchen after their talk, looking more tired and grim than ever.

Instead of listing all the ways I wanted to make Ellie pay for hurting Miles, I switched the subject to the after-party he'd asked me to host and kept him talking about what he wanted me to do. Not that I needed his input. I'd done countless appearances to endorse brands over the last three years since I got my first *Sporting News* swimsuit edition feature, and it was a set routine. Schmooze and take lots of selfies with guests, all while wearing a big smile and a little dress.

Not rocket science.

When opening night rolled around, I forced Miles home long enough to shower and change before we had to be back at the club, and I slipped into the dress and heels I'd chosen with more nerves than usual.

I'd picked them with LedgeCase—Jonah—in mind. I wanted to turn his head in a way I rarely cared about. AnnieBird, record store nerd, didn't turn heads. When I went out as my stripped-down self—no makeup, hair unstyled, in a T-shirt and shorts, people didn't pay attention to me. No one expected the woman in the baseball cap and Rams T-shirt squeezing oranges next to them at the farmer's market to be one of the most highly sought-after faces in fashion.

Truthfully, I always thought I was kind of odd-looking with my gangly legs, big mouth, and wideset eyes. Not ugly, but not conventionally pretty. Not girl-next-door pretty. Not cheerleader pretty. Until a talent scout approached me at a grocery store with my mom, I had no idea how well my vaguely odd proportions would translate on camera.

The answer: very well.

But I wanted to dazzle Jonah with the full Anneke treatment, so I used the best tricks I'd learned from years in the makeup chair. By the time I left the house with Miles to go back to the Turnaround, I was in my contoured, dramatic-eyed, full-lipped glory and a tight silver sheath dress and stilettos that would photograph well.

"You okay?" I asked Miles. His energy had keyed up the way it did before he went on stage. Ticketholders were trickling in. First, the friends and family of performers, and now, ten minutes after the designated start time for the show, the VIPs were showing up.

"Yeah, I'm okay," he said, and I recognized his professional mask slipping into place, the businessman that few music industry moguls had realized lurked inside of him. "Let's walk the red carpet, then I have to check in on the kitchen."

We exited through the delivery entrance and walked around front. A bouncer spotted us and tipped off the nearest paparazzo that owner Miles Crowe and supermodel Anneke were on the way in.

We paused and smiled for photographers from a few different outlets. There weren't many, but these guys were freelancers who would sell their snaps to multiple sites, making the media presence seem bigger online.

Inside, we slipped through the box office to take up spots at the back of the house. Once the show began, Miles would mainly work the floor, checking on guests and hitting them with some of his star power.

I periodically peeked out into the club from backstage. The dim lighting made it hard to see if Jonah had already arrived and whether his plus one was a girl. Or even a boy. I couldn't assume he was straight just because I'd decided he was my dream guy.

I tried to keep tabs on the flow of guests, but Miles wanted me here, mingling with the talent, the first night of creating the mystique of the Turnaround, where you never knew whose famous shoulders you might rub. I mostly fielded selfie requests from the musicians and dodged brass instruments as performers filed off and on stage. I loved backstage chaos. Musician show-energy was a pure adrenaline injection.

The first several acts killed it, each one building the crowd's excitement. Right now, it was a boisterous brass group, a local favorite called the Horn Dawgs, and I couldn't help sneaking to the stage wings to experience the sound up close.

As they wound down, I checked behind me for the next act, a blues duo, but instead I saw a woman about my age, twenty-five or so, standing in a classy black sheath that immediately made me feel like a disco ball. I'd have been jealous if she didn't look like she was about to pass out or puke. Or both.

I took a step toward her in case I need to catch her or some vomit—oh, please don't let it be vomit—but just then, I heard Jordan, the club manager and tonight's emcee, announce, "Miss Elle!" from the stage.

Well, well, well. That was enough to distract me from Jonah-spotting for a minute.

This should be good.

But no. No, it was not. It was not even in the same universe as good. Ellie sat at the piano, fumbled a few times, and I thought for sure the next step would be cleaning puke from the keys. But she played through a few more measures this time, and then … that was it. It was a pretty melody, but not exactly a piano solo piece. Was she supposed to sing or something? I could barely discern Jordan in the wings opposite me, and when he caught my eye, he grimaced and headed back onstage, leaning down to murmur in Ellie's ear.

She nodded and rose from the piano, Jordan taking her place as she went to stand in front of a mic. Jordan started again with the melody, and this time, Ellie began to sing.

Woooooooooow.

Her voice was gorgeous, high, effortless, but not quite pure, the faintest rasp roughing it up and making *me* want to fall in love with her a little. She was pretty in the way I'd always wanted to be as a kid, but her voice made her stunning as she sang a song clearly straight from her heart and meant to shoot straight for Miles.

If he wasn't listening—*really* listening to the second chance she was asking for in her lyrics—I would have to set him straight. Big time.

And then there he was, sliding in to replace Jordan seamlessly, Ellie never noticing as Jordan quietly exited behind her to my side.

"Tell me right now why I shouldn't kick your butt up and down Dauphine Street for not telling me about this," I hissed when he joined me. I'd gotten to know Jordan pretty well over the last several days of working beside him and Miles for hours on end. I felt entirely comfortable threatening him with his life. "You held out on me in a big way."

"Are you telling me you would have been able to keep this a secret from Miles?"

I looked at Miles, who was watching Ellie adoringly, playing the melody he'd been listening to her work on for weeks.

"No," I admitted.

"Exactly," Jordan said. "I didn't even tell my wife, and I'm going to be in even bigger trouble with her."

Ellie moved into her bridge, finally turning toward the piano. I couldn't see her face, but his softened, and when her voice trailed off, he sang the chorus back to her, words about writing a brand-new story for themselves.

"It's so perfect, I want to ..." Jordan seemed to be at a loss for words as to what this warranted.

"Scream? Cry? Gag because too much sugar?" I suggested.

"Yes. And also hug my wife, because dang. That is love right there."

"Yeah," I agreed with a murmur. Anyone could see it written all over the two of them, weaving around them like the song. Experience had taught me that dating musicians was a terrible idea, but Miles was no Erick. These two had what it took to make it. I laughed as the song ended and Miles climbed on top of the piano bench to shout, "I love you, Ellie Jones," which sent the audience into a frenzy.

All except one person.

I noticed him as I scanned the audience reaction. He was sitting at a table about a third of the way back, no beanie, but his stillness drew my attention, and then I saw his jawline. Sharp and firm, like I'd seen in the handful of pictures of him on the Ledge Records page. It was Jonah. I was sure of it.

From the sound of things, Miles and Ellie had progressed to some serious smooching, and the crowd cheered louder, but my eyes were glued to my internet crush. He was watching it all like he was thinking about it, logging, calculating, and considering. What was going through his mind? Had he been listening to the music? Focused on the love story playing out in front of him?

My eyes flickered to his table companion. He sat with a grizzled old Black man who was seventy if he was a day. It was hard to tell how tall he was, but he had at least six inches on Jonah, even seated.

Oh no. What if Jonah was short? I was 5'10, and I liked them at least as tall as me. I'd have to find out at the after-party.

I tore my eyes away from him to check on Miles and Ellie who were on a mission to break the world record for the longest kiss. I exchanged a glance with Jordan who shook his head and grinned.

"How long do you figure I need to give them before I get this show back on track?"

I thought about how miserable Miles had been for the last four days. "At least another minute."

Jordan checked his watch. "Fine, but I'm timing every second."

Miles and Ellie seemed to finally recognize that their make up didn't need an audience anymore, because they stepped apart, though their hands stayed clasped as he led her from the stage, waving to the cheering audience as they exited.

"Bout time," I said, grinning as they reached us.

"Yeah, that was a lot of kissing. Gross," Jordan said.

"I meant this dummy finally saying he loves her." I poked Miles in the arm.

"That too," Jordan agreed and headed out to the stage to do some more emcee stuff.

Miles rolled his eyes. "Ellie, I can't tell you hard I hoped this day would never come, but I guess I have to introduce you to Anneke."

"Hey." She gave me a sweet smile, her cheeks still flushed and eyes shining as she held out her hand for a shake, but I ignored it and pulled her in for a hug.

"Hey, friend. Now you and I can trauma-bond over having to put up with Miles."

"Yeah, I'm not going to regret this at all," he muttered. "Sorry about that, y'all," he said to someone behind us, and I realized that the duo Ellie had pre-empted was waiting behind us to go onstage.

"No worries, dude. Congratulations," the older man said, a grin splitting his dark brown face. "But I don't know if they're going to be much in the blues mood after that, so maybe I'll take that apology after all." He winked, and his partner, a younger white man, followed him out on stage as Jordan announced them.

"I can't wait to get to know you better," I told Ellie, squeezing her arm.

"Me too." She looked like she'd surprised herself by saying it. It didn't faze me. It always took new people in my life time to get used to my friendship with Miles, and vice versa, but it had never been like that between us, not even at the beginning, not on either side.

"We'll catch up tomorrow," I said. "I better go circulate since Miles is going to be preoccupied for a while." I winked at her and hurried toward the exit to the floor to check on guests.

Did that give me an excuse to circle closer to Jonah and scope him out?

Heck, yes. I paused before stepping through the club door, repositioning my girls to make sure they were up to the task, smoothing a hand over my hair, and pulling on the smile the camera loved, a half-flirty, half-mysterious curve of my lips.

It was *my* show time now.

4
JONAH

Big Al rumbled something, and I leaned closer to hear him over the bright blare of the brass act tearing up the stage.

"What was that?" I asked.

"Them dudes are good," he said, nodding toward the group. "Young guys. Haven't played with any of them, but I expect I will before long."

It was high praise coming from him, one of the most accomplished saxophonists to ever come out of New Orleans. And in a city where even the gutters ran with jazz, that was saying something. Big Al had forgotten more about music than I ever knew.

The act finished, and the emcee came out and announced a surprise act. A pretty young woman in a black dress walked out, and the last time I'd seen anyone look this nervous was Bailey at her fourth-grade piano recital, which she ran out of instead of playing.

Then it got really weird when Miles Crowe came out to play, and they seemed to be having a moment which ended in a Tom Cruise-jumping-on-the-piano-bench declaration of love stuff followed by some kissing.

Well, good for them. Only a grinch wouldn't have been happy for two people so clearly in love, but I was still glad when they left the stage and the emcee came out to announce the Biloxi Blues, one of my favorite regional groups.

It was a great set except for the minor distraction of a woman who kept circulating through the tables. She wore a shiny dress, and it kept catching and throwing the light as she stopped at tables to talk with people. And it was just the VIPs too, dudes who were built like they'd probably wandered over from the Superdome after roughing some passers, and a couple of actors I recognized. I could mostly ignore her except when a flash of light would catch the dress and distract me for a second.

I scowled after the third time it happened and resolved to focus harder on the stage and ignore the celebrity suck-up.

"You know that girl?" Big Al asked at one point.

"Who?"

"The one in the silver dress. She keeps looking at you."

"Nope." She was probably trying to figure out if we were high profile enough to be worth her time. If she knew her music, she'd know that Big Al was probably the most impressive person in here, but she didn't come over to our table. I had a feeling we'd be seeing her afterwards, during the party, if Big Al wanted to stay to catch up with a couple of friends who'd performed. When word spread of who he was, more people would find their way to us, and I had a feeling the social-climbing disco ball would hone in on us. That was what status-seekers did.

I shifted so she was out of my line of sight and settled in to enjoy the rest of the show. After the Biloxi Blues, Grace Kelly, an alto saxophonist and jazz vocalist from LA was taking the stage, and that was who I'd come to see. She infuriated and excited the old-school greats, and I couldn't wait to dissect her performance with Big Al, who would no doubt tell me all the ways in which I was wrong. It was one of my favorite parts of hanging out with him. As my godfather, he'd treated me to more than my fair share of shows, and it felt good to return the favor.

"You sure you don't know her?" Big Al asked, several minutes into the set. I glanced over at him, and he nodded at the girl in silver. "I caught her looking at you again."

She was talking to a movie star I recognized but couldn't name, her face in profile. She was gorgeous. She could have been a model with those high cheekbones, but that only reinforced that I didn't know her. I'd remember a face like that. Dramatic eyes. Full lips. Killer body.

"I'm sure."

The Biloxi Blues wound up their set, and I clapped with everyone else. Then the emcee announced that Grace Kelly would take the stage, and the hair on my neck rose. It had been too long since I'd come to a live show, and I couldn't wait to see her perform.

Her set was everything I hoped it would be. Acoustic but electric, her improvisations blending effortlessly with her backing band, who was incredible even by Big Al's standards. I leaned forward like it would let me lean into the music, every concern about Ledge Records and bottom lines and inventory dropping away as it wound around me.

When she ended, I surged to my feet with the rest of the audience, smiling when Big Al gave an earsplitting whistle he usually only trotted out for touchdowns in Saints games.

"That was something else," he said, when we took our seats again.

"Right?" I couldn't believe how good she was.

"Let's stay for the after-party," Big Al said.

"You sure?" He hadn't wanted to when I first invited him, saying he'd stay for the show, but he was too old to fool with parties.

"Yeah. I'd like to talk to some of these youngsters."

"All right by me." I leaned back as the emcee thanked everyone for staying for the show and reminding those of us with a blue wristband that we were invited to remain for the "post-show special."

Big Al snorted. "That's one name for a big ole booze fest."

Other attendees shuffled toward the exit while a young man took a seat at the piano and played soft jazz in the background but nothing that would get people so hyped they wanted to stay.

I people-watched, not looking forward to the socializing. I liked my interactions small and one-on-one. The energy of crowds often overwhelmed me, making me itchy to escape into the peace and quiet of my own company. It wasn't anxiety, I didn't think. More that I was a hardcore introvert the same way that Big Al was a jazzman right down to his DNA. But there was no way I'd cut this night short for him. He'd lost his wife, Letty, to a heart attack almost a year ago, and he'd been harder and harder to get ahold of. It was good to see him with something besides grief in his eyes.

It was okay. I knew exactly how to pass the time while I waited for him to circle and do his thing.

I pulled out my phone and opened my Noteworthy DMs. I couldn't wait to tell AnnieBird about the show.

5
ANNEKE

I weaved between the tables, stopping to chat with a couple of the Saints players I'd invited, smiling and obeying a wave from a TV star who filmed a weekly police procedural series here. We chatted about how the show was going, but I kept every conversation short so we didn't disrespect the performers, and ended each table stop with a reminder to come to the after-party.

I couldn't bring myself to stop at Jonah's table. A couple times, I skimmed close to it, but I couldn't figure out what I wanted to say or how I wanted to say it. A strange energy surged through me any time I got close, like every word I ever knew—in English *or* Dutch—was bubbling up at the back of my throat, like if the jitters could be turned into words, they'd come spewing out of my mouth like clowns from a car.

But ...

I kind of liked that? Liked that he could make me nervous.

That didn't mean I wanted to make a fool of myself. I needed to keep it cool, mellow, and funny, like I was in our DMs on Noteworthy. But every time I tried glancing his way, I would be overcome with this intense feeling, like my skin was stretching too tight and if he looked at me, it would split. The last time I'd had a crush like this, I'd been twelve. Paul Stansbury. He was first chair trumpet in our middle school band. I was a bad flautist. And after my ex-friend, Carie-the-oboe-player, told Paul I liked him, he'd said, "Bug eyes?" and made a face, and then she told me *and* the entire flute section at the same time.

So until the too-tight-skin feeling went away, I didn't want to get too close to his table, or I'd definitely ruin my "cool" vibe.

I couldn't resist sliding glances his way though. He was never looking at me, but once, his friend, the older gentleman, caught me looking and gave me a curious look before I flitted to a different table to talk to a movie star who'd made a big name for herself in indie film.

After about an hour, Miles reappeared and beckoned me into the kitchen hallway.

"Thanks for holding it down out here," he said as the service door muted the music. "Jordan says you've been working the floor like a pro."

"No problem, friend. Is everything fixed with Ellie?"

His whole face smiled, from his mouth to his eyes. Somehow, even his forehead got in on the action. "Like it was never broken. We just spent an hour upstairs—"

I held up my hands to cut him off. "Ew. No details."

"*Talking* in her apartment, and it's weird how having an honest conversation fixes things."

"So weird," I said. "Who'd've thought? I mean, I certainly didn't tell you that ten billion times."

"Shut up, Anneke. And go rest. Put your feet up in my office or something during this last set."

I waved my hand to brush away his concern. "I'm not tired."

"You've been on your feet all night."

"Not tired," I repeated. And it was true. Crowds energized me, whether it was a dinner party with friends or a grand opening with strangers. "I'm just getting started."

He knew me too well to bother arguing. "All right. I need to go check on the kitchen and make sure the food is ready. You want to check in with the bartenders?"

"You got it, boss."

"I'm not paying you for this, so you don't have to call me boss."

"I wouldn't let you pay me for this, and the main reason I'm doing it is so I can see the annoyed look on your face when I call you boss."

"You're the worst."

"Love you, dummy."

"Get out of here."

The bartenders were ready to serve the complimentary signature cocktail we'd designed for the night, a turnaround, named after the club. It was a twist on the most famous New Orleans cocktail—the Sazerac—but made with a splash of honey habanero moonshine because a dissonant chord in jazz was called "spicy."

I was twitchy. As far as I could tell, LedgeCase hadn't looked my way once. If he had, I would have felt it like a touch. Maybe I was twitchy because he *wasn't* looking at me. Or because words failed me. I had no idea what I would say when we eventually crossed paths.

Soon the regular crowd had cleared out, leaving about fifty VIP guests on the floor as the musicians came out to circulate and mingle. I kept trying and discarding opening lines to talk to Jonah. I thought about a simple, "Hi, I'm AnnieBird." But that would probably freak him out. One, that I knew who he was, and two, that I was here, in his city, at the club where he was.

Definitely not that one.

I could start with a simple, "How are you gentlemen enjoying your evening?" but in a fancy dress and the dim interior of the club, I sounded like the madam of a fancy brothel.

So also no.

I was talking to one of the football players, my mind only half on the conversation, when a soft arm slid through mine, and Ellie gave it a small squeeze.

"Hi," she said, giving me a shy smile. "I thought maybe we could talk instead of a drive-by intro while Miles dragged me upstairs to—"

I help up my "stop" hand.

"Talk," she finished, her smile growing to a grin.

"Absolutely." I tucked her arm in mine and grabbed a vacant table. I made sure my back was to Jonah, or I'd stare at him the whole time.

"I want to start with a confession," she said as soon as we were seated.

"Let me guess. You've been jealous about me and Miles, but after seeing us together for two seconds, you've realized there's literally nothing between us but friendship?"

Her mouth dropped open slightly before she snapped it shut and gave me a wry smile. "I guess you've been down this road before."

"A time or two," I said, signaling a server. "If it makes you feel better, I get it. And I have zero hard feelings."

"Can I apologize anyway?"

"Of course."

She leaned across the table, took my hands in hers, and looked me dead in the eye. "Anneke, you rule. I'm so glad you and Miles are friends. I want us to be friends too."

I smothered a smile. "You realize everyone who sees us right now thinks you're proposing, and that you, Miles, and me are polyamorous?"

"Absolutely," she said, her face perfectly straight.

"Oh, I like you." I tugged my hands free and threw my arms around her in a hug. "I accept."

She hugged me back, and when I settled back in my seat, she gestured for someone else to come over. "This is my roommate, Chloe. We've been friends since I was a college freshman."

I pushed out the third chair for Chloe, and we chatted about the show and what Miles and Ellie's babies would look like, which made Ellie roll her eyes.

"What about you?" Chloe asked. "You dating anyone?"

I angled toward them. "I want to be. I think. Do you see the table behind us, sort of in the center but off to the right, probably a young white guy and a tall older gentleman?"

They both scanned the floor and nodded when they had the target locked.

"I think the younger guy is named Jonah, and if I'm right, we've been DM-ing each other for a few months, and I invited him here tonight."

Chloe and Ellie exchanged glances while they both took that in. Chloe's glance flicked from me to him again. "I feel like there are some gaps in that info. You're not sure that's him?"

I shook my head. "It's a long story, but his screen name is LedgeCase, and I think he owns Ledge Records. I possibly did some more googling that makes me think that's Jonah Collier, and that we've been chatting online."

"Go talk to him," Ellie said.

"I haven't figured out how to introduce myself in a way that doesn't make me sound like a stalker."

"Don't mention the googling," she said.

I made a face at her. "Thanks, Dr. Love."

She narrowed her eyes like she was trying to study their table better in the low light. "I think that's Big Al Tatum with him."

Chloe and I both blinked at her.

"He's one of the most respected saxophonists in jazz. I'm positive it's him, actually."

"Let's go find out," Chloe said. "Ellie is the star of the night after her big moment, so I'm sure they won't mind if we approach them. We'll get an introduction to the other guy, and if it's Jonah, we'll signal you."

Ellie nodded. "Good plan. If it's him, I'll spell out his name like YMCA letters. How do you make a J?" She pretended to figure it out with her arms, and I snorted into the Diet Coke I was drinking.

"Subtle," Chloe said. "Or I was thinking like baseball signals?" She tugged an earlobe, rubbed her nose, and patted each of her shoulders.

"Probably spit and kick some dirt too," I suggested, "so I get that it's a baseball thing and not an allergic reaction to his cologne."

Chloe cracked a slight smile. "You're all right, supermodel."

Ellie pushed back from the table. "For real, I'm going to head over there. If I tuck my hair behind my ear, it's your boy."

I smiled as they left and climbed to my feet, ready to flutter to the next table and make small talk while keeping an eye on Ellie. Miles might be my best friend, but I wasn't one of those women who preferred the company of men. I heard beautiful women say that sometimes, that it was hard to make friends with women because they were intimidated. I found it was less and less true the more I grew up. It could be hard sometimes to make friends with other models, because models, ironically, were some of the most insecure people on the planet, and we were in constant competition with each other to book jobs.

But the reality was, only a small handful of models had that toxic "I'm only friends with guys" thing happening, and I always felt sorry for them, because that was clearly some trauma at play. I had lots of female friends, and I could already tell that Chloe and Ellie would climb quickly to the top of that list. I'd put myself in the hands of two very skilled—and funny—wing women.

I chatted with the director of the art museum for a few minutes, and then, there it was: Ellie tucked her hair behind her ear.

My stomach did a giant swoop, a loop-de-loop the skywriters over Venice Beach every weekend would envy. It was Jonah. And I had the perfect opportunity to go join Chloe and Ellie and get an introduction.

"I'd love to come visit your museum," I told the director. "When I'm in a new city, I try to get to know it from different angles, and you might be just the person to point me in the right direction. And if I shout it out on social media, it'll get you some extra traffic."

"That would be wonderful," she said, her eyes lighting up. "I'll look forward to seeing you."

I smiled and excused myself to go join the girls, still not sure what I would say. I would have to count on it coming to me in the moment. Stuff usually did. The key would be not to get too cute. Maybe, "Hey, we might know each other already."

Yeah. That felt simple. I'd go with that.

I approached the table, and a slight smile twitched on Big Al's mouth. Jonah's expression remained the same, like he was on the edge of slipping into boredom.

"Hey, girls," I said as I walked up.

"Hey, Anneke," Ellie said. "We came over to meet Big Al. Are you familiar with his work? One of the greatest saxophonists in jazz."

"I'm not but sounds like I need to be," I said, extending my hand to shake.

"Big Al, this is Anneke," Ellie continued. "She's a good friend of Miles's and the host of this VIP party."

"You forgot the famous supermodel part," Chloe said.

"That's interesting," Big Al said. "Would I have seen you in anything?"

"You'll have seen me in very little," I said, and when his brow wrinkled, I shrugged. "Swimsuits and undies."

This time his lips twitched into a full smile. This was a man who bought the yearly *Sporting News* swimsuit edition. "Got it."

"I'm here tonight as a music fan, though. How amazing was Grace Kelly?"

"Not bad," he said, still smiling, and I had a feeling that for him, that was the equivalent of pretty dang good. "Let me introduce you to my friend, Jonah. He's also a big music fan. Owns Ledge Records, as a matter of fact."

This was it. My stomach rolled as I reached out to shake Jonah's hand, but instead of smiling, the boredom won out on his face, and he shook my hand with a flat, "Hey."

Not the reception I was hoping for. *We might know each other already* suddenly felt like the wrong move. Inside, I was a giant guppy mouth, soundlessly flapping my lips while I tried to find something else to say instead.

"Why don't you ladies draw up a seat?" There was one empty seat at their table, and Big Al gestured to empty chairs at the next table. Jonah moved like he was going to fetch them, but Ellie waved him down.

"I need to go check on Miles, so don't bother with one for me."

"I'd like to see how he's doing too," Chloe said.

"How about you, Miss Anneke?" Big Al asked. "We have an open chair just for you."

It was a neatly executed move on Ellie and Chloe's part, but after Jonah's less than thrilled greeting, I wasn't sure I wanted the seat. But maybe he was just shy? Miles could be like that if he had to spend too much time making small talk.

I slid into the seat. "Did you guys enjoy the show?"

Jonah shrugged. "Yeah."

Big Al flicked a look at him. "Excuse my friend here, Anneke. He's ... shy."

I had a feeling that wasn't Big Al's first choice of word, and I wondered what he wanted to say for real. Because I had a sneaking suspicion I knew what was going on with Jonah, and I hoped I was wrong. But if I wasn't, he was using a tactic called "negging," a nasty brand of pickup behavior that emotionally stunted men sometimes tried. The goal was to pay a backhanded compliment to undermine a woman's confidence and increase their need to get the guy's approval. Acting disinterested in a woman was often the first step in the pattern.

Record producers used this one a lot for some reason. I'd run into it plenty of times at Miles's industry events in LA. If that's what was going on, I'd be out of here like falsies the second a photoshoot was over. I'd have to test him and see.

"Who'd you like besides Grace Kelly?" I asked Big Al.

"Horn Dawgs," he answered without hesitation. "They got something."

"That was fun," I agreed. "Great energy. Who did you like, Jonah?" It felt slightly transgressive to use his real name.

"The whole thing was a good lineup."

Holy cow. He was *not* negging me. If he was, he'd have been rude, ignored me, or found a way to pay me one of those backhanded compliments. Instead, he'd answered the question in a straightforward way, but again, kind of flat. Like …

Maybe there was something else at play here? Like autism, where he missed social cues like my cousin Tandy did? I'd watch for that next to see if there was too much or too little eye contact, and if it was with me or everyone. Maybe he was overwhelmed by all the sensory input?

"What did you think of the sound mix on the Biloxi Blues?" Big Al asked him, and Jonah turned to him, his eyes brightening.

"Good," he said, with a smile and nod. "Very good. I wonder if it's their own guy or the house sound."

He said it with full eye-contact, an immediate loosening of his body as he leaned slightly toward his friend.

I sat back, a hair shy of mortified. I could keep running through possibilities for why Jonah wasn't engaging with me; it wasn't autism. I could try ruling out social anxiety or a short list of other possibilities here, but there wasn't a need.

We were dealing with Occam's Razor here, where the simplest answer was the right one: Jonah did not like me, was not interested in me, and clearly sucked at faking like he was.

I needed an exit strategy while I figured out how to collect my exploded ego and stagger out under the weight of it. *Think, think, think.*

Oh, right. I was the host of this whole thing.

I rose and gave them my hostess smile. "Glad you could join us this evening," I said. "I need to check on other guests, but I'll send over some turnaround cocktails, and you just let the waitstaff know if you need anything else today."

"Nice to meet you, Anneke," Big Al said.

Jonah half rose to be polite, and at least I could tell he was tall. Not that it mattered now.

I walked off with my shoulders back, trying to look like I didn't care at all that I had totally humiliated myself, but I was going to need a second to recover from this. I grabbed a stuffed mushroom off a circulating platter and popped it into my mouth. It was delicious but highly garlicky, not ideal for a party host, so I slipped into Miles's office to dig a mint from my purse.

It vibrated as I picked it up, and my tummy did the flutter of anticipation it always did when I thought it might be Jonah.

"You're going to have to stop that," I said to it. "That's a dead-end road. Super dead." But it didn't stop me from checking my phone. And it only fluttered again when it was, in fact, a DM alert from LedgeCase. Which meant he was out there *right now* actively DM-ing me while ignoring me in person. I would laugh except it was too embarrassing.

I opened the DM.

LedgeCase: Caught a good show tonight. Grace Kelly headlined. Pretty killer lineup. Have you heard her Working for the Dreamers album? What did you think?

I stared at it. Seriously, he couldn't have said even a tenth of this to me out on the floor just now? What was I supposed to do with this? Did I want to keep chatting with him when I knew he wasn't feeling my real-life vibe?

I shoved my phone back into my purse.

I didn't know what I wanted to do next, at least as far as Jonah was concerned. But I did know what I needed to do next, and that was to make sure Miles's opening night continued to go smoothly. I'd modeled in all kinds of ridiculous circumstances, wearing tiny bikinis in freezing weather so that the shots could go into early spring issues. Walked a runway in an industrial culvert pipe while wearing a $1200 nightie. Even skydived in an evening gown for an Alexander McQueen shoot. I could certainly go out there and put on a party face while my crush withered and died beneath Jonah's disinterested stare.

I checked my reflection in the mirror and touched up my lip gloss before walking out, ready to fake like Jonah had never happened.

There was a whole cute boy smorgasbord of musicians and athletes out there that could overcome the aftertaste of Jonah the Stinky Cheese. I'd do my best to push him out of my mind before I got too salty and drowned in charcuterie metaphors.

6
JONAH

LedgeCase: Where are you, anyway? Like what city? We've never talked about that. Not trying to be a stalker. Just wondering what your music scene is like where you are. I'm almost embarrassed to admit where I live because I don't take as much advantage of it as I should, music-wise. But the Grace Kelly show I mentioned last night … is it weird that I wished you were there to see it too? Would have loved to talk to you about it.

I put my phone down and stared out at the store, not really seeing anything. The most recent Grace Kelly live album played over the sound system, and unsurprisingly, several people had come into the shop this morning looking for her stuff. Bailey did a good job of keeping track of the local shows and ordering the vinyl in advance when it made sense, and her instincts were largely good. She'd made sure we had enough copies of the saxophonist's catalogue.

It had been a good evening, music-wise. I could have done without the after-party. Schmoozing had never been my thing, but it had been pretty cool watching the steady stream of musicians who came by to deliver their props. But the flashy stuff—celebrities and NFL players—that wasn't my thing.

I'd come home more wiped out by the strain of making polite conversation than I had by the late hour.

I hadn't heard from AnnieBird yet, which was kind of surprising. She usually got back to me pretty fast, but I didn't know what her schedule was. Maybe she had a job that was extra busy today. Maybe she was a student. College, at least, I hoped. Or not hoped. I was twenty-nine. It would rattle me if I'd been DM-ing with a college girl.

Not that there was anything inappropriate in our DMs. We mostly talked music, but sometimes talking about music allowed you to talk about other things. Life. Philosophy. Politics. Art. Food. We'd covered a lot of ground in the last couple of months, and there was something about AnnieBird that made me think she might be around my age. She had old-soul interests, but a way of speaking that was young without being … immature?

I couldn't put my finger on it, but lately, whenever cute girls came into the store, I found myself wondering what AnnieBird would look like. Or it was like last night, where this stunning blonde had come over to the table, but she was so made up and … I don't know, glam? So *that*, and I kept thinking AnnieBird would probably have shown up in jeans, a T-shirt, and a beanie, and been chill the whole night. Not … sparkly.

Although … I glanced down at myself. I was wearing jeans, a T-shirt, and a beanie, and I'd been wearing something very similar last night, so *maybe* I was projecting.

The Noteworthy alert buzzed on my phone, and I snatched it up. AnnieBird. *Yes.*

AnnieBird: Let's see … if you went to the Grace Kelly show last night then …*Please hold for Google*… You're in NOLA. That's where she performed last night.
LedgeCase: You got me.
AnnieBird: Well, this is very interesting.
LedgeCase: Because …?
AnnieBird: View from my window.

She sent a picture, and I sucked in a sharp breath. I wasn't exactly sure which street, but she was in the French Quarter. Her picture was a view of colored shutters on a stucco building with a balcony enclosed by lacy ironwork. In the same way you could recognize any Bob Dylan song whether you'd heard it before or not, a New Orleans native would know that architecture.

LedgeCase: You're from New Orleans?
AnnieBird: I'm in New Orleans, yes

I waited for her to suggest that we meet. Or maybe that was my move, because it was my town? But who wanted to be that creepy internet guy asking for a meetup? I needed a non-threatening way to make the invitation.

LedgeCase: I know a really great record shop you should check out
AnnieBird: Yeah?
LedgeCase: Ledge Records
AnnieBird: Hmmm. Ledge Records. LedgeCase. Not trying to brag, but I think I figured out where you work.
LedgeCase: I've been told the guy who's always behind the counter looks exactly like me
AnnieBird: Weird
LedgeCase: Because it is me
AnnieBird: …
AnnieBird: …
AnnieBird: …

The dots were killing me. This was where she was supposed to say, "You know, I *have* been meaning to get the new Frank Ocean album …"
Or anything, really. Anything to suggest that she wanted to come in.
I had no time for women right now, and no money to take one out even if I had time. I also had enough pride not to wheedle her into coming over. But I couldn't resist offering her a tiny bribe when she still hadn't said anything after a full minute.

LedgeCase: I have to go, Sherlock. I need to process a signed Led Zeppelin album that just came in.

AnnieBird: !!!

I laughed at how fast her response was. Led Zeppelin was one of her favorite bands.

LedgeCase: The buyer is coming to pick it up at 3:00, so I better enjoy it while it's still here.

There. I'd put a ticking clock on her coming by the store. There was no way she could resist a signed Zeppelin album, not if her schedule allowed.

I closed the app and went to work on the invoices again and waited to see if she'd take the bait.

7
ANNEKE

Led Zeppelin?!

Oh, he was a wily man, that Jonah. Two minutes ago, I would have said nothing could make me stop by Ledge Records and embarrass myself again. One rejection was enough. But *signed* Led Zeppelin!

No. No way.

I wasn't going in there for Jonah to be like, "Hey, AnnieBi—oh, it's you." His face would fall, and we would both hear the sound of a sad trombone.

I had a full day planned doing other things, and I was ready to tackle it.

I grabbed my camera bag and sunglasses and headed out of the hotel and down two blocks to Miles's place so I could get the rest of my stuff. He'd insisted I didn't need to move to the hotel, but as cool as Ellie had been last night, I was pretty sure she wasn't going to want me living in her boyfriend's place.

He buzzed me in, and I wandered up to the kitchen. Ellie was there, dressed in a business suit and eating a yogurt.

"Hello, lovebirds."

"Why are you staying at a hotel?" Ellie asked, instead of greeting me. "Move back into the guest room."

"Good morning to you too," I said, reaching for an apple from the fruit basket on the counter.

"Move back into the guest room," she repeated.

"You guys were broken up when I got into town, but now you're not. We're cool, Ellie. I don't mind staying at the hotel."

Her eyes narrowed. "Do you think I'm threatened by your friendship with Miles?"

I paused mid-bite to look over at him at the stove. He was scrambling eggs, wearing pajama bottoms, a Turnaround T-shirt, and some serious bedhead.

"It's a trap," he confirmed.

"I …" Hard swallow. What was my move here?

"Stay in the guest room," Ellie ordered.

"Okay."

Her face transformed into a sunny smile. "Good."

"You're scary," I informed her.

"Only if you don't do what I tell you."

"That doesn't make me feel better. But you're perfect for Miles."

"He's pretty lucky," she agreed, and Miles laughed and cracked another egg. "So how did it go with Jonah last night?"

"Who?" Miles asked.

"Mind your own business," I told him. "I haven't exactly brought up this guy with him before," I explained to Ellie. "He thinks my picker is broken."

"Because it's broken. Who is this guy?"

"We've been chatting on Noteworthy, and shut up, I don't want to hear it. I'm not twelve, and I understand catfishing and basic internet safety. Turns out he's the guy from the record store."

"*That's* why you wanted to send him VIP tickets," he said. "And here I thought it was a stroke of marketing genius."

"It was marketing genius with a strong top note of curiosity," I said. "Doesn't matter, anyway. It was a bust."

"What's wrong with him?" Ellie asked.

If I hadn't liked her already, that would have clinched it. I liked that she automatically assumed Jonah was the problem, not me. "He's kind of grumpy."

"Maybe he's shy," Miles suggested. "Sometimes average guys get freaked out when a model starts talking to them."

"Shut up, never-been-an-average-guy," I said. "Quit acting like you know how the rest of us normies live."

"You're not a normie, either," Ellie pointed out. "Since Jonah and I are the only two actual normies in this situation, I get to be the expert here. But Miles is right. Maybe Jonah was overwhelmed by a supermodel talking to him."

I shrugged. "It wasn't that. I've seen that before. They either get very quiet or talk too much, or sometimes flat-out bail on the situation. He looked bored, honestly. And here's the craziest part: while he's in the club ignoring me in person, he sent me a message on Noteworthy to tell me how good the show was and that he wished I could have seen it."

Ellie grinned. "What a dummy."

"It was odd, for sure. What does it mean if he can connect with me online but in person ... *nothing*?"

"I'm sticking with him being intimidated by you," Miles said.

"He messaged me this morning too. I was going to blow him off, but then he started in about how much I would have loved the show, and I was like, '*Dude*, I was sitting right in front of you enjoying the show,' and it really bugged me, so ..."

Miles sighed when I paused. "What did you do, Anneke?"

Ellie's eyes lit with curiosity. "Do tell."

"I decided to mess with him," I confessed. "I told him I googled and figured out, based on Grace Kelly's tour schedule, that he must live in New Orleans. Then I sent him a picture from my hotel window that made it obvious I'm in the French Quarter."

"Perfect," Ellie said, grinning.

"Yeah, nothing like playing games instead of straightforward communication," Miles grumbled.

"Quiet, judgy-pants," I said.

"What did he say?" Ellie asked.

I gave a big sigh. "That he has a signed Zeppelin record waiting on customer pickup at three o'clock this afternoon."

Miles's eyes went round. "No way."

I nodded.

He gave a low whistle. "That's playing dirty."

"One of my favorite bands," I explained to Ellie.

"They're not even one of my top five, and I'd still kill to see that album." She tapped the back of my hand on the counter. "Forget Jonah. It's worth the price of a polite hello if you get to see that album."

I sighed like JoJo when we didn't give her treats. "I'm not sure I feel like getting cold-shouldered again."

"He's not going to do that to … what's your screen name?" Ellie asked.

"AnnieBird."

"He's not going to do that to AnnieBird."

"He did it to me last night."

"Nah," Miles said softly. "He didn't. Not really. Because AnnieBird wasn't at the club last night. Bombshell Anneke was. It's two different things," Miles added to Ellie. "For celebrities, anyway. A self-preservation thing. Our public and private personas."

She nodded. "I've seen it. And I definitely know what it's like to have people treat you a certain way based entirely on your public image."

I winced. That stupid meme.

She slid from her stool and walked over to Miles, wrapping her arms around his waist. "That wasn't a knock on you, baby. I'm over it, I promise. But I kind of get why Anneke's protecting herself here."

"Think about it," Miles pressed. "How long have you guys been talking?"

"Couple of months? Maybe three."

"And you click?"

I gave a reluctant nod. "Really well."

"What kind of stuff do you talk about?"

I took a bite of apple and thought about some of our chats. "It always starts with music but then leads to almost everything in the whole wide world. Maybe not sports. That doesn't come up too much."

"So," Miles said, smoothing Ellie's hair as she stayed nestled against his chest, "you've connected in a real way over real things. And you've done no catfishing, no lying about how you look or what you do?"

"It's never come up."

"Then if he rejected you now, it would be because of how you look.

Maybe you don't fit some pre-conceived idea he has of what a music nerd should look like. That's its own kind of shallow. But for real, it doesn't sound like that would happen if you went in there today."

Ellie turned slightly so she could study me while still snuggled against Miles. "Look, I'm super petty, so take this with a grain of salt, but if I were you, I'd go in and make him pay."

Miles was already groaning, but I ignored him. "Tell me more."

"Show up looking gorgeous and ask to see the album. Watch the look of horror on his face when he realizes the only way you could know about it is if you're AnnieBird."

"Orrrrr," Miles said, "go as yourself. And when you can tell he's into you, hit him with an uppercut and say something that would make him realize he met you last night."

Ellie straightened and gave him a look of admiration. "That's even better. I'm so impressed."

I grinned. "I like it. I'll think about it. But I've got a city to explore and no time for dumb boys."

"And a hotel reservation to cancel," Ellie reminded me.

"That too. I'll see you around, guys." I swooshed around the kitchen island to drop a kiss on each of their cheeks and called, "Byeeeeeeee," on my way out.

"Where's she going?" Ellie asked.

"Who knows?" Miles said. "Most likely an old maw maw's house to take pictures of her garden and charm her into making her some food."

I smiled at Ellie's muffled sound of confusion as the front door closed behind me. Miles wasn't too far off. He was one of the few people who knew about my non-work Instagram account.

I found my way to St. Ann Street and headed up to Louis Armstrong Park, a public space hedged in by simple iron gates that welcomed visitors with an elaborate arch. One of the challenges in cities with lots of tourism was that it could be hard to snap the locals doing their thing. So far, the vibe I got from the French Quarter was that eighty percent of everyone I was seeing was visiting or worked there. It was hard to get a sense of the actual residents, so I was spreading out to other sections of the city to get to know it.

I wandered for a few hours, snapping pictures of anything that interested me. The contrast of vibrant plant life against decrepit sidewalks. An old apartment building that was a burned-out hull next to a lovingly restored Victorian, exploding in bright colors. A well-tended plant bed in front of a liquor store whose windows looked as if they hadn't been cleaned since the seventies. A few times, I shot pictures of people with their permission.

A lot of photographers specialized. Landscapes or portraits. Still photography or action shots. I liked all of it, but I especially liked the way all those things came together to tell a story. It was kind of like being a photojournalist but with small, quiet stories that showed me the core of a place from its people to its food.

New Orleans was fascinating, unlike anywhere else I'd been in the US. It was more like the Caribbean, with its mashup between bright colors and European architecture. The city had clearly never heard of an HOA, and it led to a fascinating mix of new by the old, stores in between houses, houses turned into stores. Mardi Gras beads hung from trees, powerlines, and fences on many streets, and graffiti, from vandalism to street art, covered surfaces all over the Seventh Ward.

But the whole time I wandered, I also wondered. What was Jonah up to? What if I was close to Ledge Records, and I didn't even know it?

I ducked into a Rouse's Market for a banana and a protein bar and thought about Jonah and the night before. It was so weird to have him completely dismiss me, real live Anneke, sitting in front of him and trying to get to know him, and then literally a minute later have him turn around and message me like he had all the time in the world to talk about a live music experience we were sharing in person to someone he thought wasn't even there.

"What is that even about?" I stopped and asked this in the middle of a sidewalk. Out loud. A shambling woman in worn out clothes and a shopping basket full of junk stopped, eyed me, and changed direction.

I checked the time. Two o'clock. I chewed on my bottom lip, thinking. Then I did the thing I'd sworn I wouldn't do this morning and looked up Ledge Records.

It was only a mile away. I tapped my phone, debating.

And then I changed direction toward the record store. If I wanted answers, there was only one guy who could tell me.

8
JONAH

I watched the front door all morning, taking my lunch at the register so I didn't miss AnnieBird. She'd come in.

Because …

Because why, I had to ask myself when lunch was well past over, and no one had introduced herself as AnnieBird or even asked to see the Zeppelin album. Why should any woman want to meet a stranger from the internet?

Maybe because we didn't feel like strangers. We'd started messaging a couple of months ago. She started it, actually. She'd sent me a message saying she agreed with my opinion about The Doors but didn't feel like dealing with Noteworthy trolls. It was true that many dudes on the site weren't always nice to girls. At best, they dismissed them, but it often deteriorated into these guys telling women to go listen to—and then fill in the name of a female artist whose music they found unworthy. Almost any female artist would do. They found few of them worthy of respect.

But I respected AnnieBird's opinions. Even when we debated. And an invitation to come to a very public record store made sense, didn't it? I frowned.

"What's wrong?" Bailey asked.

"Nothing." I went back to browsing an online record sale to see if there was anything one of my regulars might want. "Actually ..."

She looked up from the Ledge Records sticker display she was working on, her "I'm listening" face on.

I explained about AnnieBird, and my invitation to stop in. "But she hasn't yet," I concluded.

"Are you sure?" she asked. "Maybe she took one look at your face and bailed."

I shrugged. I wasn't cocky, but I was pretty sure most women found my face okay.

"Or maybe she saw it and decided you're so far out of her league that she didn't introduce herself."

I frowned again. That *would* bother me. I wasn't a shallow man either. I could say after two months of chatting that I was attracted to AnnieBird's mind, but no matter what she looked like, it would take meeting in person to see if we had any chemistry. She could be a knockout, and we still might not click. It went like that sometimes.

All the time for me, really. No mental connection, no connection, period.

Maybe it was for the best if she didn't come in. Her picture from the French Quarter meant she was most likely here as a tourist, so then what? Would I want to click with someone if a relationship wasn't going to work anyway?

I shook my head. *Relationship.* Ha. As if I had time for one. I was barely keeping the store afloat right now.

The door opened, and I glanced up. The register was right by the front door so I could keep an eye out for shoplifters. A woman stepped in, maybe a few years younger than me. Mid-twenties, fairly tall, around 5'10, and skinny enough that my mom would try to stuff her with chowder if she saw her. I assessed her shoplifting potential. A white tank top and a camo skirt made out of T-shirt material. No good for hiding records. I stole a quick glance at her bag. It was a camera bag, too small for her to smuggle out any vinyl, and I gave her a low-key nod like I did to every customer.

She paused inside the door and glanced over the store.

"Jazz is upstairs," I said since first-timers often missed the sign. Our section was so big, it needed its own room.

"Thanks." She looked away, then wandered toward the indie rock section. I went back to browsing.

After a few minutes, she came back to the desk.

"Help you find something?" I asked, looking up.

"Led Zeppelin," she said.

My head snapped up. She had all of my attention now, and I studied her quickly but closely. She wore a messy bun and sunglasses, which she removed and tucked into the neckline of her shirt. Her eyes were a dark, startling blue. She wore a watchful look, almost with a challenge in it. Bailey had stopped and turned when she heard the album request, and her eyes flickered from the woman to me and back again, her mouth hanging open slightly.

"Are you AnnieBird?" I asked.

She hesitated then gave a short nod. "I am."

"Whoa, nice to meet you." I started to hold my hand out then retracted it. "I don't know what to do here. Shake? Hug?"

She shrugged. "You don't have to do either."

She wasn't smiling. If anything, she looked slightly confused. I understood. I was slightly confused too. She looked like this was the last place she wanted to be, but then why did she come in?

Bailey was trying to get my attention, but I ignored her. She was no doubt making faces at me or otherwise trying to bust my chops. Sometimes, with me, she acted more like twelve than twenty-two.

"Are you from New Orleans? It would be wild if we could have been having all of our online debates in person." But even as I asked, I suspected she wasn't. She would have found her way to the only record store in town before this, and the more I looked at her, the more I was sure hers wasn't a face I would forget. She was a quiet kind of pretty, with large eyes and the clearest skin I'd ever seen. She didn't even have freckles, but the more I looked at her, the more interesting her face became.

Her mouth twitched in annoyance, and I realized I'd been staring too long.

"I'm not from here," she said, and I didn't hear any kind of accent. She could be from almost anywhere. Maybe not the South or Midwest. I knew those accents.

"So you're visiting?"

"Mostly." She didn't elaborate.

She definitely didn't want to be here. I had no idea what to do next, but I wasn't going to try to force more awkward conversation.

"Uh, so would you like to see that album?" I asked.

"Yeah. That would be good." I turned to get it from the office, but I was only halfway there when she said, "Wait." I turned back. She shifted from one foot to the other. "Never mind. It's okay. I forgot about some stuff I need to do."

Then she turned and walked out. And walked right back in.

"You know we've met before, right?"

I stared at her, scanning her face again to see if it jogged a memory. "We have?" Maybe she'd come to the store before. But that face … I'd remember it.

She opened her mouth to say something, then snapped it shut, shook her head, and left.

I turned to look at Bailey who looked like she'd been clubbed over the head.

AnnieBird walked back in one more time. "Seriously? Do you not know who I am?"

This was getting slightly old. "I really don't."

She got a pinched look, huffed, and walked out again. I was trying to interpret that huff. I think it was supposed to tell me that I was dumber than dirt and had used up the last of her patience.

"That went well." My voice was dryer than … I couldn't think of a good metaphor. We were a river city in a subtropical climate. I didn't have much experience with dry.

"Do you have any idea who that was?" Bailey demanded.

"AnnieBird," I said. "She's … not what I expected?"

"I wouldn't think so," Bailey said. "I'm sure lots of people catfish as supermodels online, but you're the lucky idiot who gets the actual supermodel."

I squinted at her. My eyesight was fine, but I couldn't make sense of what she was saying. "I mean, she's pretty, but …"

"Oh my—" She sucked in a sharp breath, held it, and looked at the ceiling like she was praying for patience. Then she whipped her phone from her pocket, tapped it like it had personally offended her, stalked over, and shoved it at me. "*That* is your AnnieBird."

I took the phone from her uncertainly, not sure why she was ready to hop out of her skin. Then I glanced down at the screen and my eyes widened. It was an Instagram account full of photos of the same woman staring thoughtfully out of a window, on a beach bicycle smiling, peeking over the edge of a book, listening to earbuds and staring out of a window again, doing yoga on a beach. At least half of them were her in swimsuits or yoga clothes, and she had a banging body. But a couple were close-ups, and in those close-ups, it was easy to see that this was the woman who had just left the shop.

I read the name of the account aloud. "Anneke?" I pronounced it like "Ann-ee-kee," grappling with the spelling.

"Anneke rhymes with Danica," Bailey corrected. "Rhymes with world-famous supermodel and also with you are an idiot."

"That doesn't rhyme." I ducked when she threw a T-shirt at me. I studied the phone again. "This is definitely the chick who was just in here. But I've never seen her before today."

"Then why does she think you have?" Bailey demanded.

"I don't know," I said, scrolling through more of her pictures. "I definitely would remem—oh, damn."

I just recognized her with the help of a photo in her feed. In most of her photos, she went with a pretty natural look. But in this one, captioned "Gala time," she was in a long gold gown with a train, her hair sticking out in wild directions but like it was on purpose, her makeup heavy and dramatic.

"I did not meet her last night," I said, pointing to the door where AnnieBird had left, "but I did meet *her*." I turned the screen to show Bailey. "But her hair wasn't this crazy."

Bailey took the phone. "This was the Met Gala. The point is for everything to be over the top." She studied the phone. "You met her last night?"

"Yeah. She came up to Big Al and talked to us for a while."

"And you didn't recognize her today?"

"She didn't look like the same person." I was having a hard time reconciling it, but there was no mistaking now that the woman who had come in was the woman in these photos and also the woman I'd met at the Turnaround last night. What didn't line up was that it was also ... *AnnieBird?*

Bailey gave an annoyed scoff. "Her cheekbones alone should have given it away. I'd have guessed supermodel even if I didn't already know she's one of the most high-profile faces in the industry."

"Can you not say that like I'm an idiot?"

"No. Because you're an idiot."

"Because I didn't know the woman I've been chatting with online for months is a famous supermodel?"

Bailey pressed her lips together.

"Come on, Bay. If my online friend, AnnieBird, had told me weeks ago that she was a supermodel and I told you that, what would you say?"

Her cheeks filled with air. "Fine," she said, puffing it out. "I wouldn't have believed you. But why did she seem mad at you?"

"She's probably offended I didn't know who she was. I'm sure people recognize her all the time."

"She was mad when she walked in, before you failed to recognize her." Bailey leaned against the counter and rested her chin on her hands. "Tell me, big brother. Exactly what happened when you met last night?"

"Nothing."

"Riiiiiight."

"I'm serious. Nothing. She was the host of the after-party, and she kept walking around, and it was kind of distracting—"

"I bet," Bailey said with a smirk.

"Because she was very shiny, and it was distracting like someone shining a mirror in your eye is distracting."

Bailey collapsed her arms and dropped her head on top of them with a groan. "Jonah."

"What?" I could hear the defensiveness in my voice. "I wanted to watch the acts."

"When she came over to you and Big Al, how did that conversation go?"

"I don't know," I said, slightly frustrated. I'd been trying to recall that for the last three minutes, once I'd realized who AnnieBird was. "I don't remember much. Big Al teased me because he said she was checking me out, and I wasn't interested, but—"

She cut me off with another groan. "This is getting worse. I need to get the story out of Big Al." She straightened and called him, and I listened to her side of the conversation.

"Hey, so I was talking to Jonah about last night ... Oh, good. Glad it was a good show. Anyway, he was saying y'all met a certain supermodel ... Anneke? Oh, you remember her?" She shot me a glare. "Yes, silver dress. That's right. Anyway, it didn't make much of an impression on Jonah because—uh-huh. Agree. Total idiot." I rolled my eyes. "He doesn't remember too much about it, so I was wondering if you could tell me how it went down ... I see ... Please say he didn't ... He *did*? She was? And how did she seem? ... That's not great ... Yeah ... Uh-huh ... Can't say I blame her. All right, thank you Uncle Al. Love you."

She set her phone down and examined me like I was a case study in her marketing class. "He says you blew her off. That you ignored her every time she tried to get your attention and were borderline rude to her when she sat at your table." She pounded her hands on the counter, and I jumped. "What is wrong with you?"

"Her dress was louder than the bands," I mumbled.

"You and your 'purity of music.' Even Dad would have said you blew this one."

"I wouldn't have if I'd known it was her! And honestly, I'm not sure why she's so mad. Shouldn't she be glad I didn't want to hang out with her because of how she looks and that I was into her personality instead?"

"I'm guessing from her exit today that no, she doesn't agree with you."

"I should be scoring bonus points, not getting in trouble."

"No one likes to be rejected, Jonah. Do I really have to explain that to you?"

There was a slight warning in her tone that said she might bring up Maggie if I didn't drop this soon, and since I avoided talking about Maggie whenever possible, I changed tactics. "Okay, fine. I screwed this up. I shouldn't have been rude to her last night. But I like the way her brain works. I want to fix this, talk to her in person. How do I do that? Send her a DM? What do I say?"

Bailey sighed. "I don't know if that's enough, but it's a start."

I opened Noteworthy on my phone. "How about 'I remember you now. Sorry I didn't before,'" I said as I typed.

"Gimme that." Bailey snatched the phone from my hand. "I'll write it. Help me to understand how sorry you are. Show me on your face, and that will help me brand the message."

"Bailey ..."

"Do it, dummy."

"You and your branding."

"This is how I work. The face, Jonah. I need the inspiration."

I thought about AnnieBird walking out with that stiff look on her face, and mine fell.

"Perfect." Bailey snapped a picture.

"Hey, what are you doing?" I reached for the phone, but she held up one hand to ward me off while her thumb darted around, texting.

"There," she said, handing it back. "If that doesn't do it, nothing will."

I snatched it from her and skimmed the message she sent, then went back and read it slower. Beneath a picture of my pathetic-looking face, she'd written, "Anneke/AnnieBird, I'm sorry. I should have recognized the coolest girl on Noteworthy when I saw her in person. Forgive me and let me buy you a drink?"

"Bailey, no."

"Too late." She sounded unconcerned as she went back to the sticker display. "I'm telling you, that will work."

A few minutes later, the app buzzed.

AnnieBird: Just the coolest girl?

LedgeCase: I'm on there too.

AnnieBird: I repeat, just the coolest girl?

LedgeCase: You're going to make me work for this, aren't you?

AnnieBird: Pretty much

LedgeCase: I should have recognized the coolest PERSON on Noteworthy.

AnnieBird: Correct.

LedgeCase: So let me make it up to you with a drink?

AnnieBird: ...

AnnieBird: ...

AnnieBird: …

I watched the screen for a minute. "The typing dots just appeared and disappeared three times."

Bailey shook her head. "Sorry, bro. You're toast."

"There has to be a way to fix this."

"Nope." Bailey fluffed a T-shirt with way too much cheer.

"Bay."

"T-o-a-s-t."

"Baaaaaay. Help me."

She studied my face. "You like her."

"I like AnnieBird."

She gave a short, quick nod. "All right. But you have to let me think."

I kept my mouth shut.

She leaned over a counter to grab a duster and worked her way along the prog rock section. After a couple of minutes, she said, "Stop looking at me. I can't think."

"I'm not looking at you."

"I can feel your eyes."

I turned my back to her, getting the Zeppelin album ready for my customer. I'd been telling the truth about that.

"You have to go to the Turnaround."

"You think she'll be there?"

"No. But I think Miles will be there. And they're obviously friends or at least know each other. And you know Miles."

"Kind of."

"Enough for him to know you're not a psycho. Explain. See if he'll help. Maybe talk to Anneke for you."

I drummed my fingers on the counter and considered this. "I don't like that. I need a better idea."

"It's my only one."

I frowned at her, but the shop door opened just then and Steve, the customer I'd been waiting on, walked in.

"Hey, Jonah," he said. "I'm curious to see what you brought me down here for."

I did this with customers sometimes. It was a gamble, but if I saw something in my online browsing that I thought they would love, I'd ask them to come down to the store for a surprise. It had been Bailey's idea, and customers loved it.

"Hey, Steve. I saw something the other day that you've been wanting for a while, and I grabbed it. You ready for this?"

Steve's eyebrow rose, a glint of curiosity in them. "Sure."

I handed him disinfecting wipes for his hands so he'd know this was serious. It was a shame AnnieBird wouldn't get to see this, but I had a feeling Steve's reaction would be pretty great too.

I set the album in its plain wrapper on the countertop, then slowly began to draw it out. As soon as the first inch was showed with "Led Zeppelin" in turquoise lettering, Steve sucked in a breath, and I couldn't help a small smile. Every record hound knew that feeling. I picked up the pace and set it on the counter.

"This is the UK release. You're kidding," he said, his eyes darting over the cover, looking for signs of wear.

"It's the real deal," I promised.

"This is amazing." He lifted the album between his palms, making sure not to get his fingerprints on it, and examined it for wear and tear. There was always a certain amount with vintage records, but it was in good shape. "I'll take it," he said.

Like a true collector, he didn't ask the price. I smiled. "I thought you might." I rang him up, and he didn't flinch when I gave him a total over $1000 with tax. I packaged it in a sturdy album mailer while his credit card processed, and he practically floated out of the store with it pressed firmly to his side as if he were afraid it would disappear into thin air.

"I can't even imagine having a thousand dollars to drop on a record," Bailey said.

"For hardcore collectors, it doesn't matter," I said. I didn't get to do too many transactions like that. It had only made the store about $200, but it wasn't about that. It was about watching that guy's eyes light up and understanding the magic of finding a piece of music history that shaped you.

Maybe it was the mellow flood of dopamine that made me say it, but I thought again about AnnieBird—Anneke—and tapped the countertop a few times. I'd dismissed Anneke last night because she seemed like she was all wrapper, no package. I'd heard my dad's warning against phony types my whole life—especially the ones who hung around the music business. But AnnieBird was the opposite of phony. At least, online she'd been. And if I'd been my real self online, it was completely possible that she had too.

"All right, Bailey. I'll do it. I'll go talk to Miles at the Turnaround."

She dropped the duster and walked to the counter, leaning on it and fixing me with a satisfied grin. "All right, here's what you're going to say ..."

9
ANNEKE

I walked out of Ledge Records feeling …

I didn't know how I felt. And it bothered me. I'd expected to walk out feeling … smug, honestly. Kind of, "Ha, put you in your place, sucker. Look what you passed up."

Instead, I felt …

More irritated than ever, honestly.

Probably because no one had ever looked so perfectly at home in a record store as Jonah did, slouched behind the counter wearing a Primus T-shirt and a happy smile when he'd realized I was AnnieBird.

And then a confused—almost annoyed—one when I'd told him we'd met before.

Annoyance? How *dare* he?

Except I wasn't even sure what I was mad about. That was the most irritating part.

I stopped by my hotel to check out and rolled my suitcase the two blocks to Miles's place where I let myself in.

"Miles?" There was no answer, so I wandered around a bit, calling his name.

"In here," he finally answered from what sounded like his gym.

I walked in to find him with Ellie. They were both in their workout clothes and sounding short of breath, but I didn't see any evidence of weights in use. I decided not to ask any questions.

"Boys are the worst," I said.

"Try dating men." Miles flexed a bicep.

Ellie grinned. "I should hate that he said that, but I don't."

"Miles is annoying that way," I agreed. "He gets away with way too much because he's charming."

"Let's go to the kitchen," he said. "I need to make recovery shakes anyway."

This made Ellie blush, and I had no doubt why. "You guys are gross."

"Tell us why boys are the worst," Ellie prompted as I trailed them to the kitchen.

"I went to see Jonah at the record store."

"Yes." She did a fist pump as we walked into the kitchen.

"It did not go well."

"Tell us, buddy," Miles said as he pulled protein powder from his pantry.

"Well, I go in there to see how he reacts to the non-glam version of me. He's polite, like I'm any other customer."

"And this makes you angry?" Miles asked.

"Yes."

"Because why?"

"Because it means he's not attracted to her," Ellie explained. "He's seen her decked out and low-key and ..." She shot me a look.

"It's okay, you can say it," I promised. "Neither version worked for him."

"That," she said.

"Then I told him I was AnnieBird, and he got all excited. I mean, practically falling all over himself to say hello."

"But that's good," Miles said. "It means he's attracted to your mind, not your body or your face."

I blinked at him then looked to Ellie for help. "Would you help him understand why it's a problem that Jonah isn't attracted to me?"

But Ellie watched me with a small smile. "Did he suddenly turn on the charm when he realized who you actually are?"

I shrugged. "Yeah."

"And how did that make you feel?"

"I wanted to lean over and yell in his face. But not words. Just a yell."

"Why?"

"I don't know," I said, and it was the most frustrated I'd felt since leaving, but for some reason it made them both laugh.

"You're so messed up, Anneke." Miles dumped protein powder into a blender.

"How am I the messed up one?" I complained. "I hope you forget to put the lid on and your shake gets all over you."

Miles made a production of reaching for the lid and settling it on the blender.

"How did you two even get to be friends, anyway?" Ellie asked. "I can't imagine you two stopping bickering long enough to figure out you like each other."

"We were in this awful article for a magazine called 'Barely Legal Talent,'" I said. Ellie wrinkled her nose. "I know. So gross. But it was a batch of different people who had turned twenty-one that year, and it was a big deal to be invited. Athletes, influencers, actors, models, and music artists." I pointed to myself and Miles on the last two.

"I hated every second of that shoot." Miles scowled like we were there again.

"It was obvious," I told Ellie. "He had a bit of an attitude problem back then. But I liked that he wasn't acting fake like everyone else was, so I plopped down next to him while we were waiting for direction. The concept was a summer pool party with all the cool kids, so everyone was hanging out around a hotel pool trying to act better than everyone else."

"Except Anneke here, who started narrating the scene around us like it was a British wildlife documentary."

I busted out my British accent again. I was good with accents. It was a perk of visiting Europe since I was a kid. "Notice the female in the cheetah print bikini pretending to ignore the running back, distinguished by the racing stripes on his aquatic trunks."

Ellie had just taken a swig from her water bottle, and this prompted a spit take. Even better, it was on Miles, who grimaced and wiped the spray from his face.

"Sorry," she said, coughing and laughing at the same time.

"You see why I decided to hang out with her," he said.

"I do," she agreed. "But how come you guys never dated?"

I pretended to look scandalized. "*Miles?* You didn't tell her about our one magnificent night together?"

Ellie gave me a skeptical look. "I'm not taking the bait."

I grinned. "I like you, Ellie-girl. The truth is, we did go on one real date. It was our first and only. And excuse me for saying so, but I have no idea what you see in this dude. He has a pH of seven."

Miles looked at me blankly, and Ellie smiled. "That's neutral." Then she smiled even wider at me. "Must have used the wrong catalyst."

"Yes and no," I said. "We figured out before the end of one very awkward dinner that we didn't have any romantic chemistry, but we clicked like sugar and yeast as friends. So that's what we became. Only that date got a ton of space on the gossip blogs the next day, so …"

"You did it for the PR," Ellie said. "Got it."

"Yep," I confirmed. "It's allowed each of us to keep our real relationships mostly out of the spotlight. Until you. You guys blew that right up at the club last night."

"Not sorry," Miles said, leaning down to kiss Ellie. "Saves me the trouble of making an official announcement that I'm permanently off the market."

I mentally started picking my best man outfit for their wedding. Unless Ellie wanted me as a bridesmaid, but I sort of liked the idea of rocking a pant suit.

"Here's the thing, Anneke," Miles said, turning to me. "We've been armor for each other, but yours is getting thicker every year. Except for with Erick," he grumbled.

"Erick?" Ellie asked.

"Lead singer for Hyde and Seek. With him, she has no walls. Or like she has them, but they blow up. Explosion-style." He punched the power button on the blender like he was punctuating his point with the noise. "And then this is what's left of her when he goes storming off again." He poured the shake into two cups.

"A delicious and nutritious diet supplement?" I asked.

Ellie wrinkled her nose. "No. These are nasty." She held her breath and chugged.

"A sad, sad pulp of your former self," Miles said. Then he held his breath and chugged too.

"I changed my mind about your relationship," I said. "I'm not on board if you two are going to gang up on me."

"I'll be on your side if you're right," Ellie promised. "But you aren't this time."

"Definitely not," Miles said. "It's not fair to be mad at a guy for writing off Bombshell Anneke. It's even more unfair to be upset with him because he liked you strictly for your personality. You complain constantly about clout-chasers."

"Sounds like Jonah is the opposite," Ellie agreed. "That's a thing, you know. I forget the word for it, but there's a type of person who can't be attracted to a person until they're attracted to their personality. Maybe he's like that."

My mouth dropped slightly as I glanced between them. "How did I end up in the wrong?" I asked. "I invited him out, I introduced myself to him, I tried to make conversation with him, and he blew me off."

"You weren't up front about who you are, and you didn't meet him in person as your real self," Miles pointed out. "Stop complaining."

"Ellie," I whined. She suddenly decided she needed to drink her shake very slowly. "I can see that your glass is empty." She just kept pretending to drink.

"Okay, but how do you explain today?" I demanded.

"You mean today when you went in there as AnnieBird, but you were already mad, and then you stomped out, and he DM-ed and apologized? Did I get that right?"

"It sounds bad when you say it like that."

Miles shook his head and collected Ellie's glass so he could rinse them both.

I sighed. "What do I do? DM him back?"

"It depends on if you still want to get to know him," Ellie said.

I thought about Jonah again, leaning behind the register, as comfortable in his element as my dad was in the vineyards. "He *is* pretty cute."

"She's not as shallow as she sounds," Miles promised Ellie. "She wouldn't be giving this dude the time of day if she didn't like his personality."

"I don't think you're shallow," Ellie said. "But if you still want to get to know him—"

"Apologize," Miles finished. "In person."

"We've both had some experience with that lately," Ellie said.

"Highly recommend," Miles added. He slipped his arm around Ellie's waist and pulled her against his side to smile down at her.

"You guys make me want to throw up," I said. "I'm going up to my room."

"Y'all," Ellie called after me.

I stopped at the doorway. "What?"

"You're in Louisiana now. No you guys. The plural for a group of people is y'all."

"Y'all are ridiculous," I called over my shoulder on the way out, and their laughter followed me to my room.

Apologize to Jonah when he'd been rude to me multiple times last night?

As. Freaking. If.

10
JONAH

I thought that I was having a good day. I'd gotten a phone call that morning I could barely believe, and I'd been floating on it all day, too high on the buzz of it to even eat lunch. I thought I was having a day that could not get any better.

But the door to the shop swished open, letting in a small billow of late afternoon humidity and early spring heat.

A sandaled foot at the end of a long, smooth leg stepped in, followed by the tall, lithe form of Anneke.

I blinked. I hadn't expected to see her here again, but there she was. Bailey took one glance at her and found something to do at the far end of the store.

"Hi," Anneke said.

"Hey." I tried to think of something to add but I couldn't. I'd been planning to stop in at the Turnaround after the store closed today to see if I could catch Miles, but even then, it wasn't a sure bet that I'd be able to track her down. "You're here."

A brilliant observation. Especially from a guy who had been anything but observant in her presence.

"Yeah."

She didn't say anything else, and I hadn't thought as far as what I would say if I found her. I was just trying to get to the "find her" part.

"Sorry again about not—"

"I owe you an apolo—"

We both spoke at once and stopped. I frowned at her, confused. "I'm pretty sure I'm the one who owes you an apology here. I was rude the other night. There's really no excuse for it except …"

"Except what?" she asked, her expression curious.

I thought you were fake, and I hate fakes. Yeah, that wasn't coming out of my mouth. "I don't love crowds?"

"Is that a question?" she asked.

"No." I sighed. "I'm sorry. That's all. No excuses. I'm sorry."

"Oh."

We blinked at each other, and I wished for the easiness of Noteworthy, where there was no such thing as awkward silences.

I tucked my hair behind my ear, realizing I probably needed to get it cut. It was getting in my eyes a lot. "So what brings you in today?"

"I'm here to apologize too," she said. "I was being dramatic yesterday. Sorry. Shouldn't have come in and made a scene. I was raised better than that."

"That was a scene?" I asked. I'm not sure anyone besides Bailey and I had noticed our interaction.

"It was kind of like hanging up on you except in person."

"No big deal."

She side-eyed me. "Also, I basically said 'Don't you know who I am,' words that I swore would never come out of my mouth after I heard a co-worker say it to a server who wouldn't serve her drinks when we were underage."

I considered that and nodded. "You're right. Very dramatic. It's good you came back to apologize."

Her lips twitched at that. Suddenly I very much wanted to see the electric smile that showed in a handful of her Instagram photos yesterday. They were mostly in her candid shots. In high fashion, apparently, she had to look serious.

"If I make a good enough apology, can I see the Led Zeppelin album?" she asked.

I was already shaking my head. "My buyer came in and got it."

Her face fell, and I was annoyed with myself for pushing her in the other direction. How to get back to a smile? I snapped my fingers. "I do have something else though. I know you're not a grunge fan, but do you want to see one of Nirvana's original concert posters designed by Frank Kozik? I have a buyer coming in soon, but we have time to look at it."

"That sounds cool," she said.

"Come back to the office. Bay, take the register, please?" She was already heading our direction.

I came out from behind the counter and led Anneke to the office.

She stopped in the doorway. "Can I ask you a question?"

"Sure," I said, pausing at my desk and half-turning to face her.

"Are you showing this to me because you know I'm a big deal model now?"

"I *don't* know that. I only have your word and Bailey's to go on, and Bailey is studying marketing, so she's getting a degree in lying."

"I can hear you, dill weed," she called from the register.

Anneke and I grinned at the same time.

"Anyway, no, that's not why I'm showing you this," I said, reaching for the poster.

"Then why?"

"Because you're a music nerd, and every music nerd deserves to see this kind of music history, even if it's not your favorite genre." I opened the frame and lifted the backing out so she could see the poster with its wear and tear. "Frank Kozik was the go-to guy for alternative bands in the nineties," I said, turning the poster over so she could see it. She stepped closer and leaned in to study it, careful not to touch it. "He mainly did screen prints. A lot of people collect original concert posters, and like everything, the better the condition, the more valuable they are. But I like these kinds the best."

I pointed to some of the wear and fading, a two-inch tear in the corner, a couple of blurred bits. "This was the last hurrah of concert posters being posted outside. Now they're produced for the merch tables, so I like it when I find one that lived its full life, out in the elements, smudged by rain, wrinkly from getting dried out in the sun. It's cool."

She leaned closer, smiling at the bright colors and bubble letters before she straightened. "If I admit that this is cool, it doesn't mean that I'm going to like Nirvana any more than I did the last time we argued about them."

"Noted."

"Fine. This is cool." And she broke into a big grin, the one that was so rare in her public photos and, no lie, my knees went weak. "Can I touch it?"

"Sure." I knew I didn't have to tell her to be careful. The fact that she'd asked before touching showed that she understood she was essentially dealing with an artifact.

"Do I need gloves or something?"

I smiled. Only true music nerds asked that, like they were about to handle something sacred. "No. It's not nearly as valuable as, like, a diamond bra."

Her head flew up, and her eyes narrowed. "I guess you do know who I am."

A supermodel who had strutted down a primetime runway in a jewel-encrusted bra for the most famous lingerie brand on the planet? "I may have googled you."

She returned to the poster. "I'm not really that," she muttered.

I knew what she meant. That she was her public image. But I wasn't exactly sure she was AnnieBird either. Maybe she changed personas like she did outfits for the runway. Or maybe the real Anneke lay somewhere in the middle. But I wasn't sure I was in a place to find out. I had a feeling she didn't let people in too easily, and I'd seen enough of her "show biz" persona to feel every warning my dad had ever given me about how fame changes people. He'd tried to tell me about Maggie, and I hadn't listened. I'd gotten burned.

I reached for the frame to indicate that I was ready to put it back together, and Anneke backed up to the doorway.

"Thanks for letting me look at it," she said.

"No problem."

"I should go."

"Thanks for stopping in." I tried to think of another reason to keep her here.

I glanced up as she turned to leave and caught the way her eyes lingered on the frame with a trace of longing and wonder. It made my breath go still for a second, but I recognized that feeling in the tiny glimmer before she pulled on a friendly smile and waved goodbye. I'd felt the same sense of wonder when my dad brought me to the studio when I was nine to meet Dr. John, and I couldn't believe that I was standing in the presence of the man who had played on the records I'd listened to countless times.

Could someone who had that capacity for wonder be the kind of phony my dad had always warned us against? I finished putting the poster back together, playing her expression in my mind a few times.

Then I raced out of the office as Bailey was coming in with a scowl on her face. She yelped as I bounced off of her.

"Sorry," I called, heading for the door. "Be right back."

"You better be going after her, Jonah Martin Collier," she hollered. "You *dummy*."

I was. I pushed through the shop door and looked both ways on the street, spotting her about fifty yards up Claiborne. "Anneke?"

She stopped and turned.

"Who was in the shop today? Anneke or AnnieBird?"

She hesitated before answering, and then her face grew tight. "They're the same."

I considered that and gave a slow shake of my head. "I get the feeling they aren't."

She walked a few steps back toward me. "That was regular Anneke, not the supermodel," she answered.

I walked up the sidewalk toward her. Now only about ten yards separated us, and we didn't have to raise our voices anymore.

"Would AnnieBird like to stop in next week, Monday night after closing, for a very special signing?" This was about the call that morning, and I'd been sworn to secrecy. I couldn't even tell Bailey, because she wouldn't be able to resist turning it into a marketing opportunity.

Anneke eyed me, considering, and I got the feeling that it wasn't just about whether she wanted to come back Monday but whether she planned to come back ever.

"Who is it?" she asked.

"Even Bailey doesn't know. I'm not supposed to tell a single soul.

But ..." I checked around to see if anyone was listening to our conversation. Doubtful, but this could *not* get out. "If you were to guess it was the reclusive front man of your all-time favorite band, you wouldn't be wrong."

Her eyes widened, and her mouth formed a shocked, soundless O.

I nodded. "If you see AnnieBird, let her know to stop in around 7:00."

"Is this for real?" she demanded.

"I don't know what you're talking about." I shrugged and turned back toward the store, smiling. If ever someone deserved to meet her hero, it was the woman who'd looked at a tattered old concert poster from a band she underrated with something approaching reverence.

"Jonah," she called when I was nearly back to the store. "Ledge Records. That's where you got the name, isn't it? From their fifth album."

"I can't believe you're only now figuring that out."

We'd talked before about how we both had the same favorite band, a late-eighties alternative rock band. When I'd taken over the store, I'd changed the name of the store to the title of their best song. My Noteworthy screen name too.

I gave her a last wave and slipped back inside, grinning at the look on her face. The wonder was back, and I understood why companies were paying her millions for it. It was pure magic, and I was already verging on addiction.

11
ANNEKE

I continued up Claiborne toward Robertson. There was a boutique I wanted to check out. Or, at least, that was the excuse I'd given myself to head over to the Seventh Ward which also happened to be where Ledge Records was.

Despite Miles and Ellie and their badgering, I still hadn't been sure I was going to stop in. And when my feet took me through the door, I still had every intention of writing Jonah off after apologizing. He was one of those hardcore hipster types, so determined not to be mainstream that they became more pretentious than the people they looked down on for being pretentious.

I'd meant to pop in, say sorry, and leave the record store in my rearview mirror.

Uh, my metaphorical one. I'd been getting most places on foot, but I was going to have to look into keeping a bike at Miles's house for when I came to visit. Or making him let me borrow his classic Mustang. So far, he hadn't bought the argument that I made it look better than he did, but I'd wear him down eventually, because even for someone who didn't know much about cars, I knew that car was sexy.

But here I was, having apologized like a big girl—with a small ego—and leaving somehow with an appointment to go back? What, even?

It wasn't like I was going to say no to meeting the lead singer of my favorite band ever since I discovered one of their old records in my uncle's collection. The Placemats had reached their peak in the late eighties in Minneapolis, one of the pioneers of alternative rock. They'd broken up a few years before I was born, but I'd been obsessed since I first heard them.

How wild was it that the lead singer, Saul Vandenburg, was coming to Jonah's store to sign an album?

On the one hand, totally nuts. He'd lain low since 2015, the last time the band had performed together. And Minneapolis was a long way away from New Orleans.

On the other hand, when I thought about songs like "Jazz Club Jitters," there had been a clear interest in the lounge jazz sound. Why wouldn't Saul Vandenburg find his way to New Orleans? New Orleans was a music Mecca.

I skipped a little, hurrying toward home. Or Miles's house, anyway. I had to be in New York for a magazine shoot tomorrow, but I'd make it back in time for Saul Vandenburg.

I pulled out my phone and opened Noteworthy.

AnnieBird: Just to be clear, we're talking about Saul Vandenburg from the Placemats, right?
LedgeCase: I didn't say that. I would never say that after the lead singer of your favorite band called and said he'd stop in to sign a couple of albums if I swore to keep it completely secret until he was gone.
AnnieBird: I'm kind of freaking out. I AM DEFINITELY FREAKING OUT.
LedgeCase: ME TOO
AnnieBird: Does this happen often?
LedgeCase: Rock icons calling me up and telling me they want to drop by?
AnnieBird: Yes.
LedgeCase: Sometimes. Sometimes they just show up, and I would never know if they didn't introduce themselves when they're buying old records. But it's awesome every time.

I liked that he wasn't playing it cool. But then, I would have expected

Jonah to, not LedgeCase. LedgeCase had always been as unapologetically nerdy about this kind of stuff as I had in our DMs. I realized he'd shown a ton of restraint by not bragging about how many amazing musicians he'd met.

Kind of the opposite of pretentious.

And the reality was, I hadn't namedropped either, even though I ran into a lot of artists at parties or Miles's house. But it was hard to slip those names into conversation without sounding like a humblebrag, so I didn't. And I definitely never brought up that I had dated the lead singer to one of LedgeCase—Jonah's—favorite bands, off and on.

Off now for sure, though.

I liked how both Erick and Jonah had the same obsession with music, often spent time around the same kind of people, but with Erick, it was the first thing he liked people to know about him, and with Jonah, I might have never known if I hadn't point-blank asked.

Often, when I'd been out with Erick, he'd introduce me to people and say things like, "This is my girl, Anneke. You should check out her cover shoot on *Style Icon* last month." I'd always tell him not to do stuff like that, but he'd wave it off and be like, "I'm proud of my girl, that's all."

Nah. He wanted to brag that his girl was a cover model. *That* was all.

And then there was Jonah, who seemed to think my modeling was the least interesting thing about me.

AnnieBird: Hey, would you want to come hang out with me and some friends tomorrow? Low-key at home thing. I have to fly out in the afternoon, but maybe breakfast?

His activity icon showed that he was on, but there was no action on his end for a few minutes. Then, just when I was sure he was going to blow me off again, he answered.

LedgeCase: That sounds cool. Just tell me when and where.

A cheesy grin crept over my face, and I sent him Miles's address and the time. I knew Miles wouldn't care. If anything, he'd be annoyingly smug about me taking his advice.

He'd already left for the Turnaround by the time I got back, so I texted him that Jonah was coming for breakfast. He sent me a side-eye emoji.

I rolled my own eyes.

Anneke: I mean he's coming over in the morning. Breakfast IS the date, not an after-date.

Then I went to work making sure Miles had what I needed for cooking in the morning, hit the gym, and stayed up way too late listening to Placemats albums.

In the morning, I showered and got down to the kitchen early, getting everything chopped and prepped so it would be ready to go when Jonah arrived.

Ellie showed up first, letting herself in and calling, "Hello," to warn me she wasn't a random tourist.

"In the kitchen," I called back. "Miles isn't up yet," I informed her when she walked in. "He got back late."

She slid onto a barstool to watch me. "We're going to have to get creative with our scheduling. We're on opposite schedules. I finish work at five, and he's just getting started."

"Are you worried?"

She shook her head. "No. We're both committed to figuring it out. The club schedule is just new. It helps that I live right above it, though. He can run up to hang out for an hour here and there, depending on what's going on at the club."

"That's true," I said. "I like you guys together. I mean, y'all."

"Me too." She gave me a soft smile, her mind clearly already drifting to Miles. "Need any help?"

"Nope, I've got it." The doorbell rang, and a bolt of nervous energy shot through me.

"Is that Jonah?" she asked. "I can go let him in."

"That would be great," I said. "It'll give me a minute to figure out how to stand here looking both alluring and totally natural."

She laughed and headed down to the front door. I listened to the murmur of her voice and Jonah's deeper one as she led him back up to the kitchen, telling him the history of the house as she did. She was a real estate agent. Even though her specialty was business properties, it made sense she would have retained all the history of this place.

"Jonah's here." She stepped into the kitchen with him on her heels.

He had left off his beanie, and I liked it. He hadn't been wearing it yesterday either, and it was the first chance I'd had to study him that way. Today, his longish hair looked shower-fresh with faint comb marks. It looked like he meant to keep it shorter but hadn't gotten around to it, and now his dark brown locks were shaggy, but not in a lank, gross way. If anything, his hair looked soft, and I wanted to touch it to see as it hung around his ears and bunched on his collar.

That was the second surprise. He'd ditched his usual band T-shirt for a button-down with pearl snaps and a faded paisley print. Thrifted, probably. Designers charged a lot for that effortlessly cool look, but when guys wore them, you could tell they wanted you to know it was a five hundred dollar shirt. I had a feeling Jonah had probably paid five bucks max for it, and he still looked like a million bucks.

"Hey," I said, smiling at him. Shyness I wasn't used to crept over me, and I tried not to let it show. This was new ground for us—meeting as our Noteworthy selves. But that was my truest self, and while I was always at home in that skin with Miles, it wasn't often that I let other people see it. *You're on your turf*, I reminded myself when a buzz started along my nerves. *You've got the control here.*

"I thought we could eat some breakfast and hang out while you tell me about all the incognito musicians who've come into Ledge Records," I said.

"So I'm here as the entertainment," he said, his smile growing slightly wider.

"I make a good breakfast," I told him. "You have to earn it somehow."

"What are we having?"

"Frittata. I'm obsessed."

"A frittata good enough for me to risk looking like a tool while I name drop?" He shook his head. "I don't know."

"I hereby decree this a safe space to name drop," Ellie said, making some sort of sign in the air. "You're both allowed to say who you know, and we promise not to think it's bragging."

"Was that the sign of the cross?" I wrinkled my nose at her. "I don't think you did it right."

"No. I didn't want to be sacrilegious, so I made a fleur-de-lis." She traced the shape of the symbol that adorned the city, from the uniforms of the NFL team to the street signs.

"Good call," Jonah said. "It's practically a religious symbol anyway. All right, if I have douchebag immunity *and* you're promising an excellent frittata, I'm in."

"Better than excellent," I reassured him. "Trust me, I make this for Miles all the time, and I know how picky Louisiana people are about their food."

"So this is his place?" he asked, sliding onto a stool next to Ellie.

"Yep."

"And you're staying here?" He sounded curious, not judgmental.

"Also yep."

"And no, I don't care," Ellie said. "In fact, when Miles and I got back together, she checked into a hotel, and I made her come back here to the guest room he has for her."

"Have you been here often?" he asked. "I still can't believe we've been having all these debates on Noteworthy, and we could have just been fighting over poboys in person."

"A poboy is a sandwich," Ellie clarified for me.

"I knew that one, actually. Miles complains that he can't get a good sandwich in LA, but honestly, if you can't find good food in LA, you're just not trying."

"It could be a good sandwich, but when you want a poboy, you really just need a poboy," Ellie explained.

Jonah held up his hand for a high-five from her. "Truth."

"I'll take your word for it, but this is my first visit, so tell me where I should get a poboy."

"You don't have to. I'll take you to get the best poboy in town at Mahony's."

"Domilise's," Ellie said at the same time.

"Whoa, I mean, that's a classic, but the *best*?" Jonah shook his head. "No way."

They debated for a couple of minutes while I whisked eggs and listened, enjoying their back and forth. "You guys sound like LA people arguing over the best sushi."

The creak of floorboards indicated Miles's imminent arrival, and sure enough, he popped into the kitchen in a pair of joggers, Wonderfest T-shirt, and serious bedhead.

"Best poboys in New Orleans," Ellie said.

"Parkway," he answered, which prompted both Ellie and Jonah to boo him.

"Uh, welcome to my house?" Miles said to Jonah.

"Jonah, Miles. Miles, Jonah," I said.

"We've met," Miles said, with a relaxed smile and a "what's up" head nod, and I remembered him mentioning having gone into Ledge Records a couple of times.

"I still probably should have said hey before I booed you," Jonah said. "Sorry about that. Hey."

"You were right to boo him. Parkway Tavern? You fancy," Ellie said with an eye roll for Jonah's benefit.

"Get in anything good at the store lately?" Miles asked.

Jonah and I exchanged a smile that felt like we were keeping the best secret, because we were. Jonah kept the secret by deflecting. "We're getting some pretty cool albums for Record Store Day."

"I love Record Store Day," Miles said.

"What is it?" Ellie asked.

"It's a twice-a-year thing in April and on Black Friday at indie record stores. Artists do special releases that you can only get in a brick-and-mortar indie store on that day. It's pretty wild," Jonah said. "Long lines and wristbands and customer limits, depending on what the releases are. I have to hire all my cousins for the morning to manage crowd control."

"I got my Nancy Wilson album at the last Record Store Day," I told him. "It's my prize possession."

"That's a good one," he said.

"So what do you have coming in?" Miles asked.

Jonah named a few which led to a long discussion on the merits of different singer-songwriters while I poured the frittata into a baking dish.

"I really want to hear the Natalie Blue album," Miles said.

"No kidding. I heard she's working with Gavin Mercer for that one, and I'm interested to see what he does with her sound."

"I don't know if I'm a Mercer fan," Miles said. "He messed with Three Penny Four's sound too much."

"I can see that." Jonah nodded. "Too over compressed and muddy."

I blinked at Jonah whose cheeks turned slightly ruddy. Miles's gaze sharpened. "That sounds like more than a casual fan talking," he said. "You have a background in music?"

"I don't play," Jonah answered.

"That wasn't the question," Miles said. "But I'll be more specific. You mess around with producing?"

Jonah hesitated before giving a short nod. "I have."

"Want to come see my studio?" Miles asked.

Jonah's eyes widened slightly, and I jumped in. "This has to bake for thirty minutes. Go check it out." He looked tempted for a minute before he shifted his expression back to neutral and bit back what he was about to say.

I smiled at him. "If you're about to pass because you're here as my guest, don't worry. I'll be tagging along."

"Let's do it," Miles said, already heading out of the kitchen.

"I can't play," Ellie said. "I only wanted to pop in and say good morning before my first client."

Miles groaned. "I want to hang out. Can I come with you?"

"No. I need them to tell me what they need, not spend the whole time impressing you."

"Fiiiiiiine. I'll walk you out."

When they left, I smiled at Jonah across the counter. "Fame doesn't impress you, does it?"

"I don't know how to answer that." He wore a guarded expression, like I set a trap for him.

"Why not? It's a yes or no question, pretty much."

"No one's going to say yes to that, are they?"

"True. I'll rephrase the question. Why aren't you impressed by fame? Because even people who say they aren't are trying to play it cool. I think you might actually not care."

"I don't," he admitted. "But it's a hard question to answer when you're talking to one famous person in another famous person's kitchen."

"And yet I want to know."

Miles reappeared and saved him. "Ready for a studio tour?"

I'd get Jonah's answer out of him later, because I was super curious now, but I let it drop for the moment as we trailed him down to the studio. I'd spent lots of time in Miles's studio at his LA house before he sold it and down-sized when he decided to move here. He kept a townhome as a crash pad for his LA trips, but it didn't have a studio. He had enough music friends to use theirs if the need to record overcame him while he was in town.

For the next twenty minutes, I sat on a stool in the corner and tried not to laugh as they got deeply technical about the equipment. I was less interested in all the soundboard switches than I was in the final product, but this was like listening to my two older brothers get deep and nerdy about the Dutch Eredivisie football teams.

"So what would you do here?" Miles asked, playing a song I hadn't heard.

"Is that a new one of yours?" I asked.

"Maybe. If I can dial in the sound."

Jonah's forehead furrowed. "Play it through the chorus one more time?" he asked.

Miles obliged, and Jonah closed his eyes, his head tilted slightly toward the ceiling. "You need to notch filer and slightly compress the vocals on the chorus. Can I …" He reached toward the soundboard but didn't touch it until Miles nodded. "Headphones?" Miles handed him a pair, which he jacked in, listened hard, then made adjustments on the soundboard.

Miles's eyebrows rose a couple of times when Jonah reached for specific switches before he sat back.

"I think this is how I'd go," Jonah said, removing the headphones and resting them around his neck.

My breath hitched. It was the strangest thing. Such a simple gesture, but he did it with the air of someone who was perfectly at home doing what he was doing. I was always drawn to that, no matter who it was and what the action was. Skill. Confidence. It mesmerized me. A potter working at her wheel. My dad in the vineyard. Miles at his keyboard. A world-class photographer behind the camera.

But it made Jonah, the scruffy but cute guy from the record store, suddenly sexy. Like, I wanted to sidle over, slide into his lap, and have us each listen to one half of the headphones while we stared meaningfully into each other's eyes. And then he could kiss me with the same concentration he was focusing on the music. And I would no doubt puddle at his feet.

Well, that came out of nowhere.

For sure, I'd found him interesting before I ever saw his face. And then when I stumbled across his real identity, I'd decided he was definitely cute. But it had been more about the *potential* for attraction. This? Watching him suddenly dominate a space? That had shoved me into full-blown craving. I sat on my hands to make sure I stayed where I was.

While I was having this inconvenient lightning bolt moment, Jonah was acting as if the earth hadn't shaken, his hand barely having reached the play switch while my world tilted slightly.

Miles's song played back through the speakers, but this time there was a closeness to it, like Jonah had put Miles's voice right in my head. I wasn't totally sure what he had done, but the vibe had changed from anonymous to intimate.

Miles nodded a couple of times, a smile creeping over his face, until Jonah stopped the recording after the first chorus.

Jonah shrugged. "That's what I'd do."

Miles gave him a sharp look. "You're not new to this."

Jonah shook his head but didn't add anything.

"I like it. A lot," Miles added.

Jonah looked ... I tried to assess what I was seeing. He looked unsurprised, but not in a cocky way. More like he was acknowledging the assessment and validating *Miles*, not the other way around.

I wanted to ask questions, but I wasn't sure what. The whole point of subtext was that it was there for people who understood it and not meant for people who didn't get it. I was excluded from this silent exchange between them, but not in a mean way. In the way that a non-expert was shut out from a conversation between experts.

"Frittata is about done," I said, reluctant to break up whatever moment they were having. I liked it when people I liked also liked each other. But I also liked to feed people I liked and for my frittatas not to overcook. I headed for the studio door, and they rustled behind me as they rose to follow.

Miles waved Jonah onto a stool in the kitchen and grabbed some plates. I pulled the frittata from the oven and set it on a trivet between them. "Let it cool a couple of minutes," I ordered, then whipped up a quick omelet for myself while they talked about technical-sounding music studio equipment. I slid it onto my own plate and took a stool next to Jonah. "Dig in, boys."

"You're not having frittata?" Jonah asked in surprise.

"Can't. I made yours with all the good stuff. Cream and cheese and bacon. I have to keep it tight for work, so just an egg white omelet with fresh veggies for me."

"That's …" Jonah trailed off. "Well, now I'm going to feel guilty if I eat this."

"Don't," I told him. "I'm used to it. And here's a secret: every year, I take a two-week summer food vacation, and I make up for it all then. I pick a place or a couple of places and fully embrace the food culture there. Sometimes it's a staycation, and I eat my way through LA, trying all the dishes I didn't let myself have but wanted to. Sometimes I'll hit Italy or a different region in France. Sometimes I go up to Napa where my parents are and explore all the places around there. Since we do most of our swimsuit shoots in winter and early spring, I can get away with eating like a queen for two weeks straight in the summer, because that's when I'm doing sweater and coat shoots."

A funny look crossed his face, and I winced. "Sorry. That sounds privileged."

"It's not that," he said. "I mean, yes, it does, but I don't begrudge it or whatever."

"So what was the face you made?"

"Pure jealousy. It's the downside to owning my own business. The vacation plan sucks."

"But you get to be your own boss," I said. "That must be cool."

He made another face. "When you have customers, you're never *really* your own boss. But yeah, there are perks. Like telling the worst customers to leave."

Miles busted out laughing. "That's not what I expect a store owner to say."

"There're other perks too," Jonah said, smiling at me. "I can eat whatever I want."

"Don't gloat too hard," I told him. "I let myself have cheat meals a couple of times a month when I can work them around jobs. And anyway, I might enjoy watching people eat my food even more than I like eating it myself."

"That's your cue," Miles said. "Trust me, you won't be sorry."

Jonah took a bite of his frittata, and his eyes half-closed. "I think I'm having a religious experience.

I grinned, feeling his pleasure all the way down to my toes. "That's what a week with a *nonna* in Bologna will teach you." I stopped, registering the sound of my words. "If that's not a kid's picture book yet, someone should make it one."

We finished the rest of breakfast with more jokes, mostly from me and Miles. Jonah didn't say much, but he cracked plenty of smiles. I was coming to understand that Jonah wasn't a big talker, and that was okay. After Erick—who shared all his thoughts like they deserved the weight of proclamation—it was nice to hang out with someone who didn't feel like he needed to speak up all the time.

"I should go," Jonah said, sliding from his stool to carry his empty breakfast plate to the sink. "I need to open the store."

"I'll take care of that." Miles took the plate from him and began rinsing it.

Jonah gave a small shake of his head.

"What?" I asked, catching a bemused smile on his face.

"Just didn't expect to see platinum artists doing their own dishes."

"Stars: they're just like us," Miles and I said on cue, and that made Jonah laugh.

"We grocery shop, drive our own cars, and make our own doctor's appointments too," I told him.

"But we definitely don't brush our own teeth," Miles said. "We have people for that."

"Ditto taking our own flights. We have people who do that too."

"You might be delegating the wrong things," Jonah said.

"Nah," Miles said. "You get a 'How to Be Famous' handbook as soon as you get famous, and we follow that."

"I hate you both a little bit right now," Jonah said.

"Now *that* sounds about right," I said, grinning. "Get out of here so I can pack and catch my plane."

His half-smile appeared again, and I decided it was my favorite of his looks, but that smile lurked in his eyes too. It made him look like he was enjoying a delicious secret, and I wanted in on the joke every time I saw it, even though I'd *been* the joke at least half the times I'd seen that smile so far.

At the door, he stopped and turned, and I thought—hoped—he was going to reach out for a goodbye hug—at *least*—but he only said, "See you next week for Saul." Then he slipped out and was gone.

I collapsed against the door and closed my eyes, reviewing the highlights of his visit. The half-smiles. The way he'd come to life in the studio—not like when my inner party hostess turned on for social events, but like I felt when I was doing stuff for my passion projects. The way he'd savored my frittata.

Um, not a euphemism.

But who didn't love being appreciated for their cooking?

"He's into you."

I opened my eyes to look up at Miles who was leaning on the banister and smiling down. "You think?"

He nodded. "Surprised you didn't pick up on that. You read guys pretty well."

I pushed away from the door and climbed the stairs. "Normally, yes. Jonah's different. Doesn't help that I met him as two different people, and he only liked one of them."

Miles's lips twisted. "He seems to be coming around to your reality in the flesh."

"It's kind of a weird problem."

"Not for most people."

I rolled my eyes. "Don't sit there and act like this is a thing you've dealt with."

"I did just go through a whole thing with Ellie hating my guts on sight for a while."

"True," I murmured. "But anyway, I think I like Jonah too. He's prickly but not in a diva way. Also, why do all the negative words for fragile egos have to be lady words? Sexist much, English?"

Miles looked like he was trying to untangle my thought trail. "Diva is a word for someone with a fragile ego, and a diva is a woman, so English is sexist?"

"Obviously."

"Except diva is an Italian word, and you could have just said divo."

"Don't you go screwing up my feminist rants with conjugation."

"It's not conju—"

"Stahhhhhhp."

"You could have called him cocky. Or an egomaniac."

I glared at him as I reached the top of the stairs. "So weird that the first word I reached for to describe a difficult personality was singing-related, hm?"

Miles grinned and headed back toward the kitchen. "Get packed, and I'll drive you to the airport. It's a new service. Divo Drivers."

I packed light—I always did—fitting three days' worth of stuff in an overnight bag with room to spare. I'd be flying from New York back to LA to pack another suitcase since I was camping at Miles's house longer than I expected. I'd barely scratched the surface of New Orleans, and I planned to settle in for a couple more weeks to explore.

I'd be back in New Orleans in five days, but it felt three times as long when I measured it in impatience. To explore more of the city. And meet Saul Vandenburg.

And yeah, to see Jonah.

12
JONAH

Bailey had dragged me onto Instagram kicking and screaming, my fingers leaving horrific claw marks in the walls of my social media hermit hole.

But for the next five days, I don't think she could have dragged me *off* it. Specifically, Anneke's Instagram. She only posted once a day, but never at the same time, and I refreshed her feed like I was one of the poor saps glued to the casino's slot machines when they should be at Gambler's Anonymous. And for extra stupid points, even after she posted each day, I *still* kept refreshing in case she decided to post twice in a day.

They were curated shots, a picture of her standing beneath an electronic billboard in Times Square, her eyes wide, mouth rounded as she pointed at the photo of herself on the billboard. It was a lipstick ad, her top teeth biting her bottom lip, and it made me want to do the same thing.

Wait, what? Calm down, Jonah.

Another day, it was a selfie in a makeup mirror, her makeup done but at least three different people working on her hair as it hung or sprouted from different parts of her head.

By day four, she was clearly back in LA, this time sitting on a balcony, meditation style, in soft-looking pants and a tank top. The picture was shot from behind, looking out through the railing at the ocean not too far away over some rooftops.

Who had taken the shot? Did she put it on a timer? Was it a roommate? Had she mentioned a roommate?

Why did I care?

My list of questions was never-ending.

The thing was, we were DM-ing on Noteworthy too. She'd sent me a gif of a woman on a talk show swooning and slipping out of her chair, captioning it, "When I see Saul Vandenburg." We'd argued about why she was wrong about The Ramones (they were *not* good) and agreed that the new release from The Weather Station was the best album of the year so far.

It wasn't super hard to profile people on their music tastes. The majority of our most loyal customers at Ledge were middle-aged and older men who only liked new stuff if it a) came from bands who had been around for twenty or more years or b) sounded like it could have come from a band that was around twenty years ago. Every now and then, we got hardcore hipsters who liked getting new bands on vinyl. And, of course, in New Orleans especially, we had jazz fans who came in for everything from rare editions of old stuff to brand new pressings from upstart artists.

Anneke fit none of those categories. The one constant with her taste was that she preferred stripped-down sounds, but it didn't matter to her if it was folk, rock, or singer-songwriter. She didn't like anything that was in the realm of synth pop and had a visceral loathing for New Wave music and electronica. She was also not a big fan of EDM which surprised me most now that I knew what her job was. I sort of figured since electronic dance music was big in major party cities—Miami, Vegas, LA—that it would be her soundtrack, in a way. But nope.

I wasn't sure what that told me about her yet, but I wanted to spend more time with her, collect more clues and see how everything fit together.

Finally, on the day she'd said she was flying back, she posted a picture of a pair of feet in scuffed Vans propped on an airport seat. She'd titled it, "Flying incognito." Or at least, I assumed it was an airport chair. It looked a lot nicer than chairs I'd ever sat in at an airport. She was probably in one of the elite customer lounges.

Seeing that post come in late that night sent me to bed with a smile on my face and an even bigger one when I woke up. I sent her a DM with a gif of the dorky kid on *The Breakfast Club* sliding on a pair of sunglasses and trying to act cool. I captioned it, "When I see Saul Vandenburg."

Now it was Saul Vandenburg day. And Anneke's back-in-town day. And maybe those two feelings were bleeding together and that's what was making me so hyped to see her.

That and flashbacks to that damn lipstick billboard. I thought about asking Bailey how many times was too many to look at an Instagram picture but decided not to incriminate myself.

Saul was due in right after the store closed at seven. I told Anneke to come at six, and I wondered which version of her I should expect. Would she be the supermodel to impress her rock idol? Or low-key AnnieBird who cooked frittatas barefoot and didn't look like she'd even know what to do with false eyelashes?

She walked in right on the dot, and it was AnnieBird. "Hey," she said, and I noticed she'd dropped the "Hi." She was adapting to our New Orleans ways.

I smiled at her. "Hey. Welcome back. Have a good trip?"

She shrugged. "It was work. Which means it was whatever."

I tried not to stare too openly while drinking her in. She wore jeans, a gauzy white shirt, and leather sandals. The single braid in her hair made it look like it had all different kinds of blonde in the twisted strands.

"Hey, Anneke," Bailey said, her voice chill, like we got supermodels in here every day. "Jonah, I've been thinking about how to market this Saul thing. After he leaves," she said, holding up a hand to cut off my objection. "I mean market the signed albums."

"I'll email a few customers and offer it to them."

"That's great customer service but not great marketing," she said. "Your diehard customers aren't going anywhere. If you want to turn this place around, you need to find new customers."

Great, Bailey, I thought. *Please do let Anneke know that my store is struggling. Awesome.*

Anneke's eyebrow rose, but she didn't say anything.

"What are you thinking, Bay?" It was better to let her get it out. I hadn't figured out yet how to deter her. Ever.

"We have to position you," she said. "Really carve out your niche."

"I'm the only record store in New Orleans. I'm as niche as it gets."

"Yeah, but vinyl is exploding right now. I was reading that pressing plants can't even keep up with demand right now. You should be thriving, but you're competing with all kinds of online sellers. You have to offer something they can't."

I gave her a look.

"Quit doubting me," she said.

"I didn't say anything."

"Your face said it. So, think, Jonah. What can Ledge Records offer music nerds that online shopping can't?"

"An actual store, obviously."

"Think bigger," she said. "You can offer an *experience*."

"You *are* kind of a unique experience," Anneke added.

I narrowed my eyes at her. "Did you compliment or insult me?"

She gave me a serene smile I would have expected to see on her face if that yoga-pose-facing-the-beach picture had been shot from the front. "It's an observation. A statement of fact."

"It's not just you, although you are definitely an experience," Bailey said. "It's everything about this place. The vibe of it."

I glanced around the store. I'd put my own stamp on it since my dad's heart attack, but I wasn't striving for any particular vibe. I just put things up I liked. Flyers for local bands covered the walls on either side of the front door. My dad had put up old concert posters from shows he'd played plus interesting ones he'd run across over the years. I'd mixed in a few of my old concert shirts for bands I'd seen but didn't necessarily listen to anymore. Glossy band posters filled in the rest.

My mom had "swagged" fabrics she liked (her word) in different spots around the store that she said needed "warmth." This was not a temperature thing, which she explained after she laughed at me when I told her it was always too warm in the shop already. A few framed photos—cheap prints of iconic moments in music history—hung on the walls here and there.

"You don't get the record store smell when you shop on Discogs," Bailey said. "Or a walking music encyclopedia to nerd out on this stuff with them while they browse. Or suggest a better album if they bring a lame one up to the counter." She turned to look at Anneke. "Do you go to record stores very often?"

"I do, yeah. I like to check them out in every city I visit, if I can."

"So why record stores?" Bailey asked. I leaned farther over the counter, interested in Anneke's answer.

"Certain places give you a sense of a city's true personality. I like to know what a city is when it isn't catering to tourists. Record stores are one of those places. And I always ask the record store guys the best place to eat, and they always know," she said.

"What other kind of places do you like to visit?"

"Grocery stores," she said. "People show up in their everyday clothes, taking care of business, not putting on a show."

"That's fascinating," Bailey said, eyeing Anneke with even more interest. "Where else?"

Anneke smiled and shrugged. "That's a conversation for another day. Right now, I think you were telling Jonah how to run his business?"

"Saul Vandenburg coming in here proves my point," Bailey said. "The email said he's stopped in here a few times to pick up stuff, and you didn't even know it was him, right?"

"In my defense, I don't have a great memory for the faces of lead singers in eighties rock bands."

"No defense needed," Bailey said. "The point is, he found Ledge Records because he's a music nerd. They'll make their way here. Your job will be to provide them with a concierge experience when they show up."

"What does that even mean?" I asked.

"You already do it, I think," Anneke says. "As a veteran hotel guest, I've learned to use the concierge services to make my visits more efficient. The concierge can connect me with stuff—experiences, restaurants, whatever—I wouldn't find on my own. And I like recommendations from locals."

"Exactly," Bailey said. "Basically, for that part of things, you just need to be your usual nerdy self, and that will be enough. I'll spend time crawling through Instagram and Facebook looking for New Orleans people with interests in different kinds of music and comment on their posts, saying stuff like, 'Love this album. Just got it in.' So not saying,

'Come shop here,' but planting the idea to do it. Tweaking their curiosity, basically."

"I like any plan where I just do what I was already doing. I'm in."

Bailey rolled her eyes. "The next part will be the part you don't like. You need to do the same thing for a different audience and get more people into the store, then give them that same kind of attention."

"Bailey, no."

"No what?" Anneke said, confused.

"She wants me to grow my hip hop section."

"Yep," Bailey said. "I do."

"You don't like hip hop?" Anneke asked, her forehead wrinkling in confusion. We hadn't talked about hip hop much on Noteworthy.

"I do," I said. "But I don't know it well. I'll have zero credibility, basically."

Bailey sighed. "Either expand or go back to—"

"I got it," I said, cutting her off, knowing what she was about to say next. I didn't want to hear about how she thought the record store was a waste of my talent. "Also, thanks for making it sound like the store is going under any minute. It's not," I said to Anneke.

"But he's not making BMW money," Bailey countered.

"I don't like BMWs. I don't need to make BMW money."

"Sometimes it feels like we're barely making gas money," Bailey said.

I glared at her. *Shut up, Bailey.* Money wasn't important to me beyond making my bills, which I could always do. It was more that she was making me sound like a slacker, which I wasn't. Never had been.

"Do I need to put the two of you in a get-along shirt?" Anneke asked. "That's what my dad used to do to me and my brothers. Put us in one of his biggest T-shirts, both heads in the neck hole, and made us stay there until we agreed to get along."

"We'll be fine," I muttered. "What were you going to say about these signed Saul Vandenburg albums?"

Bailey's face brightened as she explained how we could use them to build that "concierge" brand of service but make it so that they were in-person purchases only, because it would entice people to make more impulse purchases when they were in the store. "That way, you turn customers into higher profit per transaction," she concluded.

"Okay."

"Okay what?" she said. "You made a face."

"I don't like thinking of them as transactions."

"Then you should have opened a record library instead of a record store."

Anneke had been taking a swig from her water bottle and she choked and spluttered. "Fair point," she said on a slightly hoarse gasp.

"Sorry," I told her. "This is an old argument. Should we talk about how one of your favorite singers in the world is going to be here any minute?"

"I've been practicing my cool face," she said. "What do you think?" She gave me a half-lidded blank stare, like she was in a magazine ad for a shoe brand we'd have to sell my truck to afford, and she really, really hated the shoes. Or was angry about them? I couldn't tell what emotion models in high-fashion ads were supposed to feel.

"Nah, don't play it cool," I said. "Just let your face say whatever it wants to say."

"Really? Because that's this." Her expression morphed to something that bordered between lovesick and constipated.

"Go with the cool face," I said.

She grinned, and I decided that was my favorite expression of hers so far, when her smile was for herself and not for the camera.

"Everyone practice their cool faces," she ordered. Bailey leaned against the T-shirt display looking faintly bored. "That's good, Bailey. You're practically a Banana Republic ad." Bailey grinned. "Cool face," Anneke ordered. Bailey looked bored again.

"Do your cool pose," Bailey told me.

I rolled my eyes. "This is dumb."

"Cool. Pose." Bailey punctuated each word with a clap.

I sighed. "I'm not doing a cool pose. I'm going to do a this-is-a-dumb-idea pose." I leaned on the counter and let my face say what I thought about all this.

Anneke and Bailey exchanged a look.

"It's so irritating," Bailey said.

"He's not even trying," Anneke said.

I snorted. "I told you I wouldn't."

"Because you are clearly no fun," Anneke said. "But that's not what we're complaining about. You're like a walking album cover without even trying."

"Irritating," Bailey reiterated.

Before I could defend myself, the front door opened, and a rock god walked in.

13

ANNEKE

Saul Vandenburg stepped into the store.

I couldn't have made a cool face or any other kind of face on purpose. I had no control over my face. I had no idea how my face looked, and I didn't care. Saul Vandenburg was here. Right here, six feet away from me.

Years of listening to his albums. Years of singing his lyrics. I'd used him as my yearbook quote! And here he was. Saul. Freaking. Vandenburg.

He was short and wiry, around 5'8, and he wore every one of his sixty years in the lines on his face. His messy brown hair showed more salt than pepper, and he wore sunglasses, but there was no mistaking the iconic jawline from countless *Rolling Stone* articles and album covers.

"Saul?" Jonah asked, as if anyone besides Saul Vandenburg would have walked through the door reeking of greatness.

He nodded. "You Jonah?" He held out his hand when Jonah confirmed.

"Thanks for coming in to do this," Jonah said.

"No problem. Guess I could have signed and sent them, but I wanted to poke around and see what you've got."

"Cool," Jonah said. "You want to shop or sign first?"

Cool. Like this was not the most mind-blowing thing that could ever happen to a human being. How was he staying so low-key?

"Let's get business out of the way," Saul Vandenburg said. I could not bring myself to even refer to him in my mind as Saul only. I could barely refrain from referring to him in my mind as Saul Freaking Vandenburg.

Jonah offered to bring him back to the office to sign, but Saul Vandenburg waved him off. "It's just five albums, right? I'll do that right here." So Jonah handed him a Sharpie, and he signed each cover in bold, black strokes. "If you've got any other ones, I'll do those too."

"I was hoping," Jonah said with a half-smile and reached beneath the counter and pulled out more stock. "I ordered more, because I figured people were going to want to pick up other albums too."

Saul Vandenburg smiled and signed those too, working through the stack in less than five minutes.

"Can I ask how business is?" He handed over the last album.

Jonah took it from him and looked like he was trying to find the right words. "We're getting by."

Saul Vandenburg nodded, and his face looked like the cover of his *Fifteen Songs* solo album, sort of pensive for a moment. Then he reached into the messenger bag over his shoulder. "I knew your dad."

Bailey looked at him in surprise, and Jonah's expression matched. Saul Vandenburg responded with a small smile. "I know. Very different genres, but we met at the Jazz Festival about ten years ago. He told me about this place, and I've stopped in every time I'm in town ever since. I brought you something. Maybe it'll help." He handed me a 45, the small records used for singles. "That's a song we never released," he said. "We could only afford ten pressings, and they were never sold publicly. Maybe it'll be worth something to you."

Jonah shot a quick glance at Bailey who looked like she might faint. He took the record like the Pope handed him a rosary. "Are you sure?"

Saul Vandenburg shrugged. "Yes. Karmic balance. Your dad gave me some pretty good advice at the time. Life-changing, maybe. This is my thank you. Put it up for auction. I think it'll help."

Jonah stood there, his jaw slightly open, wordless.

"You're welcome," Saul Vandenburg said, smiling slightly. "Mind if I look around?"

"Thank you!" Jonah said, and his cheeks flushed for not saying thank you first. "And yes, look around."

Saul Vandenburg nodded again and went upstairs to the jazz section.

Bailey, Jonah, and I all stared at each other wide-eyed for several seconds, then Bailey fist pumped, I did the *Home Alone* face, and Jonah threw up both hands in a victory sign. We did some very uncool silent celebration before settling down.

I walked over to where Saul Vandenburg had stood at the counter. "I'm going to stand here until I've absorbed every possible molecule he left behind."

"You're weird," Jonah said.

"I don't care. What are you doing?" I asked as he vaulted himself over the counter.

"The same thing. I want some of those molecules too." He stood right behind me. "You don't mind sharing, do you?" he asked.

"Of course not. But you'll want to put your hands up here for maximum exposure." I wasn't a dummy. I knew a golden opportunity when I saw one. I nodded at my own hands on the counter where Saul Vandenburg had leaned while signing. Jonah had me in an almost-hug in half a second, the warmth of his chest grazing my back, his arms brushing mine.

Bailey, who thought I couldn't see her, pretended to gag, then grinned and gave him a thumbs-up.

We stood that way for a few seconds before I leaned back and rested my head against his chest, because how else could I tilt my head up to ask a question? His heart beat near my ear, and it sped up a tiny bit, which made my knees think about buckling. "What do you think? Have we absorbed it all?"

His lips were so close, and his head lowered the barest fraction. I had a feeling if Bailey wasn't standing eight feet away and trying not laugh, I would have absolutely tasted them. He had that pre-kiss vibe.

He held his breath for a second then sighed and stepped back. "Yeah, I guess we probably did absorb it."

"Do you feel at least twenty percent more genius?" I asked as he walked back around to the register.

He cleared his throat and didn't meet my eyes. "At least twenty percent," he agreed.

"We need a picture of Mr. Placemat when he comes down," Bailey said. "For our socials."

"Never call him Mr. Placemat," Jonah said.

"Promise you'll ask him for a picture."

"We'll get it."

"And maybe I can get one with him?" I asked. I could feel myself making puppy dog eyes, but I couldn't help it. "I promise not to post it anywhere and treasure it forever."

"I will risk looking not cool to get you that picture," he promised.

"I appreciate your sacrifice." I made the same serious face I'd had to perfect for a shoot about Burberry career bags.

He smiled at me again, something I was beginning to crave.

We hung out, helping Bailey fold shirts, listening to the floor creak overhead as Saul Vandenburg browsed. I smiled as I traced his progress upstairs, Jonah quietly noting for me what each section was.

Saul Vandenburg came back down with about eight albums. "Ready," he said.

"Our treat," Jonah told him.

"Screw that." Saul Vandenburg's tone was mild, but he pulled cash from his pocket, like, "No arguing."

Jonah rang him up, and as he waited for the receipt to print, he asked, "Could we get a picture of you to put on our social media? Maybe with the 45? To prove it's legit?"

"Sure thing," Saul Vandenburg said, accepting his change. "On one condition. Tell me the best place to eat around here."

"Our mom's kitchen," Bailey said, "but short of that, definitely check out The Joint. And get the creole mustard on whatever you order."

"Will do."

Jonah handed back the 45 then walked around the counter to get out of Bailey's shot.

She snapped a few. "Thanks, Mr. Vandenburg."

Saul Vandenburg smiled. "In rock-and-roll, there are no misters. Just Saul."

Oh. My. GOSH. *Just Saul.* I practiced saying it in my head.

"Thanks, Saul," Bailey said.

"Can I get a shot of you and Jonah and Anneke?" she asked. I would make her a bridesmaid when I married either Jonah or Just Saul.

"Jump in," Just Saul said. Jonah and I didn't have to be told twice, taking our place on either side of him. He slid one arm behind Jonah's back and laid the other across my shoulders, flashing a peace sign.

"I better get going," he said when Bailey checked the photos and nodded. "Getting dinner at N7, but I'll try The Joint tomorrow."

"Sounds like you already know the good places to eat," Jonah said.

"I always like trying something new. See you next time I'm in town." Then he ambled out like he hadn't just blown our minds.

"I need to put together a marketing strategy to get the word out on that record," Bailey said, heading for the office.

"Airdrop the pictures first?" I begged.

"You got it." Bailey sent them and disappeared into the office.

"So," I said.

Jonah leaned against the counter. "It's good to see you."

"Yeah?"

"Yeah."

"Dinner sounds like a good idea." It was an invitation, and I badly wanted him to take it.

"I can't tonight. I need to help Bailey with this marketing thing and start spreading the word in some of the record geek forums."

"Sure, I get it." My own smile wobbled. How had I misread that? He reached up and rubbed the area over his heart almost absentmindedly. I turned toward the door like it was no big deal. "Thanks for letting me be here for that."

I walked out of the store and used my app to unlock the rental scooter I'd used to get over here. It was too much of a pain to wait for rideshares outside of the French Quarter.

I considered the last hour as I pushed off to get myself going.

That had been amazing ... until it got weird. Super weird.

What was that last exchange between me and Jonah? There was no way I was the only one vibing in there. That whole thing with him practically sidling up behind me to absorb Just Saul's molecules? Jonah felt the currents between us. I could see it in his face.

Yet here I was, cruising back to Miles's by myself on a rented scooter, no Jonah to debate greatest Placemats albums with until we found somewhere good to eat.

I did not get him. There was the strangest push/pull happening there.

It had gotten like this with Erick one too many times before our final blowout. He pushed and pulled for different reasons, wanting to "chase his muse," which meant anything in a skirt that made her way backstage at one of his shows, then always came back to me, claiming I was the only woman in his life with substance.

Substance-s, by the way, were another not-small reason we broke up. I'd always thought the amount of recreational drug use portrayed in shows set in Hollywood was exaggerated.

No. It was definitely a thing.

Anyway, we'd broken up three times over his "muse" chasing. It should have only taken once, but I'd bought into the whole tortured artist mystique. In my defense, I'd dumped him quicker each of the last two times, and there was no way he would ever talk me into taking him back again.

I didn't know why Jonah was pushing me away; he was so hard to read. Something kept a wall up between us in person that didn't exist online, and I couldn't figure it out. After today, after those breathtaking moments at the counter, his almost-touch setting me on fire enough to crave what would happen if we leaned into each other completely, I was sure it wasn't about attraction.

I pushed faster on the scooter, darting around people on the sidewalk, riding on the street if there were too many pedestrians to skim around. The most irritating part of this was that I had just met Saul Vandenburg, but all I could think about was whether a guy liked me.

A very hot guy, in an understated way. The kind of guy who knew women found him attractive but didn't know how hot he actually was.

How was anyone going to resist that?

Especially not since I knew how funny he was from Noteworthy, how sweet he was with his sister, how little status mattered to him, and how unimpressed he was with fame.

But I had just met Saul Vandenburg!

I slowed the scooter when I got to Louis Armstrong Park and leaned it against a bench so I could pull up the picture Bailey had sent me and study it. Could remember the moment that the greatest rock talent of a generation had slung his arm around my shoulders.

Bailey had sent five snaps. In all of them, Saul was giving the camera a piercing gaze. In three of them, Jonah and I smiled at the camera with slightly dazed expressions, like neither of us could quite believe it.

But in one of them, Jonah was focused on my face as I grinned at the camera. I enlarged it, a sense of satisfaction washing over me as I studied his expression. No, I'd definitely read him right. The vibe wasn't one-sided.

In the final picture, I was looking at Jonah. I remembered doing that, sneaking a look at him, hoping to exchange a look that said, "Can you believe this is for real?" But he was looking at the camera this time, and what Bailey had captured exposed me more than the *Sporting News* swimsuit edition I'd done where I'd been shot from behind wearing only Brazilian-cut swim shorts.

My eyes were on Jonah, drinking him in. Not Saul Vandenburg.

It was a model's job to manipulate the camera and project feelings or attitudes that might not reflect you in that moment or even reflect you at all. I was successful because I knew how to do that. But I also knew from being behind the lens that cameras told the truth in candid moments, when its subject couldn't construct a disguise. And this picture was telling the truth about me: I was utterly taken with Jonah.

So what did I do about a man who blew hot and cold, whose warmth inevitably cooled before long each time we hung out? I didn't want to be one of those clichés who only fell for emotionally unavailable men.

I shoved my phone in my back pocket, tightened my helmet, and pushed off hard from the sidewalk. I'd had enough of guys who couldn't make up their minds about being into me. Erick had stuck around until every Mrs. Right Now had shown up. I didn't know what Jonah's deal was, and I didn't need to. I wasn't going to spend any more energy trying to figure it out. If he wanted to see where this energy that thrummed between us could lead, the next move was all his.

14
JONAH

I was in trouble. Big trouble. The kind of trouble only women could cause. Possibly the kind of trouble only one woman had ever caused me before.

It had been two years since I'd felt a pull this strong toward someone. And I didn't want to feel it.

"That was amazing," Bailey said when she came out of the office a while later. Her forehead wrinkled. "Where's Anneke?"

"She left."

"What did you do?"

I scowled at her. "Why are you assuming I did something?"

"Because you're you." Her expression was no less accusing. "So tell me. Was this an 'I have to go' leaving or an 'I'm getting out of here' exit?"

I sucked my teeth. "How's the marketing plan going?"

She groaned. "I knew it. I'm asking again: what did you do to make my new best friend, the funny, smart supermodel leave?"

"Nothing. She asked about getting dinner, and I told her I couldn't, and she left because she was hungry."

"You're the worst."

I didn't bother arguing with her. Anneke hadn't left feeling awesome, and I knew it. I sucked at lying, so I stayed quiet.

"Fix it," Bailey demanded.

"Fix what?"

"Stop playing dumb. Whatever you broke."

I straightened and hopped over the counter to pull the iron safety gate across the store front before locking the front door. When I turned around, Bailey was still standing there, clearly not done with the discussion.

"I didn't exactly break anything," I said. "I gave her a very mild rejection. It's not a big deal. I'm sure she has a ton of men after her. She could go to the Turnaround tonight and find someone to restore her confidence in two seconds flat."

Her eyebrow went up. "Isn't the Turnaround the last time she was rejected? Also by you?"

I jabbed the register button to eject the cash drawer, grimly satisfied when it shot out with a jolt. I pulled the tray and thunked it on the counter. Hard.

"You done messed up, son."

I jerked my head up. "I'm your *older* brother."

"Then why are you acting like a high school freshman? This is ridiculous. I know Maggie hurt you, but Anneke isn't your ex. She's not going to leave you because she finds fame. She's already about as famous as it gets, and by some miracle, she's still interested in your stubborn self. Fix it."

I counted out the cash in the register, which wasn't ever much. Most of our customers paid by card. When I got to the change, I let each coin fall extra loudly into its bay. I filled out the deposit slip, sealed the bank bag, and returned the tray. The whole time, I tried to think about meeting Saul Vandenburg, but instead I kept thinking about the look of awe on Anneke's face when he wasn't looking, and the way her eyes had shuttered when I'd rejected her dinner invitation.

"Dammit," I muttered. "I messed up."

"Yeah." Bailey said it softly this time. She was good like that, knowing when to push and when to back off.

I sighed. "How do I fix this?"

"If I were her, I'd be thinking the next move was entirely yours. I'd be skeptical of it, whatever it was, waiting for you to blow me off again."

"That's a diagnosis. I need a prescription."

She tugged at her bottom lip, her habit when she strategized. She did this every time she came up with some new brainstorm for the store. She grabbed a shirt and folded it. Refolded it. It had been folded correctly the first time. She set it back. She paced. She folded some more. It made me antsy.

"Did I screw this up so bad you can't even think of a plan?"

She stopped and blinked, like she'd just remembered I was there. "It's not that. It's more that this is going to take finesse more than a grand gesture. You're not in a relationship. A grand gesture right now would be weird. And not you."

I thought back to the previous week, and Ellie standing onstage at the Turnaround grand opening, clearly terrified, laying her heart on the line for Miles. "You're right. A grand gesture at this point would be super weird."

She paced some more, then stopped and turned. "I can help you figure out how to talk to her, but if you're just going to go hermit again, I'm not helping. Are you going to hermit?"

I thought about Anneke's wide-open face, the way she seemed to absorb everything around her through every sense in her body, experiencing it all, and let it shine out in her smiles. I thought about how often she'd made me smile—even outright laugh—in our DMs. About how'd she felt inside my arms, her body brushing mine. "No. No, I'm not going to run."

Bailey gave a single, decisive nod, like it was the conclusion she'd expected me to reach. "Okay. Figure out how much you want to tell her about why you keep doing this dance with her. My advice is to tell her all of it. You have to show her literally and figuratively that you're open to her."

"That's a lot to drop in a text."

She shook her head.

"DM?" It made more sense. I should have guessed that first.

But Bailey shook her head again. "No, my read on her is that she values experiences over everything. It'll be too easy for her to blow you off if you say you want to talk, but if you offer her an experience she can't refuse, it might work. And that means …"

"Uncle Joe," we said at the same time. I was already pulling my phone out.

"What are you doing?" She sounded slightly alarmed.

"Texting Anneke."

"No, don't. We have to craft your message."

I shook my head. "I already know what to say." I tapped it out and hit send, then handed it to Bailey to read.

Jonah: Sorry about bailing on dinner. Saul Vandenburg overwhelmed all my senses. Then I came back to them and realized I was starving and should have said yes. Raincheck? Tomorrow? If you're still in town, I'm thinking dinner in the weirdest place you've ever eaten.

Bailey handed my phone back to me. "If that doesn't work, nothing will."

But an hour later when we were back at the house, and Anneke hadn't responded, I began to worry that I was facing "nothing will." Bailey had holed up in her room to study, and I was in mine to start spreading the word about our prized single in the different music forums, but I wanted to cross the hall and ask her what she thought. I refrained because I wasn't sixteen. And even when I was sixteen, I wouldn't have been asking my nine-year-old sister for advice on girls.

It was close to midnight, and even my night owl self was getting sleepy when my phone finally buzzed. I read it and sat straight, the words waking me right up.

Anneke: Bring it.

15
JONAH

I rang the buzzer at the gate in front of Miles's house, and a few seconds later, the electronic lock clicked to let me in. Anneke answered when I knocked.

"Hey," she said.

How had I not noticed how smoking hot she was that night at the club? Even standing there in flip-flops and a soft-looking, light green dress, she was kind of … spellbinding.

Spellbinding? I needed to leave the prog rock albums out of the rotation in the store for the next couple of days. I tried to interpret the expression on her face. It wasn't standoffish, exactly. It was more how she'd looked the first day she'd come into the store, like she was trying to read the situation.

"Hey," I said before it could get any more awkward. "I'm here to man up."

She pursed her lips and leaned against the doorframe. "Interesting way to open."

"I'm not very good at this, so …"

"What is 'this'?"

"Bailey says I messed up, so I'm trying to fix it."

I could tell it was the wrong thing to say. Her expression went back to watchful.

"I see."

"That was a bad explanation. Bailey pointed out that I was being an idiot when you left, because I didn't take you up on dinner. She was right. And I want to fix it, not because Bailey told me to, but because …" I trailed off here, uncomfortable with every option for finishing that sentence. That was what panic got you.

"Because why?"

"Because I'm not sure I understand you, but I think I understand AnnieBird, and I'd like to understand how it fits all together, because AnnieBird is way cool, and it would be fun to hang out with her."

She sighed. "That's me."

"I know."

"I mean, I'm not two different people. It's not like I summon that personality and then send her out to dinner with you. AnnieBird is me, all the time. I am AnnieBird all the time. You are not taking someone else out to dinner. You'd be taking me. And so far, half the time you're around me in person, you seem like you can't get rid of me fast enough."

I was on the verge of blowing this further, and suddenly, it couldn't be clearer to me that it was the last thing I wanted to do. "There's a reason for that, and that reason is that I'm a huge idiot."

Her lips twitched. "I'll buy that."

I scrambled to find the right words. "I'd like to take you to dinner in the weirdest place you've ever eaten and also explain why I've been acting like such a huge idiot."

She considered that, her eyes roaming my face for a couple of seconds. "Okay. I'm in."

I breathed a not-very-silent sigh of relief. "We'll need to drive if that's okay?"

"Sure. Let me get my bag." She returned a minute later with a small purse slung across her body. "Ready."

I led her to my Toyota pickup which I'd had to park two blocks away, and I forced myself to keep the conversation going. Silence didn't bother me, but I didn't want her to think I didn't want to talk to her.

"This is me," I said, clicking the key remote to disarm the alarm.

"You drive a pickup?"

I couldn't interpret her tone. Maybe surprised? "Yeah. I need it when I go to estate sales and purchase music lots. Have to haul back crates of albums." I opened her door then got in on my side and started the engine. Neil Diamond came blaring through the stereo, and I practically dove for the volume, trying to turn it off.

"Neil, huh? Not what I would have pegged you for." Every syllable was almost a laugh.

I cleared my throat. "Just checking the quality before I stock it."

She flicked a glance at the dashboard. "That's synced with your phone. That's coming off your Spotify."

I dropped my head back against the seat. "I need to tell you something."

"You like Neil Diamond unironically?"

"I like Neil Diamond unironically."

"Hmm. Can I see your Spotify?"

I unlocked my phone and handed it over.

"This is going to take a minute," she said. "Feel free to start driving."

I pulled onto the street, and a block later, the opening strains of "America" floated out of the speakers. Anneke leaned forward to turn up the volume. "I love this song. My mom is Dutch, and she immigrated here in her mid-twenties after she met my dad. He would blare it every Fourth of July and dance around the kitchen with her. Still does. I used to choreograph dances to this in our living room when I was a kid. I love it."

"I need to see this dance."

"Nah. But I'll sing for you." Her voice wasn't anything special—mine wasn't either—but she made up for talent with a ton of enthusiasm, punctuating the lyrics with Neil Diamond-worthy dramatic arm flairs. By the chorus, I gave in and joined her, because how could I not? It was Neil Diamond. His songs demanded singalongs.

By the time I got us to our destination in the Central Business District, we'd moved onto belting "Sweet Caroline," and we were both grinning when I pulled into a parking space.

Anneke glanced out of the window. "Mardi Gras Palace?"

It was a large neon sign, impossible to miss, and even if she had, the oversized statues from old Mardi Gras floats standing on either side of the doors probably would have tipped her off.

"Mardi Gras Palace," I confirmed. "We're going to have a picnic."

She looked around the parking lot. We were the only vehicle. "I think it's closed."

I smiled as I unbuckled. "Not if you know Uncle Joe."

She climbed out too, and I grabbed the lunch hamper I'd stowed behind the seat.

"How much do you know about Mardi Gras?" I asked as I checked my phone for the code Uncle Joe had texted me.

"Uh, I think you have to flash people to get beads? But why do I want plastic beads?"

"You're about to step behind the scenes of Mardi Gras, and I'll tell you about the beads and everything else after we eat."

Mardi Gras Palace had a storefront that catered to tourists, but I led her past the aisles full of tinsel and brightly colored plastic souvenirs to a door labeled "Krewe Only." It opened into a cavernous warehouse, and I smiled when Anneke gasped behind me.

"Wow," she said, following me in. "What is this place?"

"This is where the Mardi Gras floats are stored for all the parades. I figured since Mardi Gras is in a month, you might be interested in learning about it."

"Heck, yeah!" she said, and it was so wholesome, it made me laugh.

"I don't know why I keep expecting you to be bored and sullen, but you keep not being what I expect."

"Let me guess. You think supermodels drop F-bombs, spend all our time talking about trips to Europe in an accent that's not quite American but not British either, and punctuate our sentences by snorting coke."

"Bingo."

"Only when I'm bored."

I gave a slight shake of my head. "You might get bored, but you are never boring."

Her eyebrows rose, and she gave me an impressed look. "Smooth."

"Only on accident."

"So tell me, LedgeCase, why do you know the secret code to get into this place? And even more importantly, how did you become a closet Neil Diamond fan?"

"That's the perfect segue to what I want to talk to you about," I said, leading her toward the Prometheus bay of floats.

She stopped short. "Oh no. You didn't say we were having a 'talk.' I was lured here under false pretenses."

I turned to face her. "I'll rephrase. I brought you here to explain myself."

"Much better." She started walking again, and I waited for her to catch up.

"I love my Neil Diamond because my dad played with him a couple of times when he was in town on tour. My dad was a session musician. He died three years ago, and I've been listening to a lot of the artists he played for since he died. He's not on any Neil Diamond recordings, but that was the first concert I got to go backstage for because my dad was in the band that night."

I didn't look at her as I said all this. People reacted to parent death all kinds of ways, but somehow, most of those ways required me to make it better for them, and I didn't feel like doing it. I didn't want to see that expression in Anneke's eyes that asked me to make her feel better about my grief. Or the impending "how did he die" question. It wasn't a day I liked reliving.

But she didn't say anything. Instead, she slipped her hand into mine. "Tell me about him."

That was the only response that was ever right for me. But it made me sad, because usually only people who had lost someone close to them knew to ask it. I wondered who Anneke had lost.

I cleared my throat and thought about what I wanted to explain to her about my dad. "Like I said, he was a session musician. One of the best. He played upright bass, and he's on over three hundred tracks for dozens of musicians. He liked touring before I was born, but after that, he'd only play live if it was a performance in town. Maybe Baton Rouge at the farthest. There are a couple of famous recording studios around here, and they were always calling him to sit in on sessions. He kept a copy of every album he played on. And since he always had musician friends sending him their albums, he opened a record shop next to our house. It meant he could pay the bills if there were dry spells at the studio."

"A rooted guy. A little different than my experience with musicians."

I shot her a look. "You mean Miles?"

"No, sorry. Tell me more about your dad."

So I did, telling her about how he'd bring me to the studio sometimes to watch him work from the sound booth. Or how I grew up helping in the shop, sweeping up and doing errands until he trusted me to start running the register. How he used to dance with my mom around our house, but it was always to the Neville Brothers. I talked until we reached the Prometheus bay at the end of the warehouse. It was a long walk, and more talking than I usually did, but I was glad for all of it, because I liked the way Anneke's hand felt in mine.

Anneke stopped and stared up at the enormous float, her eyes growing wide as she tilted her head to take in the huge, fantastical dragon.

"Do you know who Prometheus was?" I asked.

"God of fire," she said.

I nodded. "The main float every year is fire-themed. This is where the king and goddess ride."

"King and goddess?" She looked slightly bewildered by it all.

"Hang on." I led her to the ladder at the back, then we climbed up and walked to the front of the float where I set up our picnic dinner. Anneke wandered around, admiring the details in the fiberglass sculpture. "My uncle Joe says that it will breathe fire when the parade is going," I said as she reached toward its fierce snout. "You ready for more than you ever wanted to know about Mardi Gras?"

"No such thing." She knocked her head lightly. "It might sound hollow, but that's a sponge in there, ready to soak up all the knowledge."

"If there is one thing I have never taken you for, it's empty-headed." Her intelligence had crackled in every message we'd exchanged over the months.

She knocked on her head again. "I'm ready. Fill it up with Mardi Gras."

"You eat and I'll talk," I said, pulling the food from the basket. "I tried to make something healthy, so I went with a salad. But I made it

Cajun-style with roasted mirliton and Gulf shrimp in a pepper-jelly vinaigrette."

"Sounds amazing. Except what's a mirliton?"

"A squash," I said. "My grandfather always grew them in his garden."

"I'm excited to try it."

I started on my impromptu history of Mardi Gras while I served everything up. "So Mardi Gras is Catholic. In the New Orleans area, school kids get the whole week off, public or private school, doesn't matter. Up around Baton Rouge, even public schools get a couple of days off too. And most towns and cities have their own Mardi Gras parades, but the big ones? That's here in New Orleans."

"How'd they start?" she asked.

I gave her a half-smile. "Bailey would tell you it was marketing. Back in the 1800s, the governor of the colony wanted to prove to a visiting French duke that New Orleans wasn't a mosquito-ridden backwater, so he decreed a parade. And since it really was a mosquito-ridden backwater, the people were thrilled for the distraction, embraced the parade, and made it a tradition that's grown ever since."

"But why Mardi Gras? Why not Christmas or New Year's or something?"

"You know we've got deep Catholic roots in Louisiana, right?"

She nodded. "Like you have parishes, not counties."

"Yeah. And again, even in public school, during Lent, they serve fish on Fridays because so few kids will eat meat. I think that old governor picked Lent because it coincided with the fancy duke's visit. Maybe if he'd come in December, we'd lose our minds over a totally different holiday. But it was February, so we do Mardi Gras, which is French for—"

"Fat Tuesday," she interrupted. "I do enough work in Paris to translate the basics."

"Right again," I said. "Ash Wednesday kicks off Lent when people sacrifice their bad habits leading up to Easter. That means Fat Tuesday is the last day to indulge them."

"And everyone throws a party to sin and excess?"

I smiled. "Yeah. It's weird, I guess. But when you do something for long enough, you don't think too much about why it's that way anymore. I guess it helps to think of Mardi Gras as a catharsis, getting it all out of your system so that you can be good during Lent. Several European countries do it and call it Carnival. We probably borrowed from them."

"People have parties for weirder things, I guess. So what's with all the beads? I've seen them everywhere, hanging off trees and power lines and people's fences."

"They'll stay there year-round too. The bead thing has been going on forever. I think it was a Renaissance tradition. But my grandma told me the flashing started in the seventies because of 'dirty hippies.'"

That made Anneke laugh. "Or maybe just Europeans. They do not care about boobs."

It wasn't in my best interests to dwell on boobs too much, so I moved on. "The colors all mean stuff too. Purple for justice, green for faith, and gold for power. I think back in the beginning, you threw the color of the bead to the person you thought had that quality. Like if you had a super religious friend, you'd throw them green. But it's not like that anymore. You throw any color. And not just beads. Every krewe has its own throws."

"I noticed some of the floats have different names. Krewe of Nyx, but k-r-e-w-e, not c-r-e-w. Krewe of Rex. Krewe of Muses."

"Yeah, Nyx and Muses are newer krewes, all women. Nyx throws hand-decorated purses, and Muses throws shoes. Rex is a super krewe, like Prometheus. They have thousands of riders and dozens of floats. Some of them are as long as a city block."

"But what's a krewe, exactly? I mean, how did all these people get together and pick a theme and make a parade? And how many are there?"

I thought about it. "There might be twenty or thirty, even. I don't know because the parades start almost a month before and go through Mardi Gras night. The smallest ones go earliest in the season. Prometheus parades on Tuesday night because it's the biggest and baddest super krewe of them all. Over three thousand riders, more than eighty floats. The krewe is men-only, specifically influential New Orleans businessmen. And that's what most krewes are."

Her forehead had wrinkled when I said "men-only."

"They're all different businessmen?"

"No, sorry. Different interest groups. Like Prometheus is made of businessmen whose businesses thrive on tourism. But Muses that I mentioned before? That's a female krewe focused on arts and sciences. They hold a design contest for school kids and the winning design is printed on their cups and revealed when they're thrown to the crowds during their parade. Some krewes focus on Black causes, others focus on family and friends. 'Tit-Rax is my favorite, because they're the anti-Rex parade where they decorate shoeboxes to look like floats and carry them. It stands for Petit Rex."

"I had no idea," she said and looked as overwhelmed as I felt when my mom once sent me to the store for "cold medicine" without warning me there were fifty billion choices. "So each parade has a group that focuses on other stuff through the year, the focuses are all different from each other, and they all throw stuff."

"Yes." I probably should have wrapped it up here, but talking about this prolonged the conversation I knew we really needed to have, and I was okay with putting it off longer. "And they all throw stuff besides beads."

"Like cups," she said.

"No, they all throw those too. And doubloons, which are plastic and stamped with the krewe's logo and year and are highly collectible and people freak out about them. You'll hear jokes about your stomp-and-bump, which is the maneuver you learn if you want to grab one that falls to the ground. But then there are signature throws."

"I feel like I should be taking notes," she said.

"We haven't even gotten to the balls."

"They throw balls? I guess that makes sense. That's one thing you're actually supposed to throw at people."

I shook my head. "Not sports balls. Think masquerade balls with elaborate decorations and ballgowns."

"Ohhhh. Wow, I want to go to there."

"It's a sight," I agreed. "But we have to talk about the other kind of throws first. Everyone does beads, cups, doubloons, and candy. But then there are the signature throws."

"Purses and high heels?"

"You're catching on." I grinned at her. "The most famous are probably the coconuts at Zulu which are hand-painted. Everyone goes nuts for those. And then there's the Prometheus throw. Want to guess what a fire-themed krewe throws?"

"Tiki torches? Matchbooks? Lighters?"

"Good guesses, but you're in Louisiana. Think harder."

Her forehead wrinkled again, and it was adorable, which felt like a weird thing to think about a stunning world-famous supermodel, but it was. Adorable.

"Hot sauce," I said, when she gave me an "I give up" shrug. "It's called Fire Sauce, and they don't sell it or tell anyone the recipe, so the only time you can get it is at the parade."

A big grin split her face. "I love that so much."

"It's a big deal," I said. "Everything Prometheus does is a big deal. The Saturday before Mardi Gras, they throw a full masquerade ball and reveal the king and goddess of the krewe at midnight. It's always some big deal celebrity with a New Orleans connection. Last year it was Sandra Bullock, because she has a house here. And my uncle is the krewe captain which is how I get the code."

"It's all coming together," she said, glancing around the warehouse again. "Except for one thing."

"What's that?" I couldn't think of anything I hadn't at least touched on about the holiday.

"You said you would explain yourself. And while that was a super fascinating explanation of Mardi Gras, I think you were maybe distracting me?"

I looked down and speared my last piece of mirliton on my fork. "Maybe," I said around a bite of it.

She gave me a knowing look and ate her salad in quiet, waiting for me to speak.

"I was hoping it would be enough to confess to being an idiot and promise not to do it anymore."

She shook her head. "Might have been if this had only happened once, but we're dealing with a pattern and not an incident, so I need an explanation."

I rubbed my hands over my face. Was I ready to do this? Willing to do this?

I thought about the deep and interesting conversations we'd had for weeks on Noteworthy before we met. About how her eyes lit up when she was loving something: Watching her friends eat. Elaborate Mardi Gras floats. Saul Vandenburg. I dropped my hands and looked at her blue eyes, full of curiosity. And her mouth. And those lips. And ...

"Okay," I said, drawing a quiet, calming breath. "Ready or not, here we go."

16
ANNEKE

Jonah's face was endlessly interesting to me. It was the kind of face cameras loved, catching light and shadow in the sharp planes and angles of his cheekbones and jawline. I liked that I had to watch for the tiniest twitches and ripples of feeling to interpret what he was thinking. Maybe I was finally figuring out how to read him.

Right now, he was deeply uncomfortable, and I was okay with that. Not that I wanted him to be uncomfortable. But I had a feeling this was what it would take to finally understand him better.

He wrapped his arms around his legs, one hand clasping his other wrist like he was relaxing into telling a story, but I wasn't fooled. I had to be an expert in body language, and what Jonah was doing here was protecting himself, curving in to keep his center safe.

"My dad being in the music business, it jaded him," he began. "He watched a lot of artists progress through their careers, starting out trying not to look intimidated by being in a recording studio for the first time, then later showing up with huge entourages, throwing fits, disrespecting people's time. He said fame changed people, and only a few people could hold onto themselves. That most of them were phonies."

He cracked a smile that was half affectionate, half rueful. "That was his biggest thing. Always telling us to watch out for phonies."

"I can relate," I said. "I think that's why Miles and I connected so well. We'd both already been in the LA scene long enough to see through the illusion, long enough to have developed our own industry personas. But we met at a photoshoot, and I could see that he was annoyed by all the attention instead of chasing it, and we clicked. It was us against the fakes after that." Something about the word "phonies" struck me. It was kind of an old-fashioned way to say it, and then it hit me. "Did your dad use the word 'phonies'? Or is that your word?"

"His," Jonah said.

"Reminds me of Holden Caulfield in *The Catcher in the Rye*. That's what he called everyone, right? Phonies?"

Jonah met my eyes for a few seconds. I sat quietly and just looked back. "Yeah, that was his word. I loved that book in high school."

"Umm ..." It was a huge red flag when a guy said he admired Holden Caulfield who was an angry, emotionally stunted adolescent misogynist.

"I outgrew it," he said. "I was never a Holden Caulfield fan. It was more that I identified with him when I went through an angsty emo phase the first couple of years of high school. I mostly saw similarities between us because of the scene when he wants to buy his little sister a record, and he's so excited to give it to her. I identified with that so much that it took me a while to realize I didn't identify with much else about Holden after a couple of years."

"That's a relief." And it was. The red flag faded.

"I promise that I recognize Holden Caulfield isn't a role model."

"Also a relief. So who is?"

"My dad," he said without hesitation. "And a lot of his friends. Mostly music guys, like my godfather, Big Al, you met the other night at the club when I was unforgivably rude to you."

"Right, which you're about to explain."

He sighed. "I brought you to the warehouse because it's a metaphor. The whole idea of Mardi Gras and the parades and the fancy masquerade, it all sounds amazing, right?"

"It does. I'm serious about wanting to get into this ball."

"I always have to work at it, or I'd take you," he said, "but it's less magical when you see behind the scenes. Uncle Joe has been involved with Prometheus my whole life, captain for the last three, and because of that, we've always heard the dirt. All the in-fighting, the backstabbing, the gossiping and politics. They do a lot of good for their causes, but I've seen people smile to Uncle Joe's face while they're twisting a knife in his gut. But the tens of thousands of people who line up for the parade don't know about any of it or care. They want to be entertained and given cheap plastic beads."

"So the metaphor here is that it's all an illusion and people are phonies."

"Basically."

I narrowed my eyes at him. "You haven't gotten to what that has to do with me, but I don't like where this is going, so tread carefully."

He groaned. "I'm screwing this up even worse than it was before I tried fixing it. I'm going to talk fast so you don't jump down and walk away from me." He waited to see if I was going to move, but I stayed where I was, hoping against my better instincts that he could dig himself out of this.

"The opening of the Turnaround was a big show," he said. "But like every piece of it, not just the performances. Miles doesn't have red carpets or supermodels hosting VIP after-parties every night, does he?"

"No, that was a grand opening thing," I acknowledged.

"I only went that night because the tickets were free. I only cared about the music. The rest of the 'show' was a distraction."

My lips twitched at how much further he was digging himself in without realizing it. "Jonah, I figured out a few days before the opening of the Turnaround who you were and made sure Miles sent you those tickets."

His jaw dropped slightly, and a dazed look came over him, chased away quickly by a look of mortification. "I'm making this worse."

"You're making this worse," I confirmed. But he kind of wasn't. The fact that he realized how snotty everything he was saying sounded and how horrified he was by it was doing him some favors.

He dropped his head to his knees. "I thought you were part of the spectacle," he said. "Like how Prometheus always brings in big deal celebrities to be parade royalty. I saw you as showmanship, not as someone who probably loved that music—"

"I did," I confirmed.

"—or as someone trying to do a favor for a friend. I am the dumbest of all the dumbasses."

I laughed. I couldn't help it. He looked so pathetic sitting there all scrunched up, looking like he wished the fiberglass dragon would eat him. "It's okay."

"It's not." He lifted his head. "You did a nice thing for me, got me tickets, tried to introduce yourself, and I blew you off because I thought …"

"You thought I was a phony," I finished when he trailed off.

He only sat there and looked about three degrees more miserable.

"Jonah?"

He sighed. "I kind of guessed you might be a hostess-type person just doing your job, and I hate small talk. If I had known it was you, Annie-Bird, I would have …" He shoved his hair, like he was frustrated. "I would have been different."

"You mean nice?"

He mimed shoving a knife in his heart, and it made me laugh again.

"It's okay, Jonah. For real. I've spent enough time around you to know that you're not a tool. I'm not sure I understand your standard for authenticity or if I can meet it. Also, full disclosure, my hang-up is people who jerk me around. I was in a relationship like that, and I'm not doing it again. I deserve better." I sort of wanted to die the second the word "relationship" came out of my mouth, but he didn't flinch, so I said nothing. Maybe he didn't notice?

"Phony for me is someone who is fake." He frowned, maybe realizing that this didn't clear up anything. "Someone who isn't themselves. Like, mainly they act differently with different groups of people, and there's no integrity. Fake nice. Fake interested. All of that."

"Okay," I said, thinking through each of his words. "Elaborate on 'acting differently with different groups,' because that can look like a lot of different things. Like a doctor has to have a good bedside manner even if his life is going to crap outside of the office. And a lawyer can't be dragging a bad mood into court with her. Is it fake if they aren't letting the bad mood show?"

"No, of course not," he said.

"Because that's what my job is, you know? I'm always the same person inside. I am always the same amount of kind to people whether it's my agent or the photographer's assistant. But some days I show up, and the client wants a carefree beach girl, and sometimes they want a hard-edged businesswoman, and some days they want sophisticated socialite. I am that thing for them that day. And sometimes my friend needs me to be the happy party girl so his new club can launch successfully, and I show up in a shiny dress and heels. But that's all an outside thing."

"Does it get confusing?" he asked. "Having to be someone else's blank slate?"

"No. On set is never the problem. It's all the stuff that happens around it, where people expect me to be a certain kind of way."

"What way?"

I shrugged. "I don't know. Cool."

"And you're not cool?" he asked, a small smile tugging at his lips.

"I'm me. But I've learned not everyone deserves access to that. So yeah, I have a persona that I trot out for parties and industry events. You'll know if you meet her. She seems vaguely bored, and depending on your point of view, as if she's only saying a quarter of what she's thinking, or as if she isn't thinking at all. I go for mysterious, but maybe I land on vapid." I rested my elbow on my knee, my chin in my palm, and leaned forward. "Is that being fake?"

"It's not being your real self, but it's not what I think of as being fake."

"So I should be my real self all the time, no matter what? Even when I'm dealing with predatory industry types who don't deserve my time?"

He squirmed. "No, I don't mean that."

"What do you mean then, Jonah? I'm all ears." And slightly angry. I was feeling judged, and I didn't like it.

"I feel like I'm taking a test and failing," he said.

I stayed quiet. He wasn't wrong.

"What you're talking about sounds more like self-preservation," he said. "Or maybe even code-switching. Like the way a bunch of musicians speak to each other compared to the way they speak to people not in the business."

"But you said that when people act differently around different people, it's fake." I was being a brat, but I couldn't help it. I'd put up with enough of Jonah's silent judgment, and now he was going to have to own it.

"You're right, I did. But I know what you're talking about. The way Bailey and I speak to each other is different when it's the two of us compared to when other people are in the store. With you, I got so confused between how you came across in all of our DMs compared to how you were at the Turnaround that night."

"And how was I?"

"I mean, the tickets literally billed you as 'Supermodel Anneke Jansen, VIP After-party Host.' Not music-arguing dork AnnieBird with questionable opinions on The Ramones."

I tilted my head slightly. "What did I say or do that night to make you think I was anything different than the person online?" The answer was nothing. I'd been myself.

"I don't know," he said. Almost muttered, really. "I wasn't paying attention."

"Right. Because you made an assumption about me before I ever opened my mouth."

"You're going to have to give me a minute. I need to process that I'm in trouble for *not* being impressed that you're a model."

"Supermodel," I corrected him.

"*Super*model," he repeated.

And then I couldn't help it anymore. I started laughing.

"You're a punk," he said, but I could tell he was trying not to smile.

"Yes. And if I'm being fair, I could have just met you by coming into your store like a regular person. So maybe I did want to impress you with my model schtick."

"Supermodel," he corrected.

I stretched out one of my legs and gave his foot a light kick. "To clarify: do you have a problem with my job?"

He leaned back on his hands and sighed. "It's a weird job, but that's not your fault. Like, it's weird that our culture makes that a job."

"I can't tell if I'm supposed to be offended or not."

"Please don't be," he said, looking anxious, and it was very cute. "I'm thinking about it more at a philosophical level. What I meant to say is that no, I don't have a problem with your job as a model."

I quirked an eyebrow at him, not sure that was enough.

"It's not my place to have an opinion about whatever you decide to do as a job."

I smiled. "That was the addendum I didn't know I needed. So we agree that I'm not fake *as a person*, even when I'm in an ad for a gross perfume any more than a grouchy doctor who is putting on a show for a patient by being nice is a fake?"

"Uh ... yes?"

"Good. What is the specific kind of fakeness you can't stand?"

"I mean fake that's more like blowing smoke up someone's ..." He trailed off with a cough.

I smothered a smile at his effort to spare my ears.

"I mean more like if someone is acting all interested in you, what you do or how you think—and I don't mean dating-wise. I mean in general. But then someone more popular or connected comes along, and you're nonexistent. No longer good enough because they've made a better connection, so you aren't useful to them anymore. They're nice to people who can do things for them and crappy to people who can't. That kind of thing."

"Yeah, that's no bueno. Who hurt you, Jonah?"

I meant it as a joke, but a shadow flickered over his face. Before I could apologize or dig deeper, he smiled and said, "It's a long, boring story. But I learned a lot from my dad's stories too, and I guess it's all made me a cynic. I never went into the music industry with illusions, so."

"Went into the music industry," I repeated. That sounded like more than selling records. I thought about him in Miles's studio. "So you're a musician too?" It would make sense. Miles. Erick. I had an affinity for them.

"Nah. I was speaking more in general." He waved his hand like he was dismissing the subject. "But now you have my full explanation for being an idiot, so I guess that leaves an apology."

He stood up and held out a hand to pull me to my feet. My heart sped up as I accepted it. If this was a move to kiss me, I was into it. He had an amazing, full lower lip, and I wanted to explore it.

But instead of pulling me toward him or leaning down, he knelt on one knee instead, still keeping hold of my hand. "Anneke AnnieBird, I'm sorry I've been a clueless, judgy tool. Will you forgive me?"

"Humorless."

"Excuse me?"

"Clueless, judgy, humorless tool."

He nodded, his face very serious. "I'm sorry I've been a clueless, judgy, humorless tool even though sometimes you are a massive brat. Will you forgive me?"

I looked down at him and sniffed. "I guess."

"Sweet."

I yanked him to his feet. If there had been a moment for a kiss, it had passed. "Now I have to get home to pack because I have a flight tomorrow."

His face fell. "Dang. You have to travel a lot."

"You say that like it's a bad thing," I said, leaning down to help scoop up the picnic remains. "I love it though."

"Yeah?"

"Yeah. I wish I had more control over the destinations, but that would be a dream life for me: going wherever I want in the world whenever I want. I usually build in an extra day on my return flight so I can explore wherever I am. Even in cities I know well, there's always something new to see."

"Where are you off to tomorrow?" he asked as he led the way to the ladder down.

"Just New York, and I lived there for a couple of years, so that'll be a quick trip."

"Then back to LA?"

Was it my imagination, or did he sound slightly bummed? I held the picnic basket while he climbed down, and I couldn't see his face to read it.

"No. I'm booked for the next four months, and I don't have to be in LA again for three more weeks. I might hang out here in between jobs."

He reached up to take the picnic basket from me so I could climb down too. When I was on the second-to-last rung, he took a light hold of my elbow, cupping his palm around it so that he could guide me down. I liked the way it felt, his palm slightly calloused against my skin, his grip sure but not intrusive. The fact that he was attuned enough to me—or enough of an old school Southern gentleman—to even do it. Maybe it was second nature. Maybe he just wanted an excuse to touch me.

Either way, I liked it.

I liked him.

A lot.

Last time I was at Ledge, I could sense strong vibes coming off him, like he wanted to touch me. On the float, I'd felt it again. Like he wanted to kiss me, even. Yet, both times, he hadn't made a move. I knew shy guys, but Jonah wasn't shy. Confidence wasn't holding him back. I didn't know what was, but I had a feeling he was fully capable of making a move if he wanted to.

I really wanted him to.

But here we were, me getting all flustered because he was touching my elbow.

My *ELBOW*.

Maybe it was for the best that he hadn't put any moves on me yet. Who knew how I would react if I was all fluttery over an ELBOW?

But even with his current non-move-making holding pattern, I liked him.

So much so that I had my Lyft driver swing me by Ledge Records on the way to the airport the next morning. Not that it was actually on the way. It was the opposite direction, but I'd thought about our talk the whole rest of the night after Jonah dropped me off. I wasn't sure what we were doing, Jonah and me. I knew exactly what I was doing at Ledge. I wanted him to see what my work was worth.

It was barely eight in the morning, so it was closed, but I hopped out of the car and snapped a selfie in front of the mural painted on the store. Then I hopped back in the car and edited and posted it on the way to the airport. "Love this funky indie record store in New Orleans. Been in four times this week already. Jonah & Bailey rule." I hashtagged it with phrases sure to catch the eye of trend followers then leaned back and smiled.

Jonah wouldn't know what hit him, and I couldn't wait.

17
JONAH

Normally, the first hour I opened the store was slow, and I spent the time managing inventory and doing grunt work, but today, there were two customers waiting when I walked around the corner.

"Hey," I said. They weren't regulars.

"Hey."

They were young, maybe Bailey's age. They didn't have anything else to say as I jiggled the key in the finicky gate lock, rattled it open, and unlocked the door. They drifted in and wandered toward the end of the store with the eighties vinyl.

"Let me know if I can help you find anything," I called, settling my messenger bag behind the counter. I'd normally get situated in the office, but I'd wait until they left.

They lingered for about a half hour, still mostly drifting, and eventually bought a couple of T-shirts and stickers, but a few more customers trickled in before they left, and I had to stay out front. People tried to rip off records all the time, and they'd do it in a second if either Bailey or I weren't watching.

By lunch, we'd had four times the traffic as usual, but it was weird. Only two were customers I'd seen before, and they were the only two who bought records. The rest of them either took selfies but didn't buy anything, or they bought T-shirts, stickers, and decals but no music.

Bailey came in close to one o'clock after her morning classes were done, and her eyebrows rose when she saw the half-dozen customers. "How's it going?" she asked, heading straight for the T-shirt display which looked like velociraptors had been checking for their sizes.

"It's been like this all morning."

"Really?" Her eyes brightened. "That's great."

"No, it's not. They're mostly buying swag, and two of my regulars got annoyed by the crowd and left without buying records."

"Only your regulars would call this a 'crowd.'"

"It definitely feels crowded in here. Can you go monitor upstairs?"

"Sure."

"But can you stow my stuff in the office first? I haven't even made it back there yet."

She accepted my messenger bag and headed to the office. I texted my mom.

Jonah: I hate to ask, but it's bananas in here. Could you bring me lunch? Will make you dinner!

Mom: Of course, baby. Run it over in a few.

Bailey walked out of the office and smiled as the door opened to admit three more customers. "You wouldn't be able to tell from your face that this is awesome for business," she said when they were out of earshot.

"Is it? I'm not selling records."

"But you're selling merch, aren't you? And the markups are better. Run a report."

I sighed and ran the totals. She was right. Barely lunch time and we'd already made what we usually made by closing.

"Well?" she asked, tapping her toe like a bossy librarian.

"Numbers look good."

"Then quit looking like they stole that much instead of bought that much. I'll be in jazz."

She disappeared up the stairs, and I went back to watching the customers and ringing up T-shirts and stickers. Another one of my regulars, Anton, walked in and stopped in surprise at the buzz of activity.

"It looks like a French Quarter souvenir shop up in here," he said.

"I know. What are you looking for today?"

"Right now? Nothing," he said as he scanned the store and took in all the people. "Did I forget it was National Record Store Day or something?"

I shook my head. "I don't know what's going on today, man."

"I'mma just wait a minute. Be back tomorrow for the Moses Boyd album. See you around." And he was gone, taking his record money with him. He always paid in crisp dollar bills, and I liked the ritual of watching him peel them off his small roll of cash and carefully count them out.

The door no sooner closed behind him than Bailey came flying down the stairs.

"It's Anneke," she said, her eyes snapping with excitement.

"What about her?" My adrenaline spiked just hearing her name.

"She posted about the store this morning. That's why we have so many customers today. Look."

She turned her phone toward me, but I was already pulling mine out to check Instagram.

There she was in a red sweatshirt and matching sweatpants, her hair in two braids, two large hoop earrings, and some bright white sneakers, and if the maker of that sweatsuit hadn't paid her at least a billion dollars to wear it, they should, because she made it look that good. She was flashing a smile and pointing at the Ledge Records mural over her shoulder. I read the caption and looked up at Bailey. "Hashtag see you around?"

"She's implying that she'll be here a lot more, and now you've made a ton of money off people who are chasing clout."

"Chasing clout?" Mom asked, stepping in to hear the last part. "Is that like catching Pokémon?"

"I'm Snapchatting that," Bailey said, giggling as her thumbs flew on her phone.

"It means people trying to get a come-up by being near someone famous."

"Or shopping where they shop," Bailey added. "Anneke gave the store a shout out on Instagram this morning, and we're busier than we can manage."

"*I'll* manage," Mom said, heading around the counter. "You go eat in the office, Jonah, and when you're done, you can eat, Bailey. I brought you some lunch too, but I know you usually grab a snack on the way in."

"You don't have to do that," I said, accepting the covered plate she handed me. "I can eat it right here."

"You could, but you don't need to. Go take a break. I'll call you if I can't handle something."

But Mom knew as much about any era of music before the 2000s as I did. She'd be fine, and we both knew it. She'd covered for me here and there when I had conflicts I couldn't get out of. Like the flu, mainly. And three bad days after my breakup with Maggie.

By the end of the day, we'd doubled our usual sales, and Bailey was gleefully restocking the shirts with the last of our backstock.

"I'll go order more, and decals too." She plopped a box of shirts down in front of me. "Put size stickers on these."

"I can't believe one photo from one person is enough to double business in a single day." I opened the box and started stickering. "But I don't think we need to buy more merch."

"I love you, dude, but you have no idea what a goldmine Anneke just turned the store into. You stumbled into it by pure, dumb luck and spray paint."

"Spray paint?"

"Yeah. The sign."

The Ledge Records sign was a mural painted by a friend from high school, Raphael, a street artist who tagged his work as V93—as in Vintage '93. He'd done it when I took over the store and some punk had busted up the old store sign. I couldn't afford to replace it, but I had some cash, and he needed it. He'd gotten pretty famous since then.

"Yes. Spray paint. She knows what works on Instagram. She let people know she hangs out here to draw in clout chasers. She used a visual that other people will want to take a picture in front of for *their* 'gram, which means even more free advertising. Text her and tell her thank you."

"Okay, but that sign has been out there for three years. Why now?"

"Are you a supermodel?"

I gave her an annoyed look.

"Exactly. So no one cares what you post. But now it's been blessed by an IG goddess, and this is making people recontextualize the sign. Did I mention the thing about how you definitely need to tell her thank you?"

I knew Anneke had been trying to do a nice thing, but Anton's comment about being a souvenir shop was feeling more like an accusation than a joke at the moment. These were rubberneckers, not customers, and I couldn't sustain a record store on T-shirts and stickers if my regulars were too annoyed to come in and buy music.

"I feel you over there pouting," Bailey said a few minutes later. "Stop."

"I'm not pouting. I'm trying to process."

"You're processing the wrong things if it's making you feel pouty. Look at the opportunities here. If we keep going at this pace, you'll be able to hire a part-timer, someone who can curate your hip-hop section and open it up to a new customer who *is* here for the music. Don't be shortsighted."

But all I could see was people listlessly flipping through records, not paying attention to the albums as they looked for photo ops or stood outside in front of the store's mural and took pictures after carefully positioning their bucket hats—so many bucket hats—and threw up peace signs. Peace for what, dummies? They were the ones disrupting the peace around here.

Like she could hear my thoughts, Bailey said, "Why don't you yell at all the customers to get off your lawn when they come in tomorrow?"

"Why don't you go away, and I'll finish all this?" I growled.

"No way. I'm invested in this store too. And if I leave, you're not going to put the T-shirts out, and while you may value your principles over money, those two things comfortably cohabitate for me in the form of merch sales." She price-stickered a tag with extra verve. "I'm increasing the shirt prices by five dollars, by the way. You're welcome."

Her words struck me harder than she meant them to, I was sure, but I felt her "I'm invested too" like a punch. "Hey, Bay? I know you love the store. You've done a lot here. I wouldn't minimize that."

She gave a grouchy sniff, her only answer another loud price stickering.

Eventually, we finished up, sealing a bank deposit bag that bulged more than usual. I shook my head as I locked it in the safe. I didn't want to grow the store's business this way. I'd need to have a conversation with Anneke about it. I'd woken up already counting down the three days until she'd be back again, but now our "Hey, glad you're back conversation" was going to have to start with "Let my business stay my business," and that was ... not awesome.

What was I even doing hanging out with her, anyway? Was a love of music enough for two people if it was our only point of connection? She lived a glamourous life, a literal jetsetter. She had a beach house and celebrity friends and enough money to hire Banksy to redo the store's mural.

And who knew? She might. She might get it into her head that it was what I needed next without asking me.

Bailey left to go study, so I locked up by myself and slid the keys into my pocket. But when I rounded the corner and saw the soft glow of lights through the house curtains, I kept walking. I needed to clear my head. Anneke had gotten in it, and I needed to get it on straight. She might not be the type who would ditch me for a better offer like Maggie had. In fact, I was sure she wasn't, because she had better offers every time she turned around and probably had for years. But that didn't mean we made sense, or that she was right for me.

I went back to my earlier question. Did we have things in common? Yes. Music.

Did we vibe?

Hell, yes.

Was that enough?

I walked for a long time, trying to figure that out.

18

ANNEKE

I only checked my Instagram message requests every couple of weeks, a quick scan to see if there was anything important I needed to respond to, but it was usually random fans and trolls whose messages I never read. They were each in their own way equally toxic. Miles and I had talked early on about how we should never believe our own hype, and reading too many fan messages was a quick way to become toxic yourself. And trolls were toxic, period, so that was a no-brainer.

But today I noticed about six in a row from an account called Crescent Bai and the spelling caught my eye. Bai like Bailey, maybe?

I squinted at the thumbnail photo. Yeah, definitely her. I opened the messages:

It's Bailey. I'm hitting up your
DMs because I
Need to tell you
That my brother is an idiot.
Sorry for all the alerts. Wanted to make sure you saw.
Let me know when you get these.

I read through the linked messages again. Interesting but also confusing. I had no idea what to make of it, so I sent a message back with my cell number and told her to text me. Within a couple of minutes, my phone buzzed.

Bailey: Saw your IG shout out for the store. You're the best.
Anneke: You're welcome. Hope it helped.
Bailey: It did. But did I mention Jonah is an idiot?
Anneke: ???
Bailey: Lots of customers, and he's kind of mad about it.
Anneke: ?!?!?!
Bailey: THAT'S WHAT I SAID
Bailey: He thinks he's mad bc he wants to keep the store pure

I rolled my eyes. I should have guessed there was a fair chance that was how Jonah would react. Music nerds tended to fall into two camps: purists, who liked clearly drawn lines between genres, and eclectics, who embraced everything, loved it all, liked the fusion of genres and dug concept albums that most fans bought out of duty then hated. Purists didn't like dabblers or newbies. Eclectics were "big tent" types who welcomed anyone interested in music, even at the most superficial level. Of course Jonah would be the guy who only wanted music nerds in his store, not tourists, never mind that their cash was worth the same amount of money.

Bailey: I'll set him straight. But I'm doing damage control and asking you to be patient with him while I get his head right.

I read her message again, considering it. In his own way, Jonah did the same sort of tortured artist thing that Erick did, so I got it. I didn't love it, but I got it. The question was whether I wanted to deal with it.

I texted Bailey a thumbs up and let it drop, not even sure what I was trying to say with the emoji. But I was tired after shooting a campaign for a new lipstick color all day that had me in everything from a white swimsuit cut to my navel to a red evening gown with my hair in a glam 1940s updo. I put my phone on the charger and climbed into my bed at my agency's crash pad, a three-bedroom apartment in Chelsea where models could stay for less than a hotel.

But I pondered the question as I met with my agent the next morning and went on two go-sees that afternoon. And all the way home on the plane the day after that. Or all the way to New Orleans, anyway. I had thought of it as going home. Hmm.

I walked in and hollered up the stairs. "Miles?"

"Yo!"

I flew up the steps to the kitchen. "Oh, good. You're here. I thought you might be at the club already." It was late afternoon, and dinner service would start in a couple hours.

"Not today," he said. "I made Jordan take the night off last night, and he's making me take tonight off."

"Doing anything fun?"

"Ellie's coming over with her crew."

"Who's her crew?"

"Her roommate and her brother. You going to be around, or you off to see your new boyfriend?"

"He's not my boyfriend. And I don't know what I want to do. I think take a nap then wake up and figure it out."

He nodded. "All right. We're hanging out here while Ellie's brother makes dinner. You're welcome to join us."

Another thing I loved about Miles was that he wasn't being polite. He meant the offer, and he also wouldn't be offended if I stayed in my room.

"Thanks, friend. Maybe I'll come out of hibernation later." I headed to my bedroom, tossed my carryon to the floor, and collapsed on the bed. I traveled so much that it rarely exhausted me. I was too used to the pace. I didn't think I even felt tired right now as much I felt pouty. I'd spent my first day in New York looking forward to coming back to New Orleans until Bailey's text had changed that. And I was annoyed with Jonah for being complicated and having feelings and opinions that were different than mine.

"You're ridiculous," I told myself out loud to make sure I was listening. Then I curled up and took a pouty nap, not waking until the smell of something delicious tickled my nose as dusk filtered through my window.

"Hey," I said, shuffling into the kitchen in my bare feet. Miles was sitting on a counter, Ellie tucked between his legs and leaning against him as she laughed at something a girl with the best hair ever was saying. I recognized her from opening night at the club. The smells were coming from whatever the guy at the stove was cooking.

"Hey," Ellie answered. "Glad you're back."

And that was a thing I liked a lot about Ellie. She meant it too.

"Ellie, you're the coolest," I said to her, grinning.

"Thanks. You've met Chloe, who is the coolest roommate ever, and Dylan, who is the coolest—" She broke off with a cough. "Well, meet Dylan, who is my brother."

Chloe hooted, and Dylan made a rude gesture at Ellie without even looking.

"Good to see you again," Chloe said.

Dylan did a quarter turn and saluted me with a wooden spatula before he turned back to the stove.

"How was New York?" Miles asked.

"Tiring," I said. "No down time, really."

"You do seem pretty tired."

I sighed. "That's not New York. That's boys."

Chloe, whose dark hair fell to her chin in a ripple of gorgeous curls, propped her chin on her hands, her face perking up. "Ooh, tell me. I'm good at boys."

Dylan snorted, and Ellie nodded. "It's true. She is."

"You want to play shrink?" I asked.

"Yes, please," Chloe answered. "Although you should know that I'm a reporter, but entertainment isn't my beat, and I would never use any of this anyway. Just don't want you to find out an hour from now that I'm a journalist and have you stressing."

"Thanks, I appreciate it, but I'm not worried." I was an excellent judge of character, and Chloe had good vibes. "So, Jonah."

"He owns Ledge Records and Anneke loves him," Miles explained.

"Do not. He's giving me problems." I explained about talking online, going out a few times and getting mixed signals, the selfie, and Bailey's text.

"I'm going to be honest, I already have an opinion here," Chloe said.

"But that's the background, so why don't you spell out the problem, so I can make sure I'm right?"

"Doesn't matter," Dylan interjected. "You're going to think you're right no matter what she says."

"Shut up, cook." Chloe threw a grape from the fruit bowl on the kitchen island at him, which he dodged. "Talk, Anneke."

I exchanged looks with Ellie, like, *What's up with those two*? Her answer was a slight shake of her head.

"I used to date this guy in a band," I began.

"Erick Hyde," Miles said with a scowl.

"Like from Hyde and Seek?" Dylan asked, looking at me, kind of startled.

"Yes, dummy," Chloe said. "Continue, Anneke."

I laid out my history of Erick, and when I finished, Miles shook his head. "She's making it sound kind of bad, but it was *really* bad. That dude was such a tool."

"*Anyway*," I said, glaring at him, "Erick exhausted me. A lot of creative types do. Except when they don't. Like Miles."

"Love you too, supermodel," he said.

"I mean, Miles has his quiet moods, for sure, when he's basically a space cadet because he's so checked out, working out new music in his brain."

"Totally," Ellie agreed. "Like his body is sitting in front of you but his thoughts are somewhere else?"

I nodded.

"Y'all, I'm right here," he said.

I ignored him. "I love that about Miles, how he takes joy in what he does, even on the days it frustrates him."

"I forgive you," Miles said.

"Stop interrupting," I said. "We're not talking about you."

"You are literally talking specifically about me and no one else right this second," he said.

Ellie patted his leg in a soft gesture that also clearly meant *be quiet*. "Yes but no," she said. "Go on, Anneke."

"I guess being around Miles made me think Erick was the same way until I realized he does more of the 'suffer for your art' thing. I didn't like that. Distracted, spacey, quiet … no problem," I said, pointing at Miles, who frowned. "Disengaged, thoughtless, sullen … just no."

Chloe nodded. "Totally get it. I can't stand temperamental creative types."

For some reason, this made Dylan frown. Were they together? I'd have to ask Ellie later. "Anyway, Jonah might sell records instead of making them, but he acts more like a temperamental creative type. The question is whether he's more Miles or Erick."

Ellie tilted her head up to look at Miles. "What do you think?"

"Me," Miles said. "Minus the part about being temperamental."

Ellie patted his leg again, and Miles pretty much pouted, which made me laugh. "You guys are so perfect together. Y'all," I corrected myself when Ellie looked like she was about to say something. "Y'all are so perfect together. You said you have an opinion?" I asked Chloe.

"She always has an opinion," Dylan said.

They were definitely dating or used to date. I was betting on used to.

Chloe ignored him. "I do. But I have a couple of questions first."

"Hit me."

"Does Jonah ever act like something he's talking about is too above you to understand? Does he talk about himself all the time and never about you? Is he overly preoccupied with his image?"

The answer to all of those was no.

Chloe pursed her lips. "I thought I was going to rule against Jonah here, but I'm going to make an exception, because he's suffered a recent trauma with his dad's death. And because my gut tells me there's more to the story about why he's so hardcore on the fake thing and letting people in. Sometimes guys do that because they're selfish and they don't want to prioritize someone else or take them into their decision-making. That's Erick. But I don't think that's what's going on here."

"I agree," Ellie said. "I think you need to give him one more shot to explain himself. But only one more."

Miles nodded, and that probably surprised me most, considering how protective of me he'd been through all the Erick drama. "Me three. But also, I wouldn't rule him out as a creative type. He was comfortable in my studio the other day, but I don't think it was just because of his dad. Dude knew what he was doing, and it was more than just because he watched growing up."

"You have an opinion on this, Dylan?"

"Don't listen to Dylan," Chloe and Ellie said at the same time, which made Miles laugh and Dylan shoot them a disgusted look.

"Never mind, Dylan," I said.

"I shouldn't feed any of you for that, but since I already made this, y'all are going to eat it and like it. Five minutes, Gabi," he said.

"That's me," Ellie said, noticing my confused expression. "Gabrielle."

"Oh, I remember now," I said, my face clearing. Miles had told me the story of how she'd gone by Gabi as a kid and Elle in college—Ellie to friends, and that's why he hadn't figured out that she was the same poor girl from the meme.

She and Miles moved to set the table without even talking about it, and Chloe and I exchanged smiles, and I knew that she was already picturing us being in their inevitable wedding, same as I was. And when I took my first bite of Dylan's glazed pork belly bowl five minutes later, I sent up a prayer that he would do the catering for it.

Dinner passed in a cloud of jokes—especially ones that Dylan and Chloe made at each other's expense—and by the time we'd helped Dylan clean up, my headspace cleared too. Bailey was sweet to go to bat for her brother, but I didn't have time in my life for someone as emotionally high maintenance as Jonah.

It was a bummer. A big one. I hadn't been this interested in someone in a long time. But this shouldn't all be so hard. How many misunderstandings could two people have in a short period of time before they had to recognize that maybe it made more sense to quit talking?

I bowed out of the game of Cutthroat Uno Ellie invited me to play with them and shut myself in my room for some meditation and mindfulness. I'd center myself and then curl up with the new Liane Moriarty novel. At least in her world, complicated people eventually sorted themselves out.

It was a good plan for the evening.

But the universe—or maybe just Jonah—had other ideas, because as I settled myself on the floor and turned on my meditation app, my phone buzzed with an alert from Noteworthy. Which meant Jonah.

I hesitated, knowing it was better to do the meditation and ignore the alert, but I sighed, knowing there was no way my brain wouldn't preoccupy itself with what the message might say.

Ugh, brain.

LedgeCase: The new Animal Collective comes out tomorrow.
AnnieBird: As if I didn't have that alert already set on my calendar.
LedgeCase: A true fan always buys vinyl.
AnnieBird: Only a true hipster believes that.
LedgeCase: Wounded to my flannel core over here.
AnnieBird: Turntables aren't travel-friendly. #StreamForTheWin
LedgeCase: If only you knew someone with a record store who would open up early for you to come listen to it in all its VINYL glory.
LedgeCase: Or even right now. I have the power. #AndTheKeys

It was after nine o'clock. If it was anyone but Jonah, I'd suspect him of a "You up?" text. But Jonah hadn't made a single move on me, so this definitely wasn't that.

I stared down at my phone and debated. He and his "flannel core" always made me smile on Noteworthy. This easy give-and-take, this was why I'd developed a crush on him two months ago. And why it had blossomed to full-blown attraction when I'd seen him in person. Um, the second time, anyway. He was quick and funny. And I'd had better conversations with him about music than I ever had with Erick, who only liked to talk about his own music, or even Miles, who liked different artists than I did.

I needed to clear my head more than ever. I wasn't going to make any rash decisions here. I responded with a simple, "Maybe," opened the meditation app, and closed my eyes as I listened to the guide's soft voice lull me into mindfulness.

It worked too well. I fell asleep on the floor, dragged myself onto the bed around midnight, and slept until mid-morning, my body waking up at what would have been eight o'clock, LA time. Los Angeles. Not Louisiana. Which mean that I'd inadvertently stood up Jonah, who would be opening the store right around now.

I hadn't said I would be there, but I'd owed him the simple courtesy of an answer, one I'd meant to give when I woke up to see if I had any more clarity.

I did.

I hauled myself out of bed and got ready for an awkward conversation.

After my mural selfie from a few days ago, fans would be on the lookout for me, so I took more care into dressing before I headed over, putting on the tangerine-colored, wide leg pants I'd just bought at my favorite Brooklyn boutique and a white corset top. I liked the play of hard and soft between structured and drapey pieces. I grabbed a pair of sandals that would work, booked a Lyft, and had my makeup routine done before it arrived five minutes later.

When the driver dropped me at the store, I paused on the sidewalk, composing my speech for Jonah. *I'm here to buy the Animal Collective album, but I can listen to it at Miles's house.* It would say, "I'm here to support your business. I don't have any bad feelings toward you. But I'm not up for whatever this is between us anymore."

I stepped into the store, and immediately three heads swiveled in my direction. Two were tourists who were clearly hoping they'd catch me here and were now fumbling out their phones for not-so-surreptitious pictures. The third was Jonah's. A smile stretched over his face the second he registered it was me and not one of the terrible tourists who wanted to give him money for things he didn't want to sell them.

But it was a great smile. One that reached his eyes. One that made me forget my pre-rehearsed lines. That made me wonder about the texture of his lips, and if they were firm or soft—or best of all—both.

"Hey," he said. "Welcome back. How was New York?" He was in a navy beanie today, and it made me realize that his eyes were that exact color. A blue so dark they were navy.

"Hey," I answered. "It's still New York. Which is always a good thing."

"You want to hear the new Animal Collective?"

"Sorry I didn't make it in earlier. My body woke up on California time, and—"

"Excuse me," one of the tourists said. She looked a couple of years younger than me, and her Lilly Pulitzer dress said she was probably a sorority girl. "I can't believe it's you. Could we get a picture?"

"Sure," I said, taking her phone and handing it to a bemused-looking Jonah. Then I put an arm around each girl and smiled, the smile I used for the Clarins sunscreen ads that invited whoever was viewing the picture to come play with me in the pool.

Jonah snapped a few pictures, and I handed back their phone with a friendly, "Nice to meet you," even as I turned away from them and toward the counter so that it wouldn't invite more conversation. They moved off toward another corner of the store, whispering punctuated by soft squeals.

Jonah shook his head. "Does that happen a lot?"

I shrugged. "More than it happens to you. But also less than you're guessing. They were expecting to see me here, so they recognized me right away. When I go around in my usual clothes, I can wear a hat or sunglasses, and people rarely realize it's me."

"A hat or sunglasses but not both?"

I shook my head. "Too obvious. It looks like you're trying to hide, and it makes people take a second look." I glanced around the store. The handful of customers wasn't by any means a throng, but it was still more than I'd seen in here at the same time on any of my previous drop-ins. "So how's business?" I asked it with a tone that said I knew we had things to talk about.

"Definitely more customers," he said.

"But ..."

He chewed on his lower lip, and I kind of wanted to, too. Chew on his lip.

This was a very stupid idea. I should have had this conversation via text. Or ignored him all together. Not come in here to stand around, wondering how he'd gotten even hotter in four days.

"Does it bother you?" he asked.

"The pictures? It comes with the territory. It's the price I pay for using my face to make money."

"I meant more how people only want pictures with you because they know you're famous and pay no attention to you when they don't know who you are."

"It would be a weirder if I wasn't famous and people were stopping me for pictures."

He gave a short laugh. "Fair."

I leaned on the counter. "What do you want to say, Jonah?"

He sighed. "I appreciate the shout out on your Instagram."

"Do you?"

He hesitated. "Let me rephrase: I appreciate your intentions in shouting out the store on social media."

I liked that he was being honest. "But?"

"But it's not really the branding I'm looking for." It was funny to hear phrases he'd picked up from Bailey coming out of his mouth.

"Haven't you heard the old saying about how all PR is good PR? Bailey says sales have been good for the last few days."

"They've been higher," he acknowledged.

"That's not good?"

"Not long-term." He scrubbed his hands over his face. "A handful of my regulars have wandered in. They put up with between zero to five minutes of these strangers in their territory, and they're gone, no records bought. I'm a record store, not a decal store. So I was wondering …" Here he took a deep breath, and I didn't step into the pause to make it any easier on him. "Could you take that post down?"

I tapped on my phone a few times then turned it around and showed him. "Done."

His shoulders sagged slightly, with relief, it looked like. "Thanks."

I didn't like the way the request felt. Like being asked to move at lunch so a different friend could take your spot. "But it's sort of ironic."

"Ironic how?"

"You and the 'keeping it real' thing."

His eyebrows crept up to nearly touch the edge of his beanie. "Still not seeing how that's ironic."

"As much as you're struggling with my job and my image, with fakes and phonies, with keeping your street cred in the store, you don't really put that much of your real self out there." It was the root of my frustration with him, I realized as the words came out of my mouth. I smiled, and it made him frown. "Brains are cool."

"What?" He looked frustrated. Or annoyed?

"Brains are cool," I repeated. "I just said something that I didn't realize had been bothering me, but it was. Clearly some part of my brain had already figured that out, it talked to the part of my brain that didn't know yet, and then it came out of my mouth. Brains are cool."

"Could you not do that?" He was scowling.

"Do what?"

"Be irresistible while you're roasting me, so I don't care that you're roasting me?"

"I'm not trying to roast you. Just speaking truth to power."

He rolled his eyes. "I have no power here," he said, pointing between the two of us. "None. Haven't since day one."

"Not true. You have a power of ..." I tried to think of the right word. "Of irresistibility," I concluded, stealing his word. "There's no other explanation for why I keep coming around even when you're—"

"What?" He cut in, his voice calm and measured. But his shoulders had tensed like he was ready to pounce. "When I'm what?"

"When you're insisting on everyone else being authentic but you don't show up as your authentic self."

His eyes narrowed now, in confusion again, but this time with a touch of anger in the tightness of the faint lines around them. "I'm not fake."

"That's not what I mean." I stayed calm. "I think everything you show is real. But you don't show all of you. It's not your full self, but it seems like you want me to be my full self all the time."

I straightened and smiled at him, happy and relieved to have worked out the thing that had been niggling at me. "Figuring that out feels like getting a pebble out of my shoe."

He sucked his teeth and watched me for a few seconds. "So you're offended that I asked you to take your picture down, and now I'm a rock in your shoe?"

Now I was getting irritated. "You're a rock in the shoe of my *soul*."

That made him blink, and when the corners of his mouth twitched, I realized how it sounded.

"Not a sole like a shoe sole. A soul like inside of my body. The one that turns into a ghost."

The twitching turned into a smile—that, to be fair, he did look like he was trying to fight—but he lost. I felt growly. I wasn't trying to make jokes right now, or even be a joke. "You couldn't possibly be a rock in my shoe, because it would mean you'd have to actually want to *touch* me." There. Brood on that, emo boy.

His smile disappeared. "You think I don't want to touch you?"

"Obviously not." This was embarrassing and not what I came to say. "I took the picture down. Good luck with the store, Jonah. It was fun getting to know you." I paused. "Mostly." I waved and walked out, glad the door was right there.

My foot hit the sidewalk, and I sighed, wondering why I had bad guy radar when I was generally a good judge of people. I guess I couldn't maintain that good judgment when there were pretty eyes and a strong jawline involved.

I had barely taken two more steps, when a hand slid around my wrist, and strangely, even in the split second before Jonah said my name and I knew who it was, I wasn't scared.

I stopped and turned. "Yeah?"

"You think I don't want to touch you?" Jonah repeated, his hand closing more firmly around my wrist. But it still didn't scare me. I knew he'd let go in a second if told him to.

I didn't answer him. I just looked at him, meeting his eyes. He stepped toward me but kept the light pressure on my wrist so I wouldn't step away.

"Now why would you think that?" he asked.

I still didn't say anything, mainly because I couldn't. I lost my voice when I saw his eyes as he took another step. It was the kind of look a man got when he wanted to kiss you, but only for starters. He took one more step, and I was forced to back up if I still wanted to see his face, but he closed the gap again. I took another step, and my back touched the mural, but Jonah kept coming until my shoulders were flat against the wall. He braced his hand on the wall beside my head and looked down at me, no smile on his face, a glint in his eye that was curious. Challenging.

Dead sexy.

"You trying to make an album cover here?" I tried for a joke. Guys made passes at me all the time. I knew what the lead up to a kiss looked like. I'd just given up thinking I'd see Jonah's version of it. I also knew how to walk away if I wanted to. I stayed right where I was.

"I asked you a question," he said, his voice soft. "Why would you think I don't want to touch you?"

"Because you don't. Didn't," I corrected myself when he gave the lightest squeeze to my wrist.

He picked it up and brought my hand to his mouth. "But I do." He pressed a kiss into my palm, never taking his eyes off mine. "Want to touch you," he added, like I wasn't very, very aware what he meant. "You okay with that?"

I let my fingers graze the line of his jaw. "I'm okay with that."

He bent the arm supporting him on the wall, so now instead of his palm holding him up, his forearm rested there instead, bringing his face so close that our noses almost touched, and I could smell him. The warm cotton of his shirt, but beneath that, the scent of cedar and nutmeg. It was so slight, but I'd done a campaign for Gucci two years ago, and I'd know the scent anywhere. It was their Last Day of Summer cologne, and if Jonah was anything, he was that in this moment: the cute boy you've flirted with all summer, the one you know you need to kiss tonight or he'll leave and you'll regret not doing it.

Would I? Or would I regret this kiss more, given how much of himself he held back? Did I want this one additional piece if I wasn't going to get all of them?

Whether my mind knew the answer or not, my body seemed to have decided as my chin tilted up ever so slightly. A dare. Or even an invitation. *Do it, Jonah.*

And he did, dipping his head down and touching my lips in the lightest graze, like he was giving me the space of a breath to say I'd changed my mind if that was what I wanted to do.

I answered with the softest possible kiss of my own, and then he was kissing me—*really* kissing me—in a way that delivered on every promise I thought I'd sensed that night in the store after Saul Vandenburg had gone upstairs, and I'd stood in the circle of Jonah's arms, giddy at the edge of possibility.

All those vibes I'd sensed, all that chemistry that had been contained in a few touches—near touches—between us, touches that I'd begun to wonder if I'd read too much into ... none of it prepared me for the sheer voltage of the electricity that leaped between us when he kissed me for real, his lips as firm and soft as I'd hoped they'd be, his mouth sure and insistent, the hand that had been around my wrist now letting go and coming up to cradle my head, his fingers tangling in my hair as he held me at exactly the right angle to deepen the kiss. How did he know this was exactly the right angle when no man had ever found it before?

My hand crept up to grab a handful of his shirt, and I strained toward him to return the very, very good kiss he was giving me, blood rushing so hard through my head that my cheeks burned and my ears thrummed, and then it all got louder as his lips opened mine, and he dipped inside to explore and taste.

Someone growled softly. I thought it was him for a second, but it was me, and he answered by pulling away with a ragged breath that made me growl again, this time in protest, but he'd only moved so he could press a kiss to the corner of my mouth, then along my jaw until he reached my ear. He brushed an open-mouthed kiss against the soft skin beneath it, stealing a taste before he pulled away again.

He pressed softly against the back of my head to bring it down so our eyes met. "You were wrong." His voice was soft but rough. "I want to touch you."

I reached up and ran a finger over his bottom lip. He nipped at it. "I'm glad I was wrong."

"You're wrong about everything you said in there."

I blinked up at him, and he straightened his supporting arm to put a slight distance between us.

"I'm not hiding anything," he said. "I'm myself. You know me about as well anyone."

I shook my head. "I don't. I know we've had really good talks in our DMs. But when you took me to the float, that was about you explaining why you don't like phonies. It still wasn't you showing more of yourself. I'm going to give you a temporary pass on that because ..." Ridiculously, considering where the tongue speaking these words had just been, I felt heat creeping up my cheeks.

A half-smile that said he guessed what I was thinking curled up one side of his mouth. "Because why?"

"Because you're a very good kisser." He leaned forward like he wanted to prove it again, but I rested my hand against his chest. It was the lightest touch, but he stopped. "That's not enough. I don't know if you've heard, but I'm a supermodel."

He pressed his lips together and shot me a look like, "Uh huh."

"I can make out whenever I want to, to be honest. It gets very boring. It got boring forever ago. So you're going to have to bring something besides a pretty face to the table."

He eyed me, his eyes growing brighter. "You think I'm pretty?"

"You know you are."

Those lips twitched again, and he shot a glance at the store's entrance. "How about an excellent record collection?"

"It doesn't hurt," I said, smiling up at him. "But it's not enough." I pressed against his chest again, and he stepped away completely, letting me straighten and create some space between us. "You've seen pretty much my whole self, Jonah."

"So have you."

I shook my head. He believed that, but I knew at a gut level that it wasn't true. "It's okay if you don't figure out how to do that, but it'll mean I'm not the right person for you. Better to know now."

I took a few steps up the sidewalk and stopped and turned. "Let me know if you figure it out. If you do, I'm here for it."

He gave me a short nod that said he'd heard and understood.

And then I turned and walked away.

19
JONAH

I let her go.
I let her go.
Why would I have let her go?
But I did. I stood there and watched her walk away. Because she'd rocked my world. Shaken me to my core. Upended everything. And all with a kiss.
A kiss.
A kiss that wrote her name on my molecules.
What ...
How ...
Just ...
I stood there, staring long after she'd turned a corner and disappeared from view.
"Jonah?"
I turned when Bailey called my name.
"What are you doing out here?"
"Discovering the meaning of life," I muttered.
"What?"
"Nothing."
"You better get back in here. I can't run the register and help with

everyone on the floor. In fact, we probably better talk about hiring another part-timer."

I walked back toward the store, already shaking my head. "Business is going to settle down real quick."

Bailey stepped back so I could walk into the store, then followed me. "What do you mean?"

"I'm making adjustments. There's no point in growing our business if we're growing it with the wrong customers."

Her hands curled into fists, and it was clear in the clench of her jaw that only a supreme act of self-control was keeping her from beating me. "I am so sick of your narrow ideas of right and wrong customers."

I was about to try to explain myself about having Anneke delete the post when a girl in a high school uniform walked in. Her eyes darted around as she adjusted to the softer light inside the store.

"Is this the store that Anneke Jansen hangs out in?"

Bailey said, "Yes," at the same time I shot her an I-told-you-so look.

"Cool," the girl said. "I follow her Instagram, because I like the work she does on eco stuff. And my grandma just died, and I got her record player, but I don't really have anything to play on it except the records she has of old Broadway musicals. Those are cool, but I was thinking I'd try some other stuff."

"You came to the right place," Bailey said, smiling at her. "And you're asking the right guy. That's Jonah. He has a music library in his head."

"What kind of music do you like?" I'd peg her for a Swiftie. Definitely some Harry Styles.

"Everything, I guess. I listen to a lot of classic rock with my parents. And I like that. I think I want more of that, but maybe … I don't know, like, less hard? Does that even make sense?" She looked anxious, like she was worried she'd asked the wrong question.

"It makes perfect sense," I promised, and the music-finding tentacles in my brain started leafing through my mental catalogue, searching for what might work. "Why don't you come over to our listening station, and I'll have you try some sixties and seventies folk rock?"

"Sure," she said, and she looked nervous, but she clasped her book bag tightly to her side and waited for me to lead her to the music while Bailey took her place behind the register.

I started her off with a Joni Mitchell album, and when she'd listened to that for a while, she came back to the register to indicate she liked it. Then I had her try EmmyLou Harris, Patti Smith, and Fleetwood Mac's *Rumors*, which she loved best of all. Thirty minutes after she walked in, she left with that plus a Patti Smith album under her arm and a huge grin on her face. I told her to come back when she was ready to try some modern artists I thought she would vibe with, and she promised she would as soon as she had more allowance.

"Tell me again about how Anneke's post brought in the wrong customers?" Bailey said. "Tell me that connecting a kid with vinyl wasn't the most fun you've had in this store in forever."

"That was pretty fun," I admitted.

"Now say you were wrong to ask Anneke to take the post down."

"Not so sure about that," I said as I changed the register tape.

"Doesn't matter," Bailey said, her voice with the same smugness she used to tell me to *Go, Fish* in. "Genie's out of the bottle." She flipped her phone around so I could see the picture of Anneke with the two tourists. They'd tagged the store, and the caption read, "When you're just out looking for new vinyl, and you run into a supermodel."

I snorted. They hadn't even looked at the records.

"Okay, Scoffy-Pants. Say what you want, but this is just going to snowball, and that's a good thing. And I'm going to the office to order more shirts. Bye, dork."

She disappeared to the back of the store, and I watched the customers milling around inside, leaning over to straighten the pile of stickers and decals. With resignation. I straightened them with so much resignation. And I thought about Anneke that whole time.

That kiss was ...

It had been ...

Damn. What a kiss.

And there would be no more kisses coming if I didn't "show my whole self," whatever that meant. She already knew I was a music-loving super nerd who lived at home and barely made the bills. What other humiliating secrets did she think I was hiding?

I rang up a few more customers over the next two hours, trying to make sense of what I wanted.

I mean, besides Anneke. Because I wanted her now more than ever.

But in what way? She was going to keep flitting in and out of New Orleans, and I'd be a stop-over for her on her way to more interesting places. Was I willing to be available in the time she had leftover between other things?

And if I was, how was I supposed to convince her that I was showing her who I really was? I didn't know how to be more real.

Except ...

Except for one thing. I glanced toward the stairs that led up to the jazz section. There was another room up there, a locked one that would look like an office or storage room to customers. But it wasn't. And I hadn't been behind that door in more than two years.

I hadn't been whole since I'd closed it. I wasn't sure I was ready to open it. Not for her. Not for anyone.

But I didn't want our kiss to be our only one.

I spent the rest of the afternoon thinking about it, and when the store quieted down an hour before closing, Bailey assured me that she was fine locking up by herself. I wanted to go home and talk to my mom before she took off for work.

She looked up from the counter where she was chopping vegetables when I walked in. "Hey, baby. You knocking off early?"

"Bailey's closing for me. I wanted to talk to you." I pulled out a chair at the kitchen table and sat down.

She immediately set down her knife and began rinsing her hands. "Of course. Something wrong?" She dried them as she came to the table and took a seat opposite me.

"Kind of."

"A girl."

"Anneke."

"Tell me."

I filled in the blanks she hadn't already gleaned from dinners with Bailey blabbing all my business, skipped over the kiss, and ended with Anneke's challenge that I needed to show up as my whole self.

"I don't get it, Mom. I always try to be my real self."

She nodded. "I know, honey. Your dad drilled that into your head plenty, that's for sure. But she said *whole*, not real."

"Same thing."

Her hand covered one of my mine, enough to give it a soft squeeze. "It's not. She sounds very perceptive, this woman of yours. I'd like to meet her some time."

"She's not my woman."

"But you want her to be." It wasn't a question. She eyed me with a soft, knowing look. The kind of look that said she saw me with all of my flaws and loved them and me anyway.

"I don't know what I want."

"Sounds like a big part of the problem." She gave my hand another squeeze and then went back to the counter to chop some more.

"If I'm already being my real self, how am I supposed to show up as my *whole* self? This doesn't make sense."

"Have you told her about your dad?"

"Yes."

"Your music?"

She didn't mean the record store, and I knew it. I kept quiet.

"Ah," she said and went back to chopping but with such a slow rhythm that it was like listening to her meditate for a minute or two. "There's your answer. You'll have to decide whether you're going to tell her about why you quit. I don't have an opinion as to whether you should or not, but whether you tell her will say everything you need to know about this Anneke."

I nodded. "Okay, Mom. Can I help with dinner?"

She put me to work, and we finished making the ratatouille together, working easily as we had for years. She'd taught Bailey and me both to cook when we turned eight. It was embarrassing to be from New Orleans and not know how to cook, so we were more of the rule, not the exception. She stayed mostly quiet, as if she sensed that I had things to consider, and I turned her advice over and over in my mind.

Did I want to tell Anneke about my music? It was a closed chapter. There didn't seem to be much of a point.

But if it wasn't a big deal, why hadn't I mentioned it before?

Bailey came home and we ate together, me in silence, Bailey chattering about the big sales today, Mom asking her questions and leaving me to mull. Bailey shot me a few looks but left me alone.

Mom started to clean up, but I shooed her away. "Go get ready for work. I'll take care of this."

She disappeared into her room, but a few minutes later, she popped back out again, holding her phone out to me. "Uncle Joe wants to talk to you."

"Hey, Uncle Joe," I said, taking the phone. He was collecting on his return favor early.

"Hey, kiddo. How was the date?" He had the same growly quality my dad's voice had had, just a little higher, and it always gave me a faint pang in my chest to hear it.

"It was great."

"Your mom says it was some kind of supermodel?"

I rolled my eyes at my mom, who without hearing Joe's question, looked confused as to why she was being eyerolled. "Something like that," I said.

"Well, is she or not? I'm going to need specifics here." His voice had a touch of urgency. This wasn't idle chitchat.

"What's up, Joe?"

He sighed. "Damn krewe. It took five straight meetings—brawls—to get them all to agree on a king and goddess. Stormi Branson and Jax Collard."

"Good choice." They were local A-listers. He was the quarterback, and she was an Oscar-winning actress and now fashion designer. They both did a ton of work in the community. People loved them.

"Yeah, you got that right. Up until their publicist called me to cancel yesterday, because the team didn't make the playoffs, and apparently Stormi is taking the whole family on an extended Caribbean vacation to help Jax recover."

"Oh, that's hard, man. I'm sorry." There was barely a month until Mardi Gras, and the other krewes would have tapped all the other possible candidates. It would be hard to get someone of the same caliber on such short notice.

"Thank you, son. But then I remembered your mother saying something about this gal you're seeing. I've seen her in the, uh …"

He was polite enough not to mention that he'd seen her walking the runway in her skivvies for the most high-profile lingerie company in the world.

"Right. Yeah, she was in that."

"Not just *in* that. She wore the jewel bra. That's what they give to the best one."

Yep, I'd seen that too. Like I wasn't going to look when she mentioned wearing a two-million-dollar corset? I didn't say anything, just waited for Joe to get to the point. I had a feeling I knew what it was.

"Anyway." He cleared his throat. "You two still seeing each other?"

I wasn't sure how to answer that. "Probably?"

"Probably?" He repeated it like he'd never heard the word. "Yes, well. I guess what I mean to ask is, do you think you could see if she'd be the goddess?"

"She doesn't have local roots," I said. That was kind of the main qualification for the job besides fame: having New Orleans roots.

"Right, but maybe she *will*?" His voice was full of suggestion, and I had to shake my head. Uncle Joe was a good guy, and I knew he was in a tough spot, grasping at straws. But there was no gold to be spun here.

"She's just passing through, unc. I'm sorry."

A heavy sigh came across the line. "It's okay, kiddo. I knew it was probably a long shot."

He sounded so stressed that I hated to leave him hanging like that. "Do you have a king?"

"No. Probably John Goodman."

He didn't add *again*, but he didn't have to. John Goodman was a New Orleans boy through and through, and people saw him around all the time. They'd be plenty happy to see him atop any Mardi Gras float, but it wouldn't have the wow factor the Prometheus krewe liked.

"I might have a suggestion there. You know Miles Crowe?"

"The singer? Sure. Who doesn't?"

"Did you know he's back in town, and he's opened a new jazz club? Maybe he'd be up for it."

"Now that's an idea," Uncle Joe said, sounding perkier than before. "That's not half-bad."

Miles hadn't chased fame as hard in the last couple of years as he had in the height of his career, but there was a time you couldn't escape his music if you wanted to. Which, in Uncle Joe's words, hadn't been half-bad for full corporate pop. But Miles was as well known in Juneau and Cape Cod as he was in New Orleans.

"I think if you call over to his place, he'd probably be open to the idea," I said, giving him the name of the club. "Good luck."

"Thanks, son."

"Sounds like krewe trouble," Mom said when I handed the phone back to her and took the rag from her hand.

"Yeah. When isn't there trouble? Now let me clean up." I shooed her out of the kitchen.

I wiped down the counters and wished that I could have given Joe a different answer about Anneke. Not just because I wanted to help him, but because it would mean that she was putting down roots here if she were eligible. But Anneke staying in New Orleans ...

I rubbed at a spot on the counter like it had personally done me dirty. Women like Anneke went on to bigger things. Was already on to bigger things. Was at a level not even contained by a single continent.

Once Mom was off to work and the kitchen was clean, I told Bailey I was going out for a while.

"Don't do anything I would." She waggled her eyebrows at me. I scowled at her and made sure to double check the locks when I left, maybe more to keep her in than anyone out.

I wandered for a couple of blocks until my feet carried me to First and Last Stop, the best dive bar in the Seventh Ward, and I slipped in to have a beer and listen to the music from a table in the back. The NOLA Gents were playing, a soul group whose mellow vibe suited my mood. They were on point tonight, and as I listened to the guitar weaving through the notes rippling from the piano, I found myself mentally making a few adjustments, thinking through how I would lay down the track in my—

I interrupted my train of thought and rubbed my hands over my face with a sigh. It was my answer, I knew.

And weirdly, I was okay with it.

I reached into my pocket and pulled out enough cash to cover my drink plus a tip for the server. Then I pulled out my phone and messaged Anneke.

"What is going on with you?" Bailey asked when my head shot up as another customer walked in.

"Nothing," I said.

"Liar. You flinch every time the door opens. Who are you waiting for?"

"No one. And I don't flinch every time the door opens." If there was anything I hated, it was feeling transparent.

"You do, and it's opening a lot. Told you the social media would take on a life of its own. People want to roll their eyes at how much influencers make, but it's for a reason. And the fact that Anneke was clearly making an organic post and not a sponsored one is huge. I wonder if she got in trouble with her agent …"

She trailed off, looking confused. "I'm surprised we're still seeing a bump since she took it down." She pulled out her phone and tapped it a couple of times before her eyes went wide. "Uhhh …"

"What?"

"Wow, Jo. Been busy." Now her lips settled into a smirk. "But I think I know why the customers are still coming in."

She handed me her phone, and there, in some ridiculous artsy filter, was a picture of me kissing Anneke against the mural, like it was the final scene of a sexy arthouse indie film.

"Who posted this?" They'd tagged Anneke and Ledge Records, but I didn't recognize the poster.

"No going back now," Bailey said.

The door opened again, and this time it was Anneke. I shoved the phone back at Bailey and smiled at Anneke. "Hey."

"Hey."

I shot a look at Bailey. "Can you handle the store by yourself for a while?"

She looked anxious as two more customers followed in right after Anneke, immediately noticed her, and started whispering to each other. "I don't know, Jo. It's been kind of busy."

"We'll be right here. Just upstairs."

She looked confused for a minute, then her eyes widened. "Oh. Yeah.

Okay." And then the look she gave Anneke was tinged with awe. "Are you magic?"

Anneke's face looked adorably confused. "What?"

"Ignore her," I said. "Bailey, text me if you need me down here."

She nodded, wordless, and fluttered her fingers as if we were leaving on a long trip, not a single flight of stairs.

The energy between Anneke and I was weird. I guess I should have expected it after the way we left things, and then me following up last night with a text saying, "Come see my whole self. Ledge. 6:00 PM. Dare you."

She'd answered after an hour with a Noteworthy link to the Jackson Five's, "I'll Be There."

I was as sure as I would ever be about what I was fixing to show her, but I didn't want this strange, hesitant energy flowing between us when I did. It was already hard, and I needed to fix this.

I stopped on the stairs and turned to face her standing two steps below me. "Does everyone feel as awkward as I do when they're about to unzip their soul and hand it over to someone?"

"No idea," she said, like it wasn't the strangest question ever. "For some people it's no big deal, because they live pretty openly. Like my dad. He practically walks around with his soul on the outside. Other people, it's a bigger deal, I think." She reached for my hand. "I don't want you to do anything you don't want to do, Jonah. That's the point of all of this. If this is something you want me to see, then I want to see it. If it's something you'd rather not show me, I get that too."

"But you'll walk away if I don't?" I asked, running my thumb over the back of her knuckles. Her skin was so soft. I hoped she had a deal for lotion and that they paid her a truckload of cash. They'd still be getting a bargain.

"I will," she said. "But not in a take-my-toys-and-go-home pout kind of a way."

"Then what kind of way?"

She climbed another step, so she was still seven inches shorter than me than usual, but much closer. She rested one hand against the wall and the other on the stair rail and looked up at me. "In the I'm-too-grown-for-games kind of way."

"You think I've been playing a game with you?" I couldn't help a small smile. I'd never been a game-playing kind of guy.

"No. But you've definitely been on defense, patrolling your emotional boundaries. So up or down, Mr. Collier?" She smiled up at me, a very slight smile, one that said she would respect whatever I chose.

The answer was down. Down into those gorgeous eyes.

I reclaimed the hand she'd braced against the wall and turned to lead her all the way up the stairs, straight to my beating heart.

20
ANNEKE

I hadn't known what to think when Jonah texted me last night, but the words "Dare you" were irresistible. I had no idea what to expect, but a trip up to the jazz section was definitely not on the list.

As he took my hand to lead me up the last few steps, heat shot up my arm from the friction of his palm. How did he do that? How did he turn me on more with that innocent touch than …

It didn't matter. I didn't want to make any comparisons in this moment. I wanted to feel everything it had to offer without intrusions from memories or anything else.

We crossed the upstairs floor full of crates of albums. The early evening light was brighter up here, and each lazy dust mote that danced in the beams caught my eye. My senses were super tuned, and I could feel the weight of the glances the few customers up here snuck our way, but I paid them no mind.

Jonah led me to a wooden door in the corner that looked fairly old and weathered except for its electronic keypad. He punched in a code then stepped aside to let me in, flipping a light as I crossed the threshold.

He didn't say anything, watching me as I turned slowly, taking it all in, but he didn't need to explain what I was looking at. Not after spending so much time with Erick and Miles.

It was a recording studio, a small one, but the room was divided into two sections by soundproof glass. On the other side of the glass was another room accessed through a second door behind Jonah. Beneath the glass on this side, a large black nylon cover hid a soundboard. I knew without looking. I'd spent a lot of time behind them, watching Miles, especially, record.

"This is yours?" I asked.

He nodded.

"When was the last time you were in here?" The room had the stuffy vibe of a place that hadn't seen people in a while, but there was no dust on the nylon covers, and the recording booth looked clean through the studio window.

He shrugged.

I tilted my head at him. I wasn't going to ask any more questions. He'd have to decide how much he wanted to say. There were two swivel chairs tucked under the soundboard, and I slid one out and sat, hands tucked beneath my thighs, waiting.

"I can play," he said. "Drums. Bass. But I'm not brilliant like my dad was. I loved being on this side of things in the studio, watching the engineers, and when I was lucky, the producers, work. That's what I studied in college. Got a degree in sound engineering, emphasis in commercial music."

It was both a surprise and not a surprise. Jonah might project to the outside world that he was a hipster slacker, but he clearly had a lot of hustle, keeping Ledge Records going.

"So this is all yours?"

"Yeah." He walked over and stared down at the soundboard, not saying anything for almost a minute. I expected him to pull off the cover and start turning things on, but instead he slid the other chair out and sat facing me.

"That day at Miles's house, in his studio? It was the first time I've touched a sound board in a long time."

"How long?" I asked it softly, wanting to let him tell his story in his own way.

"Two years." He shrugged again like he wasn't sure. "Something like that."

But I had a feeling he knew when exactly. "You looked happy in Miles's studio."

"I was."

"But you didn't come back here to your own."

"There's a story," he said. "It involves a girl."

I waved to let him know that was fine with me. I didn't want to do or say anything to disrupt the spell he was falling under. A spell of memory, possibly.

"Maggie," he said. "We met about a year before my dad died when I was running sound at one of the bars where her band was playing. They were Americana, not strange in New Orleans, but not usual either. And they were really good. I went up to talk to them after, and she asked if I had any suggestions since I probably saw a lot of acts come through the bar. So we got to talking."

He pulled off his beanie which left tufts of his hair sticking up. He ran his hand through it, an aggravated gesture that did nothing to settle it down. "You sure you don't mind listening to this?"

"I'm sure."

He shot me a look that expressed doubt.

"I'm sure," I repeated. "All the people we've known, they make us who we are. We're shaped by them. Not only does it not bother me to hear about the people who made you, I *want* to know. I always want to know. You owe something to Maggie. I'm interested in discovering which parts."

"None of the good ones," he muttered. Then a small smile tugged at his lips. "You're a different kind of girl, AnnieBird."

I shook my head. "Oh, no. Don't tell me 'I'm not like the other girls.' That's a step down the road toward misogyny, and you've already got an orange flag for your Holden Caulfield love."

The smile grew. "I misspoke. I meant to say that you're a different kind of person, Anneke. No better or worse than other girls. Just a unique human experience I haven't had before."

My tummy fluttered. I couldn't deny it. The lead singer of one of the world's most beloved indie bands had sung straight to me from the stage of a sold-out concert, and there had been no fluttering.

"I'll grant a pardon," I said.

"Also, Holden Caulfield is the literal worst?" His voice went up, like he was testing how that landed.

"Once more with feeling."

"Holden Caulfield is the literal *worst*."

"Proceed, Collier. You are on a flag-free path. Unless you keep deflecting from spilling your guts, in which case, tower control will issue another flag warning."

His eyebrow went up. "Where is this tower control?"

I tapped the side of my head.

"Got it. In that case, Maggie."

"Go ahead and dish," I prompted him.

"Maggie and I got to talking. And then to hanging out. Then to me producing two tracks for them. Then to dating." He paused. "Am I supposed to fill in all the details? Like, how intense it was? Or how much time we spent together?"

"Only what you think is important."

"It was intense." Another pause, like he was waiting for a reaction to that. I'd had intense relationships too. If I'd wanted to still be in them, I would be. I just waited. "Our work and our … just everything mixed together, spilling into each other."

"Was that good or bad?"

"Good for the work." He sighed and turned his beanie around in his hands a few times. "Very good. We collaborated well. So well that she got an offer from a label in Nashville."

It wasn't hard to see where this was going. "And she took it."

He nodded. "There's no way to talk about this without sounding like a selfish jerk. Of course I wanted her to be happy. To succeed. She wanted me to go with her, but there was no way. The offer came in about six months after my dad died. I had my mom and Bailey. The store."

"That doesn't sound selfish at all. It sounds like you stayed and did what you needed to do."

"But I didn't support her going either. I wasn't like, 'Awesome, sprout wings and fly' or whatever."

"So you broke up?" It wasn't a great look, but I kind of got it from a practical standpoint. Lots of people didn't like long-distance relationships. Which I guess I'd need to know.

"Not at first. We said we were going to do the long-distance thing. But that didn't work because she sold out." He opened a laptop and began fiddling with it.

I blinked at him. I expected to hear they didn't work for the usual reasons long-distance relationships fell apart. "Sold out?"

"Yeah. Hang on." More typing. Messing with some knobs. Typing. "This was her when we worked together." He pressed play, and about thirty seconds of a song played with a pure banjo sound overlaying an upright bass for rhythm, no drums, which was common in Americana. Her voice had a feathery timbre to it, but a purity that translated to sincerity. Like it was untrained, but more convincing for it. There was also a familiarity to it ... my forehead wrinkled as I concentrated, trying to place it.

"This is her now." He changed tracks to a song I immediately recognized. It had been all over the radio last year.

"Your Maggie is Meg and the Reconcilers?" They were a huge breakout act last year. But their sound was very different. More Lady A than Americana.

"Yeah."

"They're ..."

"More hair than wit is what my mom and Shakespeare say."

I winced. It was a rude but accurate description. Big, lush country pop sounds with strong adult contemporary crossover appeal. Not a whole lot of substance when you dug into it much. Like, if you saw the lyrics written out, you'd think you'd stumbled over someone's bad high school poetry, but you didn't notice as much when the vocals were laid down over the big, round sound.

"It's true," he said, seeing my face.

"It's true. It's a big change." I could see the problem. I was listening to stark evidence that, for him, all of his dad's predictions about stardom changing people had come true in someone Jonah had cared about. Deeply.

"This was everything we used to mock." He turned down the sound but left it playing in the background. It was like he was picking an emotional scab, and I didn't know what to do here. Wait him out?

"I feel like I should try to say something wise, but I have no Yoda nuggets for you."

He turned off the music. "You don't have to. But this is who I used to be. A producer. It's my whole self, even if it's an old part."

"So you guys broke up and you quit producing because she sold out?"

He sighed. "It sounds stupid when you put it like that. I think the whole experience confirmed what my dad had always warned me about. That fame changes people. I thought she was unchangeable. An artist all the way through. And I loved her a lot." He scrubbed his hands over his face. "You sure this is okay?"

"More than okay. I think I'm starting to get you now." And it was true. These revelations were filling in missing pieces for me.

"When she played me her new music, I could tell without her saying a word that she'd already changed more than I would have ever expected. And that we were ending. After that, being in here just hurt. So I quit coming in." His fingers moved restlessly over the soundboard, brushing against a switch then skittering away to graze a button he immediately abandoned too.

I didn't know if he even realized he was doing it. I wondered if he was mentally correcting the sound on the Reconcilers song, stripping it down to what he thought it should have been. What I knew for sure was that this wasn't even close to being an "old" part of him.

"Anyway," he said, swiveling toward me again. "That's my big, tragic backstory. Just thought you should know."

"Why?" I asked. He paused his flitting to look at me. "Why do you think I should know?"

He sat back in his chair. "Because you said I had to show you?"

He sounded so uncertain that it made me laugh. "Fair, but why were you willing to?"

"Do I get cookies for correct answers?"

I smiled. "Deflecting. Why were you willing to?"

"But I really like cookies."

"Jonah ..."

He just sighed.

"How about I take a turn now?"

"Okay. I don't understand the rules of this game."

"That's because it's not a game. We're just telling each other stuff. Sharing. No one loses, everyone wins."

"It'd still be better with cookies," he muttered.

"Everything is, I think."

"Not diabetes."

I laughed. "Yes, you're correct. Eighty bajillion points to Gryffindor."

"I'm Ravenclaw." It was the most offended I'd seen him look, ever.

"It's cute that you think you are. Now do you want me to spill my guts or not?"

"Why do you say that like it's easy?" he complained.

"I don't think it's easy. But I think when people think sharing stuff like this is hard, it's because they're worried it'll get them rejected. Like, I could sit here thinking I don't want to tell you anything I'm about to tell you because you might judge me for it and be like, bye, leave, and no cookies for you."

"You wouldn't care if I did?"

"I'd be annoyed with you but not hurt by it, I don't think. Because that would be a you thing, not a me thing. If you like who I am right now, you have to be okay with what made me that, right? And if you don't, that's not really on me. You're not rejecting *me*. You'd be rejecting …" I trailed off. I hadn't really articulated this before. "You'd be rejecting stuff you don't have the emotional capacity for, and I guess we should know that, right? About each other?"

"Man, you talk about relationships like Big Al talks about jazz."

"I think that's a compliment?"

"I think I'm out of my league. You said you have no Yoda nuggets, but the lie detector determined that was a lie. I think you ate him."

I patted my tummy. "Does it look like he would fit in here?"

Jonah smirked. "You do keep it pretty tight."

I rolled my eyes. "I'm literally immune to compliments on my looks."

"Good, because I was complimenting your brain before that anyway. How do you know all this relationship stuff?"

"I don't know. I got burned a lot. Miles did emotional first aid a few times. And then one day when the burn was pretty much third degree and even Miles couldn't do it, I ran away to the Netherlands for two weeks and hid with my oma. And we talked about a lot of stuff, and maybe she's Yoda? But I didn't eat her. She's still in Utrecht."

"Does she make cookies?"

Instead of answering him, I whipped out my phone and placed an order.

"What are you doing?" he asked.

"Postmates is life. I'm ordering you cookies so you'll stop talking about them."

"I was kidding about the cookies."

"No, you weren't."

"No, I wasn't. I can concentrate now that I know they're coming. Tell me your thing."

"I dated Erick Hyde."

"Wait, like the lead singer of Hyde and Seek?"

"Yeah."

He looked frozen, like he thought whatever might come out of his mouth next would be wrong.

"I know you like his music. It's brilliant. People with good taste always love his music. But it was rocky between us. He cheated on me, and I took him back. That is, by far, the worst thing about me."

"Seems like the worst thing about him." He had a thunder face. It was the same expression Miles had when I'd told him.

"It's definitely not a good thing about him," I said. "But I took him back, because I fell into the same trap that I hate when people fall into with me, where I felt more special for being in his reflected genius, you know? It took me a long time to see it—that's the bad part—but being with him was more about how I wanted to see myself than about him. Which is not cool."

"Are you blaming yourself for him cheating?" He sounded like I did after I got off the teacup ride at Disneyland for the first time.

"No. His cheating is about his damage. Me taking him back was about mine. Look, I don't even think it's always wrong for someone to take back someone who cheated. I can't think of examples off the top of my head where it would be okay, but I'm open to the idea that there might be. What I have to own is that *my* reasons weren't good. I didn't understand them. So I'm telling you, the worst thing about me isn't that Erick Hyde, the god of Hyde and Seek, cheated on me."

He hadn't fidgeted for several minutes. We'd been sitting across from each other, him leaning back and watching me, me sitting in my chair with my legs crossed, applesauce style. "The worst thing about me is that I took him back because I put more value on who I was when I was with him than who I was on my own."

I rested my elbows on my knees and my chin on my hands and leaned toward Jonah ever so slightly. "You're upset because Maggie changed so much. Made herself unrecognizable to you. I had the opposite experience with Erick, who was so committed to his 'artistic integrity' that it made him toxic. Nothing was off limits to him if it fed his appetite for anything that he thought would help him create. Basically, we were co-dependent. But that's past tense. Because I learned. I'm telling you because I want you to know that I'm a person who just likes to be me with someone else. To show up as myself. And that will not ever change about me, because I like who I am now. And it took Erick to make me see that."

Jonah gave a long exhale through his nose. "I'm still not buying that dude any cookies."

"He's whatever, Jonah. Honestly. But it sounds like Maggie isn't whatever? She's a thing." That would be okay. Sad, but okay.

"Maybe not?" he said slowly. "Maybe I'm not over her. Not in a want-to-get-back-with-her kind of way. I don't want that. But like an I-need-to-go-to-your-oma's-house-and-eat-cookies kind of way?"

As if on cue, a knock sounded at the door and Bailey poked her head in. "Delivery?" she asked, extending a box from the Nola Cookie Company. Her eyes darted around the studio like she couldn't quite believe she was seeing it again.

"Thanks, Bay." Jonah took the box from her.

She stayed where she was. "It's good to see you in here."

He shrugged. "Don't get used to it. I'm just making a point to Anneke."

Her eyes darted to me, and I smiled.

"Thanks for dusting in here, by the way."

"That wasn't me," she said. A bell rang by the register, and she jerked her head to let us know she had to go and disappeared. Jonah smiled.

"We're back to my original question," I said when he sat back down. "Why are you willing to show me your whole self now?"

"Seems like you're looking for a specific answer, and I don't know it," he said. "How about if I bribe you with a cookie and you just tell me?" He held out half a toffee-bit cookie.

I leaned over and broke off half of that. "I'll ask point-blank. Does your willingness to show me your whole self mean that you're willing to see where this thing between us goes?"

"I want to," he said, but every word dripped with doubt. "The thing is, I'm not a casual guy. I throw myself into things completely, which is why I'm picky about what I throw myself into. I'm busy enough with my family and the store. But you …"

I held my breath as he scrubbed a hand through his hair. I didn't know what he was thinking. I … what? Made him want to rethink all of that?

"You're going to leave," he said, his voice blunt. "What am I supposed to do with that? You're going to find somewhere more interesting to be than New Orleans. Someone more interesting to be with than me. And I don't take loss well, Anneke. Not at all."

Part of me wanted to throttle him for being stubborn. But surrounded by the evidence of what he'd given up the last time he'd been hurt, I reached for compassion instead. "I understand. But remember, every ticket I've booked out of New Orleans lately has been round trip."

I stood up and leaned down to press a kiss against his forehead, a soft one that I hoped communicated patience and understanding. "I don't make promises I can't keep, Jonah, so I won't make one now. You're playing for keeps, and I respect that. Maybe I need to go think about what I want too. About what I have to offer. About what this is, and what I want it to be."

He started to rise when I stepped around him toward the door, but I pressed lightly on his shoulder, an unspoken message to stay. Jonah had his own thinking to do, and my gut told me that his abandoned studio was the very best place for him to do it.

21
JONAH

The door clicked closed behind me. Was that finality? Or was I being as dramatic as Anneke's ex-boyfriend, Erick Hyde, aka Lord Emo?

Did anyone besides a total idiot let Anneke walk out like that?

But I couldn't make myself get up and go after her, and I didn't think she wanted me to. If there was anything I was learning about her, it was that she meant exactly what she said. She was the opposite of drama. I thought she might mean it when she told me to take some time to think.

I turned up the volume on Maggie's song but paused it and switched to a track I hadn't listened to in forever. Two years, maybe? It was one of the old ones we'd laid down together, one that I hadn't quite figured out when she'd gotten the offer in Nashville.

I let it play through with just her vocals and the acoustic guitar, getting a little lost in Maggie's voice the way I always had. I leaned back and closed my eyes, listening to her sing about the simple pleasures of home. When it played through, I switched it to the big label version, once again met by a wall of sound pouring from the speakers.

I sighed. Yeah, they'd ruined it. They'd made it into a corporate product that would do well on country radio, but that's not what Maggie and her band had stood for just a few years ago. Back then, she'd wanted to break into Nashville and bring back a pure sound to the country charts. Not sing the mass-produced country pop she'd always ridiculed.

I scrolled through some of the older tracks in my files, pulling up one from a young guy I'd met at Sweet Lorraine's Jazz Club, a guy named Travell who had flashed me a grin and told me he was a one-man blues revival. I'd recorded a couple of tracks for him to make a demo, and I replayed them now, closing my eyes and disappearing into the soft growl of his voice and the lyrics that spoke of heartache that I only understood now. In fact, if I were to record these with him again—

I straightened, and my hands flew over the sound board, sliding faders and tweaking the EQ.

An hour later, I jumped about a mile when a soft hand touched my shoulder, and I twisted to find my mom there, smiling at me.

"Bailey said you were up here. I wanted to see it for myself."

I paused the music and set my headphones down. "Have you been dusting in here?"

She smiled but didn't answer, her eyes running over every square inch of the studio. "You got any of your dad's stuff?"

I nodded and pulled the other seat back for her to sit, already calling up the old tracks my dad and I had worked on.

"This is him and Al just messing around one day," I said as the saxophone began to wail. "I was on drums. Does it make you sad?"

She shook her head. "It would make me sad if I couldn't hear him every time I wanted to."

We sat in silence for a long time, listening to three more tracks before the recordings from that session ended.

I closed my laptop and let the silence envelop us.

"You look good in here," she said after a minute.

I could feel her windup pitch coming. "This is just a one-time thing."

She was shaking her head before I could even finish. "It shouldn't be. This should be your all-the-time thing. This should be your every-spare-second thing. This should be your sell-the-store-and-do-only-this thing."

I stirred, uncomfortable with that. "Mom, he loved the store. I wouldn't sell it."

"He loved you more. And if it keeps you too busy to be up here, then he'd say to hell with the store." She said the last part in an imitation of my dad's gruff voice that almost made me smile.

"He'd want me to keep paying the bills."

"You have enough talent in your little finger to turn into one of the finest producers in New Orleans. It would be more than enough to pay the bills. I didn't realize how much it was breaking my heart for you to leave this studio empty until I saw you in it again."

I shut down the laptop and turned off the soundboard. "Time to go eat."

"Jo—"

"I'm hungry," I said with the tiniest whine. No Southern mom could stand to think a child of hers was hungry.

She knew I was playing her, but she couldn't resist the bait. "All right. I made rosemary chicken. Let's get you fed."

The subject of the studio stayed dropped until she left for work, but in my room, I pulled out my phone and looked up a number I hadn't used in forever. I didn't know if it was even still current, but I texted it to see. The reply came back in less than a minute. "Yoooooooooooo! What's good, man?!"

And just like that, I turned back time.

———

LedgeCase: I'm dropping a link. Your mission, should you choose to accept it, is to listen and respond.
AnnieBird: Jesse McCartney? Is he related to Sir Paul?
LedgeCase: He wishes. Just listen. I had to go to the Way Back Machine to find that.
AnnieBird: Pressing play.
AnnieBird: Hmmm. Did he just say he doesn't want my pretty face but my beautiful soul?
AnnieBird: This has very strong boy band energy.
LedgeCase: l i s t e n
AnnieBird: Okay. I listened.
LedgeCase: To the part where he said, uh …
AnnieBird: Said w-h-a-t

LedgeCase: This is ridiculous. I can't do this via some stupid pop song that came out when I was in third grade.
AnnieBird: DO W-H-A-T
LedgeCase: You're killing me.
AnnieBird: I'm definitely going to kill you.
AnnieBird: Hang on …

I'd never broken a sweat as hard as the one I broke while I waited for her to respond. I had no idea what to expect. I mean, I'd sent her the cheesiest lyrics of all time from a kid who looked like he escaped a third-rate boy band and stole a mic at karaoke before his manager could stop him. But every other song I'd tried to think of to send her was too … much? Too much. Too serious. Too metaphorical. Too overworked. Trying too hard.

Anneke wasn't angst. She was simple and uncomplicated but in the way the best things are. And I wanted to state my case plainly.

So dumb. What was I thinking?

Her typing dots appeared, and then a few seconds later, a link of her own. I clicked it open to Ariana Grande's "Into You."

I wasn't super familiar with Ariana Grande's work, but as I skimmed the lyrics, my eyes grew wider. A sudden flurry of DM alerts came in, telling me that Anneke had just spammed me with a bunch of messages.

AnnieBird: Wait
AnnieBird: Unsend unsend unsend
AnnieBird: Why isn't it unsending?!
AnnieBird: Jonah, don't open that link! I messed up.
LedgeCase: You mean you don't want me to do all the touching your body stuff?
AnnieBird: Yes!
AnnieBird: I mean no!
AnnieBird: GAH
AnnieBird: I sort of forgot that part of the song.
LedgeCase: Which part did you mean exactly?
AnnieBird: Doesn't matter. I've died of embarrassment. This account is no longer active.

I listened all the way through the song as I re-read our messages despite three more messages from Anneke telling me to stop. There was something adorable about her panic. She was so laid back in person that I wouldn't have even thought her capable of this level of being flustered.

LedgeCase: Listened to it. I think I'm a superfan of Ariana Grande now.
AnnieBird: I TOLD YOU THIS ACCOUNT IS NO LONGER ACTIVE
LedgeCase: Who am I talking to then?
AnnieBird: A bot.
LedgeCase: An Anniebot? I'm intrigued.
AnnieBird: Stop. You're making it sound dirty.
LedgeCase: I'm not the one who sent lyrics about *checks notes*
AnnieBird: STOP
LedgeCase: Wanting me to 'light you up'? Did I hear that right?
AnnieBird: This is karma for when Kjarsten Jorgenson fell off her heels in the Givenchy show and I laughed.
LedgeCase: I'm judging you hard. Definitely karma.
AnnieBird: She ripped the seam on one of the other model's dresses so that she couldn't walk the runway.
LedgeCase: Then I hope you laughed loud. Why don't you tell me which part of those lyrics you meant then?
AnnieBird: Basically the first verse before the light me up stuff?
LedgeCase: Rewinding.
LedgeCase: Listening.
LedgeCase: So, you want us to cross the line?
AnnieBird: No! I mean the part about waiting for you to make a move.

I grinned down at the screen. I knew that was what she'd meant, but teasing her was so fun. I'd so rarely had the upper hand between us that it was hard to let it go. I texted her that I was about to call, then opened FaceTime.

She answered with a pillowcase over her head. "Hey."

"Hey," I said. "Is Anneke there?"

"No. She left the country. She's never coming back."

"That's too bad. Who are you? Do you like conversations with strangers?"

She tugged the pillowcase up so it revealed her face and hung from her head like a nun's wimple. "Sometimes. Are you a nice stranger?"

"Define nice."

"Nice like if someone did a mess-up on song lyrics she sent you, you wouldn't bring them up?"

I pretended to think about it. "I could be that kind of nice."

"If you aren't, I have to go."

"Okay, I'm that kind of nice."

"Then I'll stay."

I grinned at her and flopped back on my bed, my stack of three pillows settling nicely behind me.

"Are you in your room?" She craned her neck like it would let her see better.

"Yeah."

"Show it to me."

"It's not very exciting."

"I want to see it anyway."

I flipped the camera and panned around. It was a good-sized room, smaller than a master suite but it fit my queen bed comfortably, along with a desk, an easy chair, and an armoire. Lots of older New Orleans houses didn't have built-in closets.

"Is that armoire just full of band T-shirts?" she teased.

I opened the doors. "I have at least six that aren't band shirts," I said. "Maybe seven."

"So fancy. How many pairs of jeans?"

"Six."

"And beanies?"

"One hundred and four."

She gave a serious nod. "Sounds right. Now, you want to tell me why you've summoned me?"

"Let's say that I never sent you any lyrics from a nineties throwback boy band escapee. Let's say instead that I give you the following phrase, and your job is to respond to it."

She saluted. "I can do that."

I flopped back down on the bed and settled my arm behind my head, angling the phone so I could still see her clearly. It didn't seem to matter what angle or light she was in, she always looked … luminous? Was that a word? I'd have to ask some songwriting friends.

"I'm into you."

She blinked at me. "That's the phrase?"

"That's the phrase."

She seemed to be sitting cross-legged on a bed, and now she unfolded her deliciously long legs and stretched them behind her, settling on her stomach with her free hand propping up her chin. "I say, 'Good.'"

"Good?"

"Yeah. Good."

I wasn't going to get any more than that out of her, and that was my fault. It was my turn to give a little. "What do we do about that?"

She arched an eyebrow, and I wished I could reach through and trace it, the way it flared just so above the outer corner of her eye. "What do you *want* to do about that?"

I groaned and flopped my head against the pillow, smiling when I heard her laugh. "I want to spend every free second I have with you. Take you to all my favorite places. Show you all my favorite things. Feed you all my favorite foods. Introduce you to all my favorite people."

"Even though I'm leaving?"

I straightened a little. "Yeah. Even though you're leaving. I wish you weren't, but if it's a choice between some of you or none of you, I'll take what I can get. You should probably look away if you don't want to see a man losing the last shreds of his pride."

She smiled, slow and sweet. "Humility looks good on you."

"So when can I see you? Now?"

She laughed again. "This is quite a turnaround."

I shrugged. "Maybe. Maybe it's me leaning into the inevitable. If I'm going to think about you, whether you're here or gone, then I may as well get as much time with you when you're in town. So? What are you doing right now?"

The smile she gave me this time was regretful as she crept back up to sitting. "This, unfortunately." She reversed her camera so I could see the suitcase she was packing. "I have a shoot in Utah in two days."

"Utah? This is not where I expected to hear about a supermodel jetting off to. Going skiing?"

She flipped the camera back to herself. "No, but I'll be in an evening gown in the snow for a fragrance campaign in this fall's *J'Adore* holiday issue. Like nine months from now? And when that print campaign is running, I'll be on the Miami Swim Week runways for next spring's looks."

"Sounds cold."

"Kind of. I'm pretty much always dressed the opposite of the weather." She raised and dropped a single shoulder. "You get used to it."

I couldn't imagine it, so I didn't have anything to contribute to the conversation. When another beat of silence fell between us, I cleared my throat. "I'll let you get back to packing then."

She sighed. "I guess I better. But Jonah?"

Her breath caressed the syllables of my name so nicely, making them round and full. "Yeah?"

"When I get back home, I want to steal all of your free seconds. Go to your favorite places, see your favorite things, meet your favorite people. And taste …"

She trailed off, and I swallowed. "My favorite foods?" I supplied.

With a slow smiled, she shook her head, waved goodbye, and ended the call.

Lord, have mercy.

22
ANNEKE

"I did not expect that," I announced to the room.

The room didn't answer because I was the only one in it.

"Jonah Collier is into me," I tried again. The room did not respond.

But I did. I squealed and flopped back against the bed.

"Hey, Anneke, can I—" Ellie had knocked and popped her head in only to stop in the middle of her sentence as she took in the sight of me staring goofily off into nothing. "What's going on?"

"Jonah Collier is into me," I said, eyes on the ceiling, still not seeing anything but the replay of his face as he'd said it.

"Duh."

That got me upright. "It was surprisingly not obvious," I informed her.

"Maybe not to you," she said coming in and settling into the armchair in the corner. "But it was to anyone else. Everyone else. Literally *all* of the other people who have ever seen you two together."

"Yeah?" I liked hearing the confirmation.

"Oh, yeah," she said. "But tell me why you're just figuring it out."

So I did, all the way up to our FaceTime.

She frowned at me. "You left out some important details."

"Like?" I couldn't think of anything I'd skipped.

"Is he a good kisser?"

My only answer was to grin and flop back against the bed.

"All righty then," she said, the trace of a laugh in her voice. "Good for you, girl. I came in here for a favor, and I got a hot gossip bonus."

I raised myself up to my elbows. "What can I do for you?"

She sighed. "Can I borrow a dress? I told Miles I'd do a song with him tonight, and I only have one good dress for a performance like that, and I already used it."

"Absolutely." I bounded from the bed to my closet and threw it open, leafing through the hangers.

"Wow. You have more stuff here than I would have expected," she said, eyeing the closet's contents.

I paused and looked over my shoulder. "Is that weird? Does it bother you that I have all this stuff in your boyfriend's house? Because I don't normally give a rat's Aunt Fanny what Miles's dates think about me being around, but I *like* you, and I don't want you to be bothered."

She laughed and waved a hand like she was brushing off my concerns. "No, sorry, that's not what I meant. I'm glad you and Miles are doing your usual thing. I just mean you have almost half as much stuff in your closet here as I do at my house."

"Yeah, I've kind of been bringing an extra suitcase back with me every time I stop over in LA."

"Oh?" she said it with a note of interest. "And why is that?"

"Because I'm going to move in and steal your man," I said, more confident now that I could get away with the joke.

"You wouldn't want him."

"True," I said, turning to face her with a dress in my hand. "But why are you so sure?"

"Because if you guys were ever going to happen, you'd have happened by now."

I grinned at her. "How come all the other geniuses he's dated could never figure that out?" When she shrugged, I laughed. "And, P.S., it was never going to happen at all. Miles and I have never had that energy."

"I know," she said. "Watching you two around each other is how I sound with Dylan." She accepted the dress I handed to her, and her eyes widened when she saw the label. "Whoa, are you sure? I don't think it'll even fit."

I smiled at the silky gold slip dress in her hands. "Very sure. It'll look amazing under a spotlight. And it'll be fitted instead of loose on you, but it'll work. Spanx if you're self-conscious."

She hugged me. "Thank you." On her way out of the room, she paused and turned. "I'll make sure Miles orders a bigger dresser for this room."

I shook my head. "No, don't. Not that I don't appreciate it."

She took another step back into the room. "Then why do you keep bringing back more clothes?"

"I ... don't know." She gave me a look like, *Yeah, right*. "I guess wherever Miles is feels like home."

"Hmm," she said, heading back toward the door. "Interesting that he was here for six months before you figured that out, isn't it?"

"El—" But she shut the door before I could set her straight. I'd been busy, that was all. I'd have been out here sooner if my schedule wasn't always packed with shoots and shows, and—

I plopped on the bed. I knew what she was implying. That my steadily-filling closet had more to do with Jonah than Miles.

One of the things that Oma had taught me when I hid in her cottage for two weeks was that there was no such thing as hiding. Whether you confronted them or not, your troubles always followed you. No amount of running or numbing would make them go away. "Ga ermee zitten," she'd said, and waited until I looked it up in Google Translate. *Sit with it*.

So I sat in front of my open closet, noting the hangers filling more than half of it, the dresser close to running out of space.

These were not the signs of a woman passing through. These were the signs of a woman settling in.

I wasn't the settling-in type. My LA townhouse was a shared model apartment with a rotating cast of faces, because I didn't need my own place there. I wasn't there long enough to ever feel restless about the constantly-changing roommates. And in New York, I only had the model crash pad or a semi-permanent room in my friend Ilse's apartment if someone else hadn't claimed it while I was in town.

But here ... here I had my favorite shoes lined up on the floor of the closet, the ones I wore the most.

Miles was the longest-term friendship I had. That was why I felt comfortable here. I rose to finish packing, throwing in a pair of black leather booties, leggings, and a gray cashmere tunic. It was the kind of effortless style models developed to communicate low-key good taste without a strong personal fashion point of view that might interfere with the client's vision when we showed up on set. Or slope, as the case would be tomorrow.

Except ... I sank down on the bed again. It wasn't just Miles who made me comfortable here. We'd always clicked from the very first time we met, because—as he'd explained to his parents once when they came to LA for a visit—real recognized real. I had that same feeling of recognition with Ellie. And Chloe. Possibly even Dylan.

And definitely with Jonah.

So why just bring another suitcase home after my next LA trip?

And then I heard it. I'd thought of New Orleans as "home."

When had that happened?

And what did I want to do about it?

———

Utah was beautiful. I think. I didn't pay too much attention, because if I wasn't looking into the camera—or just past it for an artsy pose as the photographer requested—then I was looking at my phone.

Jonah and I had fallen into a pattern in the way we communicated: if it had anything to do with music, it was on Noteworthy. If it was text, then it was everything else. And that night, as I was curling up in my hotel room to rest for another long day of shooting, I learned what FaceTime was for: when we weren't in the same city and really wanted to be.

At least, that was how it felt to me when Jonah's FaceTime call trilled on my phone.

I opened it and smiled at him. "Hey, you."

"How's Utah?" he asked.

"Cold. Where are you?" I squinted at the background. It didn't look like his bedroom. It looked like ...

"The studio."

"Really? And no one emotionally blackmailed you to be there?"

He smiled. "You didn't emotionally blackmail me."

"I kind of did."

He shook his head. "You provided an incentive. I made a choice. I'm glad I did."

My stomach flipped at that. "Yeah?"

"Yeah." He glanced around, and I wished I could see all of it. "Yeah. I closed up the shop about twenty minutes ago, and now I'm waiting for a friend of mine. Travell. We used to work together. He's going to drop in, and we'll see."

I wanted to push him on that. See what? If he still loved making music? Of course he did. It was written into his DNA. But he'd tell me when he was ready.

"How was the shoot today?" he asked, clearly wanting to change the subject.

"It was fine. I had to frolic in the snow without smiling, but I like snow, so it was hard not to smile."

He shook his head. "Can you even frolic if you don't smile? If there's no smiling, then I think you have to call it something else."

"You make an interesting argument. What's it called if you're not smiling?"

He thought for a second. "Prancing."

"Prancing?"

"Yeah."

"I think you have to smile when you prance too."

"No. I'm sure about this. People who prance take themselves too seriously. So if you're doing the same motion while smiling, it's frolicking. No smiling, it's prancing."

I leaned back against the fluffy hotel pillows. "I can't believe I'm buying this argument."

He tapped the side of his head solemnly. "What else about Utah?"

"I only drove from the airport straight to Park City, but I can tell you pretty much all those bits are pretty. It's kind of wild that in two days, I'll be stepping off a plane in New Orleans again and it'll be seventy-five and humid. Kind of blows my mind that all of that exists in one country."

We talked for another hour about unreasonable demands the photographer had made, about customers he'd had in the record store that day, about when he would put the signed Placemats vinyl up for sale. I'd nudged him about that a couple of times. I wanted to bid on it anonymously as soon as it went up.

Jonah's eyes darted to something off camera, and he turned back to smile at me.

"My friend Travell is here. I better go. When do you get back Thursday?"

"In the afternoon," I said.

"I'll call you when I close the store. Sound good?"

Yes and no. Any call from him sounded good, but I wished he would call tomorrow. And text in between. And send me Noteworthy DMs between all of that.

I thought about him all the next day, and then I thought about how much I was thinking about him. I liked having Jonah on my mind, liked having my thoughts wandering to him every few minutes. Okay, every couple of minutes.

Fine, all the time.

In fact, by the time I made it back to my hotel room the next day, I didn't want to wait anymore. There weren't any direct flights from Salt Lake to New Orleans until the one I was already booked on the next day, but if I flew down to LAX, I could get an early flight to New Orleans that would have me landing around breakfast time.

I didn't think too hard about it, just made the changes and called a Lyft for the airport. In LA, I swung by the condo, patted JoJo on the head, loaded up another suitcase, slept for four hours, and headed right back to the airport.

My Lyft driver in New Orleans deposited me in front of Miles's house at least two hours before his alarm was even thinking about going off. I walked in to find Ellie in the kitchen, dressed for work, a cup of coffee in her hand and a magazine open in front of her.

"You coming in late or getting up early?" she asked.

"Just landed."

"You must be tired."

"Yes and no." I was the tired that came from taking a string of flights, but beneath all that was a restless energy, like I was counting down until the earliest possible minute I could get away with calling Jonah.

"Have some coffee," she said, standing and pouring me a cup.

"Thanks. How's life?"

She told me about a new deal she was closing on, a retail property in the Central Business District. I didn't understand much about commercial real estate, but I always liked listening to people who were good at things talk about that thing.

She'd just moved on to talking about needing to lease the apartment across from her when she rose, walked to the fridge, and pulled out a purple and green monstrosity that made me lose the thread of our conversation.

"What is that?" I asked as she set it on the counter.

"King cake." She reached for a knife.

"You say that like I know what it means."

She paused, knife hovering over the cake. "You don't know what king cake is?"

I shook my head and stared at the … thing. It was ring-shaped and frosted with purple, gold, and green icing and colored sugar. "I'm guessing it has to do with Mardi Gras."

"I'm ashamed of Miles right now. I can't believe you've known him all these years, and he never told you about king cake."

"Don't deprive me of knowledge for another second. What is it?"

"We eat this during Carnival"—she pronounced it almost in a French way, with the accent on the last syllable, which she gave a short A sound—"which runs from Twelfth Night until Lent. Although, honestly, bakers sell these year-round here because of tourists, and I don't blame them."

"So it means something."

She nodded. "You know what the Mardi Gras colors mean?" I nodded, remembering Jonah's explanation. "So that's the main thing. It's always ring-shaped, but I don't know why. Kind of everything comes down to good luck. It's cinnamon dough, twisted, frosted, sugared. And if you're smart, which I am, you buy the kind with the cream cheese filling."

"That sounds amazing."

"You're about to find out," she said, setting out two plates. "Watch out for the baby."

I wrinkled my forehead at her, and she smiled as she set a second slice on a plate and handed it over. "There's a plastic baby baked into each cake. Well, not anymore. Now the bakers put them on the outside of the cakes so they don't get sued for a choking hazard, which is why I don't get mine from a bakery. I get them from an old maw maw in the Bywater who sells them out of her house, and she still bakes the baby inside. If you get it, it means you'll have good luck. And it also means you have to buy the next king cake."

Ellie picked up her slice and ate with her fingers, like a pastry, so I did the same, giving a happy grunt when the cream cheese and cinnamon flavor hit my tongue. "Oh, this is good."

She nodded, savoring her own piece. "Not all king cakes are created equal. There's some dry, mass-produced ones out there, so watch out for those. I'll tell you where to get the real deal if you want to buy your own."

I finished off my piece. "Go ahead and tell me. I want to pick one up for Jonah on my way over. That's okay, right?" It struck me that there might be some kind of significance attached to it that I didn't know about. "I'm not accidentally proposing marriage or declaring my love if I show up with a king cake, am I?"

"No more than if you brought donuts. Although why anyone would show up with donuts during king-cake season, I don't know. I'll text you the address for this place. Trust me, after one of Maw Maw Gautreaux's king cakes, everything else is a letdown."

She boxed up the rest of the cake, and I scooped up my bags and headed for my room, tired but too wired to sleep. Instead, I jumped in the shower to knock the travel funk off me, then considered my closet before pulling on a black sleeveless jumpsuit with a soft blue hoodie designed to look like it had been worn a hundred times. I added stacked flat sandals that gave me two more inches, and a simple fleur-de-lis gold pendant that had caught my eye in the airport gift shop.

Forty minutes later, I was standing in front of a house with a box of king cake under my arm, hoping I'd listened well enough to guess right.

Anneke: Is your house turquoise with bright yellow shutters and a cherry red door?
Jonah: No.

My heart sank as I looked at the house in front of me. He'd said it was right next to the store, hadn't he? This was the only house close enough.

"It's tomato red," Jonah said, stepping onto the front porch.

He wore flannel pajama bottoms and a wrinkled white undershirt, his hair sticking up in more directions than a compass could identify, and he'd never looked better as he gave me a sleepy smile. "What are you doing here?"

I held up the white bakery box. "I was in the neighborhood."

He blinked at it. "King cake? You're turning native," he warned when I nodded.

"That feels okay."

"Come on in."

He stepped back, like he was making room for me to pass him through the door, but when I climbed up the steps, he took the box from my hands, set it aside, and gathered me into a hug. His movements were slow and deliberate, and he held me against him fully. I breathed him in, the scent of sleep-warmed cotton and Jonah, and I relaxed against him completely, every bit of me resting against him like I'd been painted there.

"It's good to see you," he murmured next to my ear, and he turned his head slightly, like he was going to kiss me, when he paused and listened to the creaking of the house.

A few seconds later, Bailey came out, fully dressed, with a backpack slung over one shoulder.

"Oh, hey," she said, stopping to blink at me. "Good to see you, Anneke."

"You too, Bay."

"Off to school," she said with a salute, and then disappeared through the front door.

Jonah took my hand and led me to the stairs, not even bothering with the king cake. "My room," he said, and my heart thumped harder than it did during the reptile photoshoot I'd done with a real boa slung around my shoulders instead of a feather one.

"Welcome." He drew me in and closed the door, leaning against it to smile at me.

"Thanks. Looks just like FaceTime." I glanced around the room, noticing that he kept it neat. No piles of dirty clothes hiding in the corner. Only his bed was rumpled, and I swallowed and looked away from it, back toward him. But maybe that was a mistake too, because the way he was studying me from his heavy-lidded eyes made me feel like I had just crawled out of the covers with him.

"Glad you're back." He straightened and reached toward me. I crossed a few steps and took his hand, letting him reel me in slowly, watching the smile fade from his face as his eyes turned a darker shade of navy.

He slid his other hand around my waist and drew me against him. I settled my hands against his chest, feeling the solid wall of those lean muscles. "It's good to be back," I said softly, and goosebumps popped up along his neck when my breath feathered over his lips.

He leaned down, and his lips brushed mine, turning my knees liquid, and he held me tighter against him but kept the kiss as soft. "Hey," he murmured against them.

"Hey," I murmured back, and I'd just caught his bottom lip teasingly between my teeth when another voice floated up the stairs.

"Jonah? You got king cake?"

He groaned and dropped his head to my shoulder. "Nothing like living with your mom to set a mood." He opened the door and called down to her. "Yeah, Mom. Anneke did. Have a slice."

There was a beat of silence. "Anneke?" There was undisguised curiosity in her voice, and he grinned at me.

"We'll be down in a minute."

I cleared my throat. "Not how I was planning to meet your mom."

"You're fine. Trust me, you don't look like we got up to anything interesting. Yet." He ran his fingers through my hair and pressed his forehead to mine. "But let's get you out of here before we do have some 'splaining to do."

We found his mom in the kitchen, taking the king cake from the box. Jonah performed the introductions, and Mrs. Collier gave me a warm smile.

"Nice to meet you," she said. "King cake is a nice touch."

"I just learned about them this morning," I said. "My friend Ellie sent me to an old woman's house in the Bywater to buy this. She said it's the best."

"If the house didn't have a sign, and the old woman fussed at you over something, then Ellie is right," Mrs. Collier said.

"She told me I was too skinny," I admitted.

She grinned. "This is going to be some good king cake."

When she took three plates down, I held up a hand. "None for me, thanks. I'm …" I wasn't sure how to finish that sentence. "In training."

"For what?" she asked, pausing with the third plate in her hand.

"Anneke's a model, Mom," Jonah said.

"And I've got Fashion Week coming up. Except it's more like a month. And I have to stay at runway weight."

Mrs. Collier shook her head as she put the plate back. "Forgive me for saying so, but that sounds miserable."

"Mom …"

"It's okay," I told Jonah. "It is, to be honest. But that's the tradeoff with this job."

Mrs. Collier put the other two plates back too. "How about some … egg whites?"

I nodded that egg whites fit the bill.

"Mom, I'm still going to have a piece." Jonah said it half-complaining as he reached for the knife.

She smacked his hand. "You are most certainly *not* eating that in front of your friend. Boy, sit down and wait for your omelet."

"It's no problem, Mrs. Collier."

"Miss Marina," she corrected me.

"I … what?" I looked at Jonah, lost.

"That's how we call our elders here," he said. "Mister or miss plus their first name. My mom's name is Marina."

"Oh. Okay. Miss Marina, it's fine, truly. I had a piece already this morning which is how I knew what king cake to get."

She looked mildly appeased. "All right, but Jonah still can't have a piece until you get an omelet."

"That's fair," he said, sinking into a kitchen chair, and I smiled at how this tall, grouchy hipster was so easily bulldozed by his tiny mom.

She waved him off. "I know you don't want to hang out in the kitchen with me."

"I always want to hang out in the kitchen with you," he objected.

"But you'd rather be hanging out with your *friend* anywhere I'm not. Go somewhere else. I'll bring your breakfast when it's done."

"You don't have to do that—" I started to object, but Jonah was already shaking his head.

"You won't talk her out of it. Let's go over to the studio."

"Good plan," his mom said. "Bye." She gave us a cheeky wave and pointed in the direction of the front door.

Jonah didn't bother changing, just grabbed a key from a hook on the way out, then slid his hand into mine and walked with me down the front path, to the sidewalk, around the corner, and to the store. I forced my eyes not to travel to the mural and the scene of that bone-melting kiss.

23

ANNEKE

Jonah opened the security grill and unlocked the door, then locked it behind me, and we climbed up to the studio.

It had a different vibe in it the second I stepped in. The covers had been stripped off the soundboard, and a pair of headphones hung on the mic in the recording booth like they'd been used recently. But it was more than that. There was a different energy in the air, like the molecules had gotten a good workout recently, stirring and moving like they hadn't in a long time.

"Been busy?" I asked.

He shrugged. "Been messing around."

"How's it feel?"

"Pretty good," he confessed with a small smile. He reached for me again, but I dodged out of reach. Another kiss from him would make me lose track of everything, and the store was supposed to open in an hour.

He settled against the soundboard and crossed his arms to study me, his eyes more alert now as they skimmed over me. "I thought you weren't getting back until this afternoon."

"I changed my flight." I left it at that. He didn't need to know the lengths I'd gone to.

"Why?"

"I didn't want to hang out in Park City all day. Too cold."

He nodded. "So you decided to come back early and surprise your new guy with a make-out that would make his mother blush?"

That made *me* blush. "I didn't—"

"I'm kidding," he said before I could get fully indignant. "And maybe trying to cover up how uncool I feel about being interrupted by my mother, who I live with. Bet not too many guys can offer you that."

He was embarrassed, I realized. "Lots of people still live with their parents. Life is expensive."

He sighed. "If it helps, I moved in after my dad died. I lived on my own for a long time before that. She won't really need help with the bills once Bailey graduates in May, and she's not covering tuition anymore."

"I didn't mind your situation before, but now I think it's sexy," I said.

"That I live with my mom?" He clearly doubted my sincerity.

"That you stepped up like a man to help after your dad died."

He considered that, then nodded. "You're right. I'm pretty sexy."

The funny thing was that even sitting there in pajamas with bedhead, he totally was. So much so that I had to distract myself, or I'd reach for him to show him how much. "What have you been up to in here?" I ran my eyes over the soundboard, like it would magically tell me the answer.

"Got together with my friend, Travell. Worked on a new song of his."

"That so?"

"Don't sound so smug."

"Do I have a reason to be smug?"

His lips twitched. "Maybe." A full smile opened up. "It felt pretty good being in here the last couple of days. So yeah, thanks for dragging me in here."

"I didn't drag you anywhere. I nudged you toward the place you already wanted to be but you'd just sort of forgotten."

"Settle down, Dr. Phil." He took my hands, pulling me to stand between his legs as he looped his arms around my waist. "So tell me why you came over to see me at early o'clock?"

His head was lowering like he was going to nuzzle my neck, and I'd go up in a column of smoke if he did, so I stuck my phone in his face, forcing him to pause.

"Because of this?"

He paused and squinted at my phone, then leaned back to study it better. "What am I looking at?"

"My secret Instagram account."

"Secret?" He took the phone from me, and I backed off the few paces the small studio allowed me.

"Yeah. This is my grand plan to off-ramp from modeling when the next younger, thinner girl comes along." I needed the space between us, because even though none of the pictures he was looking at showed me, they made me feel more naked than my *Sporting News* swimsuit issue.

"This is really cool stuff." He was looking at pictures from my travels, people I'd met, food I'd made with them, small slices of life that didn't show up in glossy travel magazines. "Why do you need to keep it secret?" he said. "Is it even secret when you have over forty thousand followers?"

"Look at the account name."

"No Beaten Path," he read. "Like off the beaten path, kind of?"

I nodded. "I wanted something from the Frost poem about the road less traveled, but pretty much every iteration was taken. So I picked that one."

He was quiet for several moments, scrolling through pictures, stopping to read posts here and there. My nerves stretched thinner with every second ticking by. "This is a travelgram?"

"Yeah." I hesitated. "Do you like it?"

His nod was absentminded, like he'd almost forgotten I was there. I relaxed a fraction. If he was getting absorbed in the feed, then it was doing its work.

"Wait, I know this house," he said, pausing. He turned the screen to show me the small bungalow with lime green paint and dark purple trim.

"Yeah. It's in the Marigny." That was one of the gentrifying neighborhoods near the French Quarter.

"How do you know all this stuff about it?" His eyes were still on the screen, reading the description.

"I got curious, so I knocked on the door and asked questions." An elderly Black woman name Jacinda had answered. She was eighty and had lived in the Lower Ninth Ward her whole life. She'd told me about how she and her husband had saved for ten years to afford the house, and then raised kids, grandkids, and great grandkids in it. I'd listened to her for two hours the previous week, sitting on her floral sofa and eating a bowl of red beans and rice which she explained she always made on Monday to use up the ham from Sunday dinner.

He looked up from the phone. "Your writing is so good. I can smell the red beans and rice from the way you describe it. And that house, I've seen it hundreds of times. I always liked the colors, but I never thought about why she picked them. Thought it was a Mardi Gras thing. But you just knocked on the door and asked?"

"Yeah. It's kind of what I do. Every city I go to, I have questions. And I ask them. Then I take pictures. Then I post them."

"'It's purple and green, because it reminded her of her mother's brooch she always wore to church on Easter,'" he read from my caption. "This is pretty amazing, AnnieBird."

My screen name sounded like an endearment on his lips, and my whole body relaxed. I hadn't realized I'd been clenching so many muscles so tightly. "Thanks," I said. It was simple, but I meant it with every part of me.

"You mentioned this is your offramp?"

I nodded. "You know who Chrissy Teigen is?"

"Sure. Married to John Legend?"

That made me smile. Of course he would know one of the biggest supermodels of the decade by her musician husband. "Yes, married to John Legend. But also, a television host, producer, social media personality, and the author of two cookbooks."

"You put some emphasis on the last part. You want to write cookbooks?" he asked.

"No. But she gets to do that and not starve herself ten months out of the year if she doesn't want to. She figured out how to carve out a life separate from runways and photoshoots. But she couldn't have done any of that if she hadn't used her modeling as a springboard."

"So you want a Chrissy Teigen career, and your secret Instagram is part of that plan?"

"More like an Anthony Bourdain career. Remember him?"

"Yeah. That chef guy. He traveled all over the world, eating food."

"Right. But it was more than that. He explored places through the food. And I want to do that too, but in my own way. Like New Orleans.

Everyone knows New Orleans. Everyone knows the food is good. You've got Emeril and all that. But you've lived here your whole life, and you didn't know about Miss Jacinda or why her house is purple and green."

"So why keep it secret?" he asked. "Wouldn't it grow faster if you put your name on it? And put your face in it?"

"Yes. And I will, eventually. But this isn't my brand right now. My brand is fantasy. Perfect. Untouchable. It's luxury. Thirty-dollar lipsticks. Ten-thousand-dollar evening gowns. Two-thousand-dollar ski parkas." I pointed at the phone in his hand. "It's not Miss Jacinda and her red beans and rice, even if she's worth more than all of them put together."

"But this is so much cooler," he said, holding up the phone.

"But it doesn't pay the bills. This does." I framed my face and gave him a dead-eyed pout. "More than pays the bills, honestly. I don't spend much. Designers give me clothes, and clients pay for my travel. So I save. Save, save, save. And I'm going to do the thing that business gurus say never to do, and I'm going to invest it all in myself as a brand and build this Instagram to the point where it's got major traction before I even put my name on it. Then I'm going to pitch a show to the cable networks with me as the host and producer, and it will basically be turning these posts into full episodes."

I'd gotten a little breathless as I talked, and I took a calming breath. "Sorry about the monologue."

He didn't say anything for a minute. Then, in a flash, he crossed the room in two steps and had me up against the wall, kissing me before I even knew what was happening.

It didn't seem possible, but it was even better than that first insane kiss against the mural. Slower but hotter, like he had all the time in the world to explore my mouth, and I tasted every texture of his.

"You're amazing," he murmured into the soft hollow beneath my ear after a while. I had no idea how long we'd kissed, and his words barely penetrated the haze his kiss had woven around me. The warm puff of his breath made the small hairs at my nape stand up. "Every time I think I've found the peak of your awesomeness, you show me a new level."

He was making his way back to my lips, and I was tugging on his hair to get him there faster when an alarm on his phone went off.

He cursed and let get of me so he could grab it where it buzzed and sang on the soundboard.

I made a small sound of protest as he stepped away, but he kept going, sweeping the phone up and silencing it with a curse.

"That's the alarm to open the store," he said. "And normally I'd say screw it, but a certain someone has put this place on the map lately, and there are always customers waiting as soon as we open."

I sighed. "All right. But you've got a small problem."

"What's that?"

I waved a hand to encompass him from head to toe. "I don't think bedhead and pajama pants are the look you're going for."

He glanced down at himself and laughed. "Yeah, all right. Will you be at Miles's tonight? I'll come over when Bailey gets in."

"Is she going to mind running the store by herself?"

"Normally, yeah. But not when I tell her what I'm up to tonight."

"And what's that?" My stomach did a delicious curl at the smile on his face.

"Just a DTR talk with a supermodel to see if she wants to be my girlfriend."

My stomach did a whole flip. "Really? What do you think she'll say?"

"Bailey? That it's about time."

"I meant the supermodel."

His face grew serious. "I don't know, but I'm going to give her my best pitch."

I walked to the door and threw him a smile over my shoulder. "I like your chances."

24
JONAH

"Why haven't you put the Placemats album up for auction?"

I blinked at Bailey, who hadn't even made it all the way into the store before asking the question. I had to switch mental gears because mine had been idling on Anneke and nothing else all day.

"Hello to you too," I said.

"Answer the question."

"Why are you firing that question at me like a bazooka?"

"Why are you hiding in a bunker to avoid it?"

"Go dust something."

"Go to—"

"All right." I held up my hands in surrender. "I don't know." Which wasn't exactly true. I did know why I wasn't putting the album up for auction. But it was a stupid reason, and I didn't want to tell it to Bailey.

"If you sell it for even close to what's it worth, we could hire a part-timer for six months. And if you'd take my suggestion and pick up someone who knows their hip-hop, they'll more than earn their keep. I say you bring back Isaiah. He was our best holiday hire, and he knows his stuff."

"It's not that easy." Also a lie. It was exactly that easy. It wouldn't be hard to talk Isaiah into coming to work. If I promised to let him choose the music we played in the store on his shifts, he'd start tomorrow.

"Why isn't it? I'm going to drop my book bag in the office, and you better have an answer for me when I come back out."

She stalked toward the back of the store, and I looked around at the customers. The reality was that we could hire a part-timer now, even if I didn't put the Placemats record up for auction. We'd seen such a steady increase in business since Anneke's selfie, and then our kissing picture, had gone viral that we might actually be losing a few sales each day because Bailey and I were spread too thin to work the floor effectively.

"I'll call Isaiah," I said when she reappeared from the back. She snapped her mouth shut on whatever she'd been about to say and nodded with a pleased look. I was glad because it meant she didn't ask anymore follow up questions about the record.

How was I supposed to explain to her that I hated the idea of anyone owning it after seeing Anneke's face when she'd held it in her hands? That it felt like it belonged to Anneke and only Anneke, but the only way I could afford to give it to her was to revisit a part of my life I'd thought I was done with?

No, not even revisit it. Revisiting was what I'd done for the last couple of days to keep myself busy while I waited for her to come back from Utah. It would take reopening that part of my life completely. Four days ago, that had been unthinkable. And now …

I couldn't stop thinking about it. About her. About the studio. About kissing her in the studio. This morning. About how soon I could do it again.

All of it. Kissing her.

And the music.

I couldn't sort out how that was making me feel. In the mornings, we always had jazz albums playing because that was when those customers came in. In the afternoon, we often played acoustic or indie rock. The last two hours was usually harder rock or classic metal since that was when our metalheads were finally stirring for the day, often starting off with a wander through Ledge Records.

But even though it was time to switch over to some Black Sabbath or

Dream Theater, I put on Radiohead instead, the dissonance of *OK Computer* perfectly suited to my mood and the jangle of nerves inside me.

Anneke's visit this morning had been ... confusing. It made me more sure than ever that I wanted her. Not just to see if supermodels got bedhead too. But because she was a never-ending surprise, catching me off guard again with her secret Instagram. I'd spent more time than I should have scrolling through it today while Bailey was in class, reading her descriptions. Her photography was amazing, but her words brought her subjects to life even more. The photos concentrated on objects and parts of people but did very little portraiture, which I thought was interesting, considering she was probably an expert in it.

Instead, she seemed drawn to bits and pieces that told bigger stories, like you could feel so much in the frame, but then you were hungry for what was just beyond it too. In her pictures from Miss Jacinda, there were only two. The house, which she had captured as a defiant bright spot against the cracked and weed-wrecked sidewalk the city had let decay in front of her home. And then there was a picture of Miss Jacinda standing at the stove over a pot of red beans, but you could see only the roundness of her apron-covered belly and her cracked and wrinkled hand sprinkling salt into the pot.

Bailey growled at the depleted T-shirt inventory and dragged a box from behind the counter to replenish them. I ignored her and flipped to Anneke's personal Instagram, the one with more than four million followers. I'd checked it while she was gone, so I already knew what I would see: a picture of her in profile, a three-quarter shot of her gazing into the distance with a snow-covered mountain behind her that made you wonder what could be holding her attention instead of a mountain peak.

A canvas, she'd called herself. And as I looked at the picture, I understood her job less than ever. The Anneke I'd gotten to know—not just for the couple of weeks she'd been in and out of town but for months on Noteworthy—wasn't anywhere in these pictures. She looked cool and mysterious, but Anneke was warm and funny, mischief and curiosity constantly chasing across her expression.

I didn't understand how it didn't drive her crazy to have other people constantly projecting their "fantasy" on her, making her into whatever they wanted her to be.

"I'm going to go, Bailey," I said, sliding my phone into my pocket. "Call Isaiah. See how soon he can start. Tell Mom I won't be home for dinner."

She'd stopped in the middle of folding a bright pink Ledge Records shirt that made me want to rip it up and use it for a dust rag. There was never a shortage of dust in a record shop.

"Sorry, what? You're leaving?"

"Yeah. I'm going to Anneke's. You good closing up?"

She shoved the T-shirt into a size cubby without folding it. "I'm great. Go. I'll call Isaiah." Then, as if to make sure I wouldn't change my mind, she added, "I'll have Mom come over and help if it gets too busy."

I nodded and headed out, driving to Anneke as fast as I could, which was never fast on the narrow streets of New Orleans. I'd texted that I was coming, and the door opened as soon as I hit the gate buzzer.

"Hey," she said.

"Hey. I'm here to see my girlfriend. Is that you?"

"Yes, I hope." She chewed on her lip, something I'd never seen her do before.

My stomach dropped, and I stopped short on the walkway, halfway to the front door. "You hope?"

She closed the gap between us and hooked both of her index fingers into my front belt loops. "Let me revise. I meant to say yes."

I narrowed my eyes down at her, noticing for the first time that she *did* have freckles, two very faint ones on one cheek. "Yes, you're my girlfriend?"

"Yes. Now let's go inside." She tugged my belt loops enough to pull me slightly off-balance and stole a short, hard kiss.

"Yes, ma'am."

"Miles is at the club, and I told him I'd drop in tonight, but we've got some time." She shut the door behind us.

I tried not to think about time for *what*, but as a living, breathing, red-blooded male, I failed completely.

She led me into a living room. Or something. Miles's house was so huge it might have five living rooms, and they probably each had some other, fancier name than living room. But it had three couches and some armchairs. She waved me toward one of the couches, then sat in the opposite corner of it, cross-legged.

"So you want me to be your girlfriend?"

"Yes. But now that sounds like fourth grade, so maybe no?"

"Best idea I've heard in forever," she said, but no sooner did I feel like I'd just injected Mountain Dew into my veins than she added, "but that means we have to start dealing with reality. Specifically, my schedule."

"I'm a business owner. I'm good at schedules."

She tugged at the tassel of a throw pillow, and her eyes kept skittering to mine and away again. She sighed and settled into her corner. "Do you know what tomorrow is?"

"Friday?"

"Also the first day of February. Do you know what that means in the fashion world?"

"At first I thought you were asking me easy questions to make me feel smart, but now I feel like you're asking hard questions to make me feel dumb."

"Have you heard of Fashion Week?"

"Vaguely? You mentioned it to my mom."

"All the major fashion capitals have them, so it's more like fashion month. And it happens in February for the fall collections and in September for the spring collections."

I nodded. "Right, because fashion runs opposite of the rest of the world."

"More like it runs six months ahead, so buyers from major retailers can put in their orders. It goes New York, London, Milan, and then wraps up in Paris. And I have to be at all of them."

"*All* of them? So you're going to be traveling a lot." I'd already been bracing for that reality, seeing how often she'd had to fly out in the short time since I'd met her.

"Even more than usual. Most of the top tier girls go straight from one fashion week to the next, because it's the only way to get any rest. Airport hopping, living out of a suitcase. And if you walk in more than one show each week, forget about sleeping, eating, or peeing. You're in and out of fittings and listening to the creative directors have meltdowns because they suddenly hate the walk they hired you for."

"That sounds ..."

"Insane." She sighed. "I know."

"Are you one of the two-show models?" It wouldn't surprise me.

"For every week except Paris."

I didn't know what to say to someone who I suddenly realized was so far out of my league that I felt dumber than a box of rocks for that never occurring to me until this moment.

"I knew it." She tossed the pillow aside like she was making a point.

"Knew what?"

"That my schedule would be too much for you. This happened to Miles. None of his relationships ever survived his tours."

"I didn't say it was too hard for me. I'm taking it in. Processing. Figuring out how all the pieces fit."

"Do you think it's bad that we're barely getting started, and it's already complicated?" She shoved another throw pillow behind her with enough malice to make me feel sorry for it. "I'm twenty-six. I thought this is when my prefrontal cortex was supposed to finally be fully functioning."

"I ... what?" Why were we talking about brains now?

"I moved too fast with us. Was too impulsive. Again."

"Impulse isn't always bad. Sometimes it helps us make leaps we wouldn't otherwise." It was a very not-me thing to say, but it was true, and it seemed like it might help her. She was so jumpy, her movements short and jerky where I was used to thinking of her as more fluid. I didn't know how to set her at ease, but I tried to give her some breathing room. "I'll give you major points for style."

"What do you mean?"

"'I definitely would be your girlfriend except for, you know, schedules and stuff.'" I gave my hair a girly flip.

She threw a pillow at me. "That is *not* what I mean," she said, a hint of laughter lurking in her voice.

"Then what? Tell me why you're so nervous. I've never seen you like this."

She stood up and paced over to a window, but it faced the interior courtyard and there wasn't much to see. She fiddled with the curtains before she turned, crossed her arms, and met my eyes like was ready to face her doom. "Been a minute since I liked a boy this much."

I melted the way I usually reserved for puppies and baby cousins, but I tried to stay cool. "If it helps, I know the feeling."

She smiled a little. "Okay." She uncrossed her arms. "Okay, yeah, I'm being weird." She did an arm stretch, crossing them back and forth in front of her like a boxer. "Let me loosen up."

"Okay, weirdo."

"The timing here is so bad. Why can't it be March? In March, there's no problem. I get down time. Room to breathe. A couple open weeks in my schedule. Time to start something new and give it an actual chance."

"Is February really going to be that bad?"

"*Yes*." There was no hesitation as she practically punched the word out. "Besides all the other stuff I told you, there's photo shoots and after parties, wash, rinse, repeat until you want to scream."

I tried to take that all in. It sounded … intense.

She frowned at me. "Whatever you're thinking, you're wrong."

"What do you mean?"

She shrugged. "You have a look on your face. Some people get like that. I'm normal to them one minute, and then someone tells them who I am, and suddenly they're weird and forget how to talk, and it makes me weird and awkward. Don't do that."

I swallowed. "I don't want to. But right this second, I don't know how not to do that. The reality of you is kind of setting in."

"You said your dad hated it when people got famous and started acting different, right?"

"Right …"

"I hate it when people start treating me differently because I'm famous. So, I don't know. Channel your dad or something and get over it."

She said it so matter-of-factly that I could only blink at her and then bust up laughing.

"What?" she scowled.

"You invoked my dead father to give me a lecture from the grave, and it worked. I'm cured. You're still the same dork with an incomprehensible love for The Ramones that I've been talking to for months."

"Damn straight. Take it back about The Ramones."

"No."

"Then suffer the consequences." She made like she was going to lunge for me, but I jumped off the sofa.

"You can come at me if you want, but be warned that you might be starting something you don't mean to."

Her mouth formed a surprised O, and then she eyed me speculatively for a couple of seconds before she sat on the chair nearest her, looking prim, legs neatly crossed at the ankles.

"Smart girl," I said.

"Only dumb people accuse me of being dumb."

"I'm not that dumb."

"It's one of the things I like best about you."

"Like it enough to be my girlfriend, hm? Except for not really, because you're trying to get out of it."

She heaved a long-suffering sigh and rose from the chair to stand in front of me and slide her arms around my waist. "Here's my confession: before Erick, I don't think I'd had a boyfriend since high school. My job makes it hard. And then with all Erick's cheating and how hard it was to find time for each other ... I don't know. I told myself that a relationship wasn't in the cards for me until I was done with this part of my career. The thing is," she said, clasping her arms behind my back as she smiled up at me, "this part of my career still has a few years to go. So what do we do about that?"

I ran my fingers through her hair. I was never going to get over the way the blonde strands flowed through them like silk. "It sounds to me like you might need a patient boyfriend."

"Do you know any?"

I bent down and kissed her, soft, only stealing the smallest taste. "Yeah. I do."

She brought her hands up to close around my wrists and sighed softly against my mouth. "Jonah ..."

I groaned.

"What?" she asked.

"Your tone. I can tell I won't like what's coming next."

She pulled my hands down and stepped back, still holding them. "I've never been great at commitment. I'm a good friend to Miles because he understands me. His schedule used to be this crazy too. But my word means something to me, and I don't want to get into something only to see it fail. *Us* fail. The thing is, I get so swept up when I'm with you …"

I smirked at her despite the hollow feeling in my chest, and she squeezed my hands, a warning to take this seriously.

"It's a great thing but also a bad thing. I've still got plans to wander the world. It's not fair to leave you sitting around, waiting for me until I feel like coming back. I do a lot of things on instinct, but this, us," she squeezed my hands again, "can't be an impulse. Do you understand?"

"I don't know," I said, and it was the honest answer. "Maybe I don't. I'm not sure if you're trying to warn me or negotiate with me."

"Negotiate, I think." She studied my face for a few seconds.

"I can work with a negotiation. How about if we don't put a label on us until you're done with Fashion Decade?"

"It's a week."

"It's a month that's going to feel like a decade."

She smirked. "All right. No label during Fashion We—"

"Let's just call it February."

"No label during February. Then what?"

"Then you have to decide if you still want me." It stung, and I tried not to show it.

"I will," she said her voice firm. "But you get to decide that too. You might hate how the next month feels. That would suck, but it's valid."

I glanced around the room, taking in the subtle marks of money and good taste, then let me eyes settle on Anneke. Anneke, whose face had gone from interesting the first time she'd walked into my store to stunningly beautiful now. Despite her claim that her superpower was to be a blank canvas for other people's projections, to me it spoke volumes even when she herself was quiet. It was an open book, flashes of humor appearing in her eyes, the quirk of her eyebrows when she was curious about something, tiny movements in her lips as she processed and considered information. What I read in there now was a plea to give this a shot on bad terms, and a willingness to accept it if I said no.

I sighed, plopping onto the sofa. "I'm in, but only because it's my moral obligation to change your mind about Radiohead."

"They suck," she said.

"See? This is why I need to stick around. Who else will show you the light?"

"So just to be clear, we'll keep doing whatever this thing is, and then in a month—"

"In a month, you tell me if you're keeping me around. I have never been this pathetic," I said.

"That's not the deal at all," she said. "The deal is we both need to think. Especially you, because I *know* what you're signing up for, and you don't yet. And I have to think about the current state of my life and what adjustments I can make. And I can't do any of that when I'm with you."

I glanced over at her, her knees inches from my thigh, her body half an arm's-length away, and smiled. "Why is that?"

"Because all I want to do is this." She slipped onto my lap and twined her fingers through my hair, pulling me down for a kiss that only made me more sure of how I would feel about all of this at the end of the month, no matter what she decided. But it also made me sure that it would suck, big time, if she decided to walk away.

I kissed her back, trying to fuse it with everything I felt, even if they were feelings I wasn't ready to name yet. I needed her to remember it for the next four weeks.

Rational thought slipped away as the kiss grew hotter. I had no idea where all of this was taking us, and I didn't care. She felt so—

The front door opened and shut loudly followed by the sound of a heavy tread climbing the stairs.

Anneke froze then slid from my lap. "Hello?" she called.

"Hey."

"Hey, Miles," Anneke said, coloring slightly as he walked into the living room.

"Hey, y'all. What's good?"

"Everything," Anneke said. "I thought you were at the club."

"I was. But I forgot my favorite guitar pick, so I came back to get it." He glanced at me. "Actually, I'm glad you're here, Jonah. I was working on something last night, and it's not quite right. I'd love to get a second set of ears on it. You got a minute?"

"He does." Anneke stood and reached a hand out to pull me from the sofa.

"Great," Miles said, already turning in the direction of his studio.

I furrowed my forehead at her, a question that I hoped she took to mean, *Why are you shoving me out of here?*

"I can't behave when I'm with you," she said, her voice low. "Go help Miles."

I swear no one had ever made me smirk as much in this life as this woman did. She rolled her eyes and gave me the lightest of shoves in the direction of the studio. "Go."

I followed Miles in and listened as he explained the song he was working on, but part of my attention was still with Anneke in the other room. It had been like that for days now. Weeks. Some part of me was always focused on her, wondering what she was doing. Seeing. Feeling. But if I couldn't be out there, drinking in her kisses like a man dying of thirst, then some distance was probably the next best thing as I tried to put our conversation in perspective, turning it over in my mind as I listened to Miles.

Before long, his music had almost all my undivided attention. Almost. "This is good," I told him when it had played through.

"But?"

I nodded. "It needs something. Try ..." And in the way they always seemed to, my hands instinctively reached for the right knobs and faders. "It needs some delay on the guitar."

I let it play with the guitar's slight echo filling in the empty spaces, and Miles was nodding by the chorus. "You're right. That's what it needs."

We were in his studio for two more hours before Anneke stuck her head in, her face looking like the clouds that had been gathering all morning with the promise of a rousing storm to come.

"Stole your man," Miles said, seeing her face. "Sorry. I'll give him back."

"It's not that. My agent called." She looked at me like this was supposed to mean something to me.

I gave her "And..." eyebrows.

"I have to go into New York two days early. She booked me into the Carolina Herrera show because Giselle Laurent dropped out, and I have to go in for a fitting because I'm almost two inches taller than her."

"Oh," I said.

"I ... need to be somewhere else," Miles said, and left the studio. Anneke came in and took his chair.

"When do you leave?" I asked.

"Tomorrow morning. First flight out."

She looked so bummed that I only wanted to make her feel better, but I didn't know what would do that. "The experiment begins early, I guess."

"I don't want to leave."

I smiled. "I'm glad."

"Rude."

"I just don't want to be the only one who feels that way."

That won a small smile. "You're not."

I pulled the edge of her chair closer. "Gotta figure out how to fill the time between now and then."

Her eyes went slightly heavy, a look I was learning meant that she wanted to be kissed immediately, but even as I reached for her, she pressed her hands lightly to my chest. "I told Miles I'd go to the Turnaround tonight. He wants to promote a jazz player from Jordan's afterschool mentoring program and make him seem like a big deal, because even supermodels are showing up to listen."

I sighed. "You made the one case I can't argue with. I'm never going to stand in the way of a new act getting some love."

"I'm sorry," she said, and I could hear how much she meant it. "When I agreed to do it, I thought I'd be around for two more days to hang with you."

"It's okay," I said, resting my forehead against hers.

"Come with me. It'll be fun."

"I can promise you that if I came with you tonight, I'd be doing my very best to distract you. You better go solo." And I kissed her, thoroughly, to make sure she got the point.

"Yeah, okay." She was slightly breathless when she drew away. "Slow and steady feels like the smarter play here, because this is wild." She brushed her thumb over my bottom lip to make sure I understood exactly what was wild.

"So now you have to go? And I have to go? And I won't see you for a month?"

She stood and pulled me to my feet. "Pretty much. You still want to do this?"

"Wait around to see if you can make up your mind about me?" I rolled my eyes. "Yes. Thrilled. Can't wait."

"I'm sorry," she said. "For once, I'm trying to make the careful choice, not the impulsive one."

"I've liked impulsive Anneke up to now, but I'll respect what you're asking for here. It's not like I don't have a million things to keep me busy."

"And I'm always just a FaceTime away." She sighed. "Although to be honest, once I get to Europe, it might be down to texts, with time differences and the way they cram my schedule."

"It's fine, Anneke. Go. We'll figure this out."

"I can't believe you're being so patient about this."

"Hey," I said, catching her jaw and cradling it softly. "Good guys always will be, okay?"

She nodded. "You're way more of a Miles than an Erick. Except I've never once wanted to make out with Miles."

"I'm going to collect on a make-out for every day you're gone, when you get back."

Her eyes widened. "Wow. That almost makes me want to be gone twice as long."

I pulled her into a hug with something between a growl and a laugh, and then did my best to give her a kiss that would haunt her for the next thirty days the way she already haunted me.

25
DAY ONE

Anneke: Hey. Did the stupid fitting. You've never seen people freak out so much over the hem of a dress.
Jonah: It's probably like me trying to get the perfect reverb for a particular singer.
Anneke: Unless you are also poking the artist with pins and treating them like you're doing them the biggest favor with every poke, then no. I don't think it's the same.
Jonah: *sad face emoji*

DAY TWO

LedgeCase: Hey, listen to this when you get a chance, would you?
AnnieBird: Is this a new one from Miles? I love it. It's like his sound but cooler.
LedgeCase: Yeah, tooled with it a little.
AnnieBird: Just texted him. He digs it. Did he tell you he digs it?
LedgeCase: He mentioned it.
AnnieBird: He says you're a genius.
LedgeCase: I mean, I know some stuff. Genius is strong.
AnnieBird: G-E-N-I-U-S

DAY FIVE

Jonah: I saw some highlights from your show on a YouTube fashion channel.
Anneke: I'm sorry I didn't call. I kept thinking time would open up, and then I was falling into bed half-dead at midnight.
Jonah: Don't worry about it. Get some rest.
Anneke: Can't. On the way to the next fitting. Fashion Week is why so many models do coke.
Jonah: Maybe just do Coke.
Anneke: *woozy face emoji*

DAY SEVEN

Anneke: London is not great in February.
Jonah: It's rainy here too. But no one cares. Mardi Gras craziness has started. And Uncle Joe is the craziest.
Anneke: I wish I was there.
Jonah: Where are you right this second?
Anneke: In a warehouse that's being used for a show with "industrial" vibes.
Jonah: What are you wearing?
Anneke: JONAH
Jonah: IN THE SHOW
Anneke: Oh. I'll send a picture.
Jonah: Wow. You look like …
Anneke: I'm about to supervise a construction crew on a spaceship?
Jonah: Maybe
Anneke: My job is stupid sometimes

DAY NINE

Anneke: It was good to see you on FaceTime yesterday.
Jonah: Sorry I couldn't talk longer.
Anneke: Sounds like the store is doing well?
Jonah: Yeah. And I've been in the studio a lot.
Anneke: …
Anneke: …
Anneke: …
Jonah: What?
Anneke: Nothing.
Anneke: I'm afraid to say how awesome that is in case you're like a feral cat and it spooks you into not talking about it.
Jonah: I had no idea feral cats were so into producing music.
Anneke: I'm just going to play it cool. Glad you're back in the studio.
Jonah: Me too.

DAY TWELVE

Jonah: Guess who just came into the store?
Anneke: It's after midnight. I have no brain cells for guessing.
Jonah: It's not even dinnertime here.
Anneke: Let me tell you about a little thing called time zones
Jonah: Draw me a diagram later. Now GUESS.
Anneke: Beyoncé? Jay-Z?
Jonah: Both, actually.
Anneke: Really?!
Jonah: Yes.
Anneke: I was just naming people who I know have houses there! They really, for real, came in?
Jonah: Yes. And Isaiah talked to Jay-Z for twenty minutes, and I'm pretty sure he's too good to work for us now. I'll find out when he comes out of his trance.
Anneke: Lol
Jonah: You laugh, but he's legit been staring into space for an hour.
Anneke: You might never get him back.
Jonah: Going to have to. Bailey is going to put them on our IG.
Anneke: *Laugh/cry emoji*
Jonah: Exactly. I'll be spending the rest of the night ordering more stock

for the rap and hip-hop sections and seeing if Isaiah has any friends who can come in and work.

Anneke: I'm happy for you.

Jonah: I just hope the sales justify another hire.

Anneke: You know you could solve this if you just put the album up for auction …

Jonah: I will. I just … want to hold onto it for a little longer. I need to listen to it a hundred more times. Then I'll be ready.

Anneke: I get it. Growing pains, right?

Jonah: I'm happy for Bailey. She's never gotten to say, "I told you so," so many times in one day.

Anneke: Wish I was there to hear it.

Jonah: And hang out with Queen Bey and Mr. Carter?

Anneke: Nah. They'll be at the Lune show in Paris, special guests.

Jonah: Tell them I said hey.

26
JONAH

"Talking to Anneke again?" Bailey asked, passing me with a big stack of freshly folded Ledge Records shirts.

"Mind your business," I said.

"This *is* my business. And it sort of feels like I'm the only one running it lately."

I sighed. "Fair. I'm sorry, Bay. I've been distracted."

"It's fine. It's how we do. But I'm sliding into the last half of my final college semester ever, and it's a lot with the store in the mix."

"Do you need to cut back your hours?"

"No. Yes." She dropped the shirts on their shelf and ran her fingers through her hair. "I don't know. I feel overwhelmed, but if I wasn't helping in the store, I'd still feel overwhelmed, plus I'd feel guilty."

"I'll hire that other part-timer."

"That could take a couple of weeks. It's fine. I'll make it work. Times and seasons."

That was one of my dad's phrases, a reference to how sometimes life asked more of you and sometimes asked less, but that it all evened out in the end.

"Times and seasons," I agreed.

If we could just hold out a little longer, I could make all of this work.

217

In the two weeks since Anneke had left, I'd been spending every minute the store wasn't open in the studio. Travell had told a few friends I was opening it back up, and I had a couple of bands trying to book me for some producing. I'd been resisting the idea, but ...

I felt good in the studio. And the money would help. Not fast enough to make the semester easier for Bailey though.

As much as I'd tried to avoid what was coming, up to this point, there was no way around it now. "Watch the front, yeah?"

She nodded, and I went back to the office, pulled out the Saul Vandenburg record, and took the pictures. It felt like when I was a kid, and our old dog, Maisie, had birthed her one and only litter before we got her spayed. We'd found homes for all the puppies, and I knew they were going to people who were thrilled to have them, but it had been hard to watch them go.

Only, this record was rock-and-roll history. Myth. Maybe even legend. And I was holding it right in my hands. I was so close to being able to give this to Anneke. But I pictured the tired slope of Bailey's shoulders, and I uploaded it to eBay and put the word out on our social media.

The only play I had here was to keep the bidding open for as long as possible and try to earn enough money to offset what it would cost to keep it. If I could set it for a 30-day auction, then keep putting the word out that I was back to producing ...

Maybe. Maybe this would work. I'd have to have the studio booked pretty much every night, but I might be able to earn enough to float the store and keep the album for Anneke. In the meantime, I'd create a dummy account and keep driving up the bidding to discourage buyers, and if I made the producing work, I could just pull it from auction. I'd pay the store what it would have gotten in auction. If I didn't, then I could sell it and supplement the store that way.

When I had the auction open, I went back to the floor. "We're hiring someone. ASAP. Let's get you through the next two months of school. Work when you can."

Bailey looked at me wide-eyed from behind the register. "Are you sure?"

"Positive." And I was.

"Great, because I need to ask another huge favor."

I shook my head. "You never take an inch when you can take a mile."

"You love me." I waved for her to continue. "I have to do a senior capstone project and partner with an actual business to rework their branding. I want to use the store."

"Bay, it's already February. Isn't it kind of late to get started on this?"

Her face was the yikes emoji, complete with a toothy, frozen grin.

"Bailey …"

"Maybe I've already submitted this as my project and started on it? And maybe I did that last semester? But also, maybe now I'm just getting to the point where I need to make bigger moves that I have to get your approval for, and so now I have to tell you that you've already been my branding project?"

I couldn't even say anything to that, just glared at her.

"So that's a yes?" she asked, her voice bright.

"Is there any other business you can ask to let you do this in the amount of time you need?"

"No."

"This was underhanded."

"Me *helping*? Not underhanded at all. Loving. So full of love. All the love."

"It was manipulative."

She twirled a strand of her hair around her finger. "It didn't start that way. But I knew you wouldn't consider it unless I could show you some results already, so I started doing a few things quietly to gather proof that these strategies work. And then I got so busy with everything that I didn't have time to put together a really good pitch to sell you on the idea, and then suddenly we're almost halfway through the semester and now …"

"Now you have to do this or flunk?"

"Kind of. Yes."

"Of course I'm going to say yes, Bailey."

She squealed and clapped her hands. "Best brother!"

"No. Not best brother. Very grumpy brother. Very unhappy brother. Very, very reluctant brother. A brother who is going to lay down some ground rules."

"Anything," she said.

"You can't change anything that will be too hard to change back."

"Like ..."

"Like no painting things. Or making major investments on fixtures. You have to spend as little as possible to make this happen."

"But—"

"Those are the terms, Bailey."

"But you have to spend money to make money."

"Take it or leave it," I told her.

"That's like saying fail or graduate."

I looked at her, letting the silence do my speaking.

"Okay, okay," she said. "But honestly, a big part of the capital outlay I had earmarked was for hiring another part-timer. So can I do the hiring?"

I threw up my hands, not wanting to let her know that she would actually be doing me a big favor by taking over that part. It was so time-consuming.

"Yay, best brother!" she said. "Don't worry, I have such a good plan. You're already halfway through it, and you've been doing great."

"I am? I have?"

"Jonah, when's the last time you ran the store numbers?"

It had been a while. They always stayed in such a predictable range that I only ever worried if sales felt soft, but they hadn't. "I don't know. A month."

I should have tackled them the previous week, but I'd been in the studio with Travell instead.

Bailey rested her forearms on the counter, a small smile playing around her mouth. "Then I should let you know that sales are up forty percent over this time last year, and sixty percent of that is from sales of Ledge Records merchandise. Of the increased music sales, almost eighty percent is in hip-hop and rap, thanks to Isaiah, who is cultivating a new customer base, and you really need to take every single one of his recommendations on what to stock."

My jaw dropped. "Are you serious?"

"Yes, dude. You've been wandering around with your head in a fog. Welcome to earth. Ledge Records is looking good, thanks to your little sister." She stopped and looked thoughtful for a second. "And a certain supermodel selfie didn't hurt."

"That kinda blows my mind a little."

"That she's into you? Me too."

I shot her a dirty look. "No, the sales numbers. Good job, Bailey."

"You can thank me by never complaining about merch again."

"Deal." I didn't point out that the bump from Anneke's selfie would only last so long. She'd earned the right to gloat about the store's current trend. "I'm going to see if Isaiah can come in. I need to run some errands."

"Sounds good. And brace yourself, because when I post Queen Bey and Jay-Z, there's no going back." And she went back to her shirts.

Isaiah couldn't make it in, but I was so anxious to kick my new plan into gear that I asked my mom to come in, and she did, happy to help Bailey for a couple of hours on the promise that I would grab some takeout to feed everyone. Then I jumped in my truck and headed over to the Turnaround to see if I could catch Miles.

"He says to go on back," the hostess informed me after she called back to the office to let him know I was looking for him.

"Hey, man," he said, when I stood in his open doorway and knocked. "What can I do for you?"

"A big favor," I said. "I'm reopening my studio. If you hear of people looking for an affordable producer and studio time, would you give them my name? I'm only doing evening hours right now, but I'm pretty open."

Miles smiled. "I don't think you will be for long. I'd be glad to put the word out. And I'd like to come check out your setup myself, but I'm tied up here most evenings. Let me know if you get some other hours."

"I'm hiring someone else for the store, and if we can get them on board soon, I'll have more flexibility."

"Sounds great, man. Give me your contact info and keep me posted."

I went from there to Satsuma Cafe to get some dinner for Bailey and Mom, and Isaiah called me on the way to let me know he'd be willing to flex up to full-time for a while.

I smiled as I hung up from that call. Everything was lining up so perfectly that it felt a little like fate. The way things went when the universe wanted you to win. After dropping dinner off in the store, I went up to the studio and spent the next hour sending out texts to all my old music contacts, asking them, like I had with Miles, to put the word out that Seventh Ward Studios was open again for business.

Right around closing time, Anneke texted.

Anneke: Sorry I couldn't get back to you. It's insanity this week. Stomach flu is sweeping through Milan Fashion Week, and most of the models don't have anything to throw up, so they're triaging them for hydration IVs.
Jonah: Are you okay?
Anneke: Exhausted but not sick. I had to walk in a show this afternoon with two hours' notice because this bug took out too many of their models.
Jonah: Sounds like the worst.
Anneke: I don't know. I feel bad about the girls getting sick, but I'm sort of loving the pace. No dull moments.
Jonah: It's so late there.
Anneke: Trying not think about the time. Have to be up for a fitting in five hours. How's it going there?
Jonah: Great. Put the Placemats record up for auction.
Anneke: *sad face emoji*
Jonah: It's okay. It was time. And I'm reopening the studio.
Anneke: WHAT? That's amazing. I'm calling you right now!
Jonah: I'd love that, but don't. Go to sleep. We'll catch up when it's not so wild.
Anneke: K. *Three snoring emojis*

I set the phone down and sighed. The last couple of days had been quick exchanges like this. Yesterday, I hadn't heard from her at all, but I'd caught a glimpse of her walking the runway for some designer in cable-knit shorts, an oversized shirt, and a fur cap. It was a testament to Anneke's beauty that she somehow made the whole thing look good.

I would hate keeping a pace like that, but so far, every time I heard from her, she sounded like the text: frazzled but in happy ways.

She would be gone another two weeks, and I resolved to keep equally busy, mainly because it gave me less time to sit around, thinking about how long it felt like she'd already been gone and how long it felt like it would be before she got back.

The next couple of days, it was hard to fill the time, but then I got a text from a local jazz band Miles referred. They asked for studio time the next day, and that kept me busy for three nights straight.

And then it kept going. Just one new group or singer a night, but the music community in New Orleans was small, and when word of my lower rates started going around, the texts and calls kept coming in. I'd raise my rates in a few months, but for now, I needed to get people in the door and convinced of my abilities. Word would spread.

On top of everything else, Uncle Joe kept calling for favors. There were only ten days until Mardi Gras, and the weekend crowds were swelling so much that tourists were spilling out of the French Quarter into the quieter wards, taking pictures of colorful houses and street graffiti. It was good for Ledge Records too, Bailey reassured me. We were seeing an uptick in social media tags, and she said sales were good.

I was glad she seemed comfortable handling it all with Isaiah's help, because Joe had me running errands all over town. It was like this every year, and I'd been patient about it, because the closer it got to the Prometheus parade, the less he trusted other people to get stuff done. Driving out to Luling to pick up the hot sauce bottles for the krewe to throw so no one could smuggle them out early. Running the sound on one of the floats that was too far behind the marching band, so they needed their own music. And ... checking on the king.

Who turned out to be Miles. Normally, Joe wouldn't tell a soul outside of the krewe committee who the royalty were, but he was so stressed after losing his original royalty that he tasked me with being Miles's unofficial handler. Neither of them would tell me who the goddess was; Miles, because he didn't know, and Joe, because he was being cagey.

When I texted Miles to tell him that Joe had put me in charge of him and to let me know if he needed anything, he'd responded that all he needed was to come check out my studio, which led to him coming in mid-morning the week before Mardi Gras to lay down a track and see how he liked my setup. And then he kept coming back every morning, which Isaiah didn't mind because Big Al had agreed to help out in the store until Mardi Gras was over, and he and Isaiah had taken to each other, in Big Al's words, "like white on rice."

Miles was probably my favorite to work with because he was as picky as I was, only he had the ear to back it up, unlike a lot of artists.

All of it helped to pass the time while I waited for Anneke. With the flu situation, Milan was new heights of insanity. Every day, I'd been getting short texts in the wee hours of the Italian morning with messages like, "Sorry, will call tomorrow." "Sorry, couldn't call. Tonight!" "Sorry, it's crazy here."

And by "helped to pass the time," I meant "didn't help at all."

In fact, I could feel my grip slipping on her. Or, no … that wasn't right. I wasn't trying to keep hold of her. She was free to go as she pleased, and I would never interfere with that. It was more that I wanted her to want to be back in New Orleans. With me. But the connection between us was thinning, like long threads of molten glass becoming more brittle as she moved farther away.

I tried to hold onto the fact that she would be back in one more week, but every week she'd been gone already felt twice as long as the week before it. By the end of this final week, it would feel like she'd been gone a year, not a month.

I wondered if it felt like an eternity or a flash to her. Maybe being busy made it go fast. Or maybe it just made New Orleans feel more and more like a distant memory.

I had to be okay with it, either way. She'd made me no promises before she left, and she owed me nothing. I'd been too much of an idiot to give her a compelling reason to stay. For example, acting like an emotionally mature adult and telling her how I felt. If Anneke came back and decided she wanted to see if we were worth exploring, it would be in spite of me, not because of me. And honestly, as her messages had grown more sporadic and shorter, I had to wonder: why would she?

I was picking up collaborations faster than I had hoped I would, but I was still just a local dude with a medium-grade studio and only a few interesting credits to my name. Worse, I seemed to be dealing with some serious emotional constipation. I wasn't a prize.

I spent a long night in the studio, working with a young female jazz trio who were covering some of the standards but giving them a modern update, and they were cool, but not enough to keep my mind off Anneke.

She was the first thing on my mind when I woke up the next morning and reached for my phone, shooting straight up when I saw a text waiting from her.

Anneke: Huge day today. Will update when I can.

That was it. I flopped against the pillow and stared at my ceiling, thinking of all the things I wished she had said. *I miss you. Can't wait to see you. I'm carving out a few minutes to call you. Run away to Paris with me.*

Not that I could. Big Al and my mom were holding the store together pretty well in the afternoons and giving Bailey time to work on her marketing plans while I spent time in the studio or out networking with my music contacts, spreading the word that I was back in the game, as far as I could through the city. And so far, every night this week was booked. I'd left open Friday and Saturday, because everyone would be at Mardi Gras parties or booked performing at bars and clubs. And Saturday was the Prometheus Ball, which I told Joe I'd run sound for, same as I always did. Although, Anneke seemed so interested in the pomp and spectacle during our picnic on the float. Maybe …

Jonah: Still coming back Saturday?
Anneke: Yeah. Red-eye from Paris to NYC Friday night, sleep at model house, catch mid-morning flight to NOLA.

I bit my lip, trying to decide if my invitation would feel cute or pathetic to her. After a couple of minutes of debate, I decided to shoot my shot.

Jonah: Do you have a fancy dress? Like the long kind? You could hang out with the reasonably handsome guy at the soundboard of the Prometheus Ball and spy on the fancy people with me.

I pressed send and regretted it immediately. Anneke *was* the fancy people. She was hanging out with movie stars and moguls as I typed. Why did she need to hang out in the sound booth of a Mardi Gras party for kicks and giggles?

Anneke: I wish I could! *crying emoji* Miles is expecting massive crowds at the club and asked me to host again. Meet up after at late o'clock?

I sent her a thumb's up emoji. And pulled my pillow over my head to growl into it. What a surprise that "come hang out with the AV guy" didn't butter her bread.

Eventually, I stuffed down my humiliation enough to shower and pull on cleanish clothes before opening up the store. I worked through lunch every day, then Isaiah or Big Al came in and took over until Bailey came in mid-afternoon after class and studying to work until closing with one of them.

But today, she popped in before noon, meaning she'd come straight from class. "Did you hear?"

"Hear what?" I asked as I rang up another hoodie for a customer who wanted to know if Beyoncé would be in today.

"Look." She handed me her phone which was open to a fashion news website. My heart gave an extra hard bang against my chest when Anneke's unsmiling face stared back at me from an ad. She'd told me it was her Blue Steel smolder, but she liked a more feminine image and called it Blue Diamond. "That's the moneymaker," she'd said, hitting me with it.

The picture just said "Lune" in fancy lettering across the bottom, but the headline beneath it gave more information: "Iconic brand signs new ambassador."

"That's a big deal, I'm guessing?"

Bailey gaped at me. Like, fish-mouthed and everything, for three full seconds before she wheezed, "YES," with more exasperation than I'd heard from her since she was five and I was twelve and turned off her Barbie movie so I could watch the Grammys.

"This is huge. Fashion houses don't do this often. It means they're declaring that Anneke is the face that will define their image, and very, very few models have ever reached that level. Every now and then, a movie star does, like Audrey Hepburn and Dior. But seriously. They rarely hang their brand on a single model. Lune is making *her* iconic."

This weird feeling rippled through me. Or two feelings at once, and I couldn't separate them. There was pride that Anneke had gotten that kind of recognition. And there was ...

Despair.

Disappointment was too weak of a word for how fast and hard my heart sank. Because a brand-new deal like that was not the sign of a woman who was thinking about slowing down and spending more time in New Orleans, far away from the fashion centers that kept Anneke working.

It hurt that she hadn't warned me it was coming, but she hadn't owed me any explanation. She'd been upfront about wanting me to be fully present, with her, in every moment we shared, but she'd never talked about the future. Never in terms of us. Just said she'd see how she felt after Fashion Week. Month.

It became so obvious as I stared at the screen. A hot wave of humiliation clawed its way up from the pit in my stomach. I cleared my throat and handed Bailey her phone. "Can you handle the store until Isaiah comes in? I need to do something in the studio."

The excitement on her face faded to concern. "Are you okay?"

"Yeah, fine. Just forgot to do something, that's all."

"Sure, I can handle it. Tuesdays are slow anyway, so I can get some work done while I man the register."

"Thanks." It was hard to get the word out of my tight throat, and I didn't try to say anything else, just walked around the counter and straight up to the studio. Then I closed myself in the soundproof booth and cussed myself out, ending with, "You loser simp."

Isaiah had taught me that word the other day when it played in one of the rap tracks he'd chosen for the PA. It meant a man who wouldn't take a hint when a woman wasn't interested and kept trying to buy her affection with lavish gestures and lapdog behavior.

What had become clear as day when Bailey explained Anneke's new role was that Anneke had been trying to let me down gently for almost a month. From the gradually tapering FaceTimes and texts to the polite decline of my invitation to the Prometheus Ball, she'd had time to rethink us, to remind herself of all the opportunities she had everywhere *besides* New Orleans, and she was setting me up for a brushoff.

How could I have been so blind? I was usually so good at detecting someone's vibe, seeing more than people often wanted me to. But I'd seen only what I wanted to see. She'd even tried to warn me before she left, not wanting to commit to anything specific but to talk instead when she got back.

Of course.

I was a guy with a recording studio in the back of a recently floundering record store.

She had just become an icon. Icons didn't date emotionally-stunted guys who still lived with their moms.

I opened my laptop and logged into the auction website. It was time to let the Placemats record go. Anneke deserved better than the desperate gesture of a simp who had borderline bankrupted himself to buy her something to impress her. I entered a "buy now" price of five thousand dollars higher than the current high bid. I'd let the other bidder have it, but not without making it hurt.

Once that was done, I closed the laptop, stared into space, and wished I wrote music so I could vent the crappy feelings brewing inside me. I'd produced three songs this week alone for different artists who'd let theirs out that way, but mine were destined to stay right where they were, eating away at me until enough time passed that I was too numb to feel them. I'd survived my dad's death and Maggie leaving that way.

It was the only thing I knew to do to survive the loss of the woman who'd brought me back to life.

27

ANNEKE

I frowned down at my phone, and Gigi, Lune's makeup artist, tsked at me.

"No frown lines," she said. Her French accent made it sound like *froon.*

"Sorry," I said, trying to relax the muscles of my face so she could continue her contouring.

"Why you are frowning? You should be top of ze world, non? You are now an icon. *Icon,*" she repeated, swishing a blending brush over each cheek to emphasize each syllable.

I sighed, too tired to explain.

"Ah," she said, her face clearing. "It's a man."

"A record, actually."

"A what?"

"I just won an online auction for a record I've been wanting to buy. I was bidding against this jerk who kept driving the price up, but the seller finally set a reserve, and I got it first."

"And this is bad?"

"It should be good."

"Then why isn't it?"

"Because I was trying to buy it for my …" I wasn't sure how to finish that sentence. A week ago, I would have known. But after Jonah's silence the last two days …

Gigi gave me a knowing look. "So it *is* about a man."

I didn't bother denying it.

"Tell Gigi," she insisted. "The French, we are good at love."

"Uh, yeah. Hopeless, nihilistic love."

"Is there any other kind?" She arched an eyebrow at me, and I laughed.

"Laugh lines are better than frown lines," she said. "But no lines are best of all. Be still."

"Talk or be still?"

"You can do both. Tell Gigi."

"I started … something with a guy. Recently. But also a while ago?"

"How it can be both? Is this an English phrase I do not understand?"

"No. I … we met chatting on an app."

"Ah, Tinder!" she said, triumphant to finally be following.

"No, for music. Not dating. And we talked for months. First, we argued about music in the discussion forums, then we started sending private messages." She waggled her eyebrows at that, and I ignored her. "We talked about music but other stuff too. Books. Movies. Food. And then I accidentally figured out who he was in real life. And that he lives in the same city as my best friend."

"Oooh, kismet! What city?" she asked.

"New Orleans. I thought so. At first. But it was start and stop a lot. He was pretty closed off with his feelings, and I'm just not that way."

"Ah, that is the French influence in New Orleans," she said. "We like to suffer with our feelings. It's more interesting and dramatic than sharing them, which we only do when yelling and throwing things. He is French at heart, so I will know how to fix this. Continue," she ordered as she yanked my chin up to work on my eyes.

"I went to visit my best friend—"

"Mais bien sur."

"—and it was a rough start, but then we started vibing."

"What is vibing? Like …" She paused lining my eye long enough to make a scandalous gesture with her hands.

"No!"

She frowned. "You don't blush. The blush I give you is better than real blush. You are all red now. Stop it."

It was not possible to stop blushing just because someone said to, it turned out. Her frown deepened. I tried to think of non-cringey things like puppies and ice cream until her frown faded.

"Continue," she said, wielding her liquid eyeliner again.

"We were ... simpatico?" I tried.

"Ah, yes. Good."

"I've never clicked"—I snapped to illustrate—"with someone so easily in some ways. But then he was difficult in other ways. Into me. Then not into me. Hot and cold?" I tried.

"Yes, I understand. He is scared."

I widened my eyes at how quickly she'd divined the problem, and she tsked at me for impeding her eye-lining. "Yes."

"So this is what he is doing now? He is cold?"

"Yeah. I thought we'd gotten past this. We had such a good talk"—Gigi rolled her eyes at this—"and we agreed to explore what's between us when I finish in Paris."

"But?"

"He hasn't texted in two days. Which isn't like him. We text at least once a day, even if it's been too busy for me to do more than that."

"What did he last text you?"

"He asked if I could go to a big Mardi Gras ball with him, but I told him I couldn't."

"You hurt his pride. That will bother him more than if you hurt his feelings."

"Yes, but I couldn't say yes, because I'm going to surprise him!" It came out almost as a wail.

Her forehead wrinkled, and I resisted the urge to scold her for it. "C'est quoi?"

"Did you know I only signed the Lune contract two days ago?"

"Oui. There was quite a lot of consternation"—which was apparently the same word in French but with more syllables the way she said it—"that you would not sign."

"I wasn't going to," I admitted. "I prefer to be a free agent. Or I thought that's what I wanted. But after shuffling from one city to the next, from hotel to tent to warehouse to the next, for show after show, I realized I was more tired in my bones than I have ever been. It wasn't fun. It wasn't exciting. The parties bored me."

"Ooh, poor bebe," she said, her tone teasing.

"I know. That's the thing. Shouldn't it be fun? Shouldn't the parties be exciting? They used to be. But all I wanted ..." I trailed off.

"All you wanted was to be with your hot and cold man?"

"Yeah." I sighed. "So maybe it was exhaustion, but I decided to sign the Lune contract because it forces me to be exclusive."

"And it pays very well," she said, waggling her eyebrows again. Those kinds of details never stayed secret. No doubt someone at the agency had leaked the number to brag about landing it.

"Yes. Not quite as well as freelancing would have, but it frees up more time."

Gigi paused and stepped back to meet my eyes. "That will always be worth more."

"Yes. I only want to have to fly out to Paris this September for Fashion Week, only walk a single show, only have to make an appearance at one party." I smiled at her for the first time. "I can't believe I almost didn't take the deal. I feel drunk on all the time I'll have now." But it faded as I remembered the person I'd freed up a lot of that time for wasn't returning my messages.

"So what is the problem?" she asked.

"I'm supposed to be the goddess of the ball he invited me to, but it's top secret. You're not supposed to reveal to anyone if you're chosen. And you can only be chosen if you're deeply connected to New Orleans, which I will be. The reveal was going to be my way to tell him that I've reprioritized. That I want to follow this thing between us wherever it goes."

Gigi gave me a happy sigh. "I approve."

"Thanks, but that doesn't do me any good if he's not even talking to me."

"Perhaps he is as busy as you are?"

I shook my head. "I know he's been busier than usual, but this feels like more than that. This feels like I'm being ghosted."

"Ghosted?"

"Fading away without telling me."

"Ah. I see." She gave a very Gallic shrug full of the insouciance only a Parisian could muster. "Zis is nothing. You go to see him in New Orleans. You say why you are not answering. Then you either kiss or throw things. But what you do *not* do, Mademoiselle Icône, is sit in my chair and pout and ruin my palette."

I shut my iconic mouth and let her finish making up my iconic face. I wanted to believe that Gigi was right, but I had no messages, missed calls, or DMs waiting for me after each of my several photo shoots for the Lune fall campaigns over the next three days, nor after walking their runway in their showstopper evening gown, and not when I boarded the plane Friday evening at Charles de Gaulle airport to leave Paris.

This was a ghosting. I'd tried calling Jonah and had been sent to voicemail. I'd sent a DM in Noteworthy, asking what was wrong, that he saw but didn't answer. By Friday morning, I'd given up trying to reach him and let anger fuel my fiercest catwalk ever. Léo Duval, Lune's creative director, was so thrilled, he gifted me with a pink gold Patek Phillippe watch so expensive that I'd have to keep it in a vault and hire a guard for it if I ever wanted to sleep easy again.

I tried to sleep on the flight, but I couldn't. Instead, I stared out at the night sky for hours, wondering what the hell I had done with my life. Had I really just signed a binding two-year contract so I could spend time with a man who didn't even want me?

I teetered at the edge of a spiral, something I hadn't experienced since my last fight with Erick, something I'd worked on mindfully, to avoid ever experiencing again. But here I was.

I'd told Jonah the one thing I wouldn't tolerate was someone who was less invested in me than I was in him. Jonah had seen more of the real Anneke than Erick ever had. With Erick, I'd been too intimidated to express strong opinions about music, because I'd figured mine counted for less than his. I'd put up with crappy behavior, because I'd thought, at first, that it was par for the course when dating a musical genius.

Miles had finally straightened me out, and with my growing anger at Erick treating me like a convenience when the mood suited him, I also had a deep sense of shame for ever making myself smaller for him. For making myself *convenient* to him.

I hated the feeling, and somehow, here I was again. I forced myself back from the brink somewhere over the middle of the Atlantic Ocean, forcing myself to remember all the other benefits of becoming the face of Lune.

You won't have to work as hard for the money. You'll have more time to travel. You can put your free time into practicing your photography and building your IG. You won't have to diet as often. You can hang out with Miles and Ellie more. Jonah was A factor, not THE factor.

I looked out at the night sky again, the eastern seaboard appearing as a soft distant glow that grew brighter as we neared New York. By the time we landed in New York just after 1:00 AM, I had calmed my mind to a single point of clarity: Jonah would still be getting the surprise of his life tomorrow night, but when I met his eyes from the stage across the crowd at the Prometheus Ball, I'd be channeling my inner Julia Roberts to shoot him a smile that said, *Big mistake. Big! HUGE.*

I'd hear him out if he even bothered to explain himself, but Oma had taught me, "When someone shows you who they are, believe them." I had thought Jonah was showing me himself on Noteworthy, that he was a thoughtful, funny guy with the tiniest streak of sadness that gave him the illusion of depth.

But he was as broken as Erick had been, and just like I'd meant my final warning to Erick and stuck by it when he disrespected my boundaries, I would do the same with Jonah. I should have believed him when he'd disappeared behind his walls the first time. Keeping himself unhurt mattered more to him than our connection did. This wasn't an Anneke problem; this was a Jonah problem, and I refused to let myself feel like less for it.

I turned to the window of the plane as I waited to disembark and practiced my Julia Roberts smile for him one more time.

Big mistake, Jonah. Big. HUGE.

28

JONAH

I was beginning to dread every sound my phone made, because if it was Anneke, it would mean nothing short of a wrestle with my soul.

And at least once a day, it was, and the ensuing fight I had with myself not to return the call or text or DM made me wonder if this was how heroin addicts felt. It was like carving out my insides with a rusty spoon not to answer her.

But the messages, they weren't real, any more than the high that addicts chased was real happiness. The messages were more of the kindness I'd seen in Anneke in her every interaction, from her sweetness with Big Al that first night I'd met her to the patience she'd shown fans at the store.

To be on the receiving end of that kindness was far too close to pity. She was used to men falling for her, had learned to let them down gently, but her basic decency would keep her checking in on them anyway.

Her message this morning had nearly broken my resolve. *Is everything okay?*

No. But that wasn't her fault, and I wouldn't make it her problem. I'd get through the Prometheus Ball for Uncle Joe, then I'd brace myself for her gentle rejection.

I even left my phone at the house before I opened the store on Friday, then went straight up to the studio to work, playing back the tracks I'd laid down with the jazz trio the night before. I wouldn't have any time to work on music tomorrow, because as soon as Big Al and Isaiah came at noon, I belonged to Uncle Joe for the rest of the day, overseeing the sound and light rigging in the massive ballroom they'd rented at the Grand Duke Hotel for the ball.

I'd been in the studio for an hour, trying not to think about how Anneke would probably be landing in New Orleans tomorrow, about how she would be so close and yet totally out of reach. It wasn't working.

After another hour, there was a knock at the studio door, and I opened it to find a ghost.

"Hey," it said. It was Maggie, both the same and so different from the woman I'd been involved with for a very intense two years. The brown hair that had run more to frizz was now full of smooth curls. Her brown eyes had much longer, thicker eyelashes than before. And she'd traded her thrifted clothes for stuff that looked ... expensive. But her smile, though tentative, was still the same, and so was her soft voice.

"Hey." She was the last person I would have expected.

"Can I come in?"

"Uh, sure." I stepped back to make room for her. I studied her quietly as I took my seat and waved her toward the other one, cataloging more changes even as we sat in the chairs we'd spent hours in together. The rings on her fingers. Her expensive-looking shoes.

"So ..." She glanced around the studio, brushing her hair from her eyes. She'd always kept short bangs before, but they were long now and seemed to be in her way. "Looks the same in here."

"Yeah." *Why are you here? What do you want?* But I kept the questions inside.

"I ran into Travell at the Turnaround. He said you're producing again."

"I am."

"How's that going?"

This time I didn't answer. It was unreal to sit here with her, making small talk. "You doing okay, Maggie?" Something about her was off. A restlessness in the way her fingers kept busy, fiddling with the string bracelets on her wrist, creasing and smoothing the fabric of her pants above her knee.

"Sure, great," she said. "Nashville is busy. Label keeps me hopping."

I nodded. "You had a good year."

"Yeah, great." But there was a false brightness to her tone.

"Maggie …" I wasn't sure what to say here. We'd meant so much to each other once, and we'd hurt each other too. But I'd never wanted anything bad for her, and her restlessness was starting to change the vibe in the studio, bending the air a little, making it buzz in a way that kept making me want to scratch, but I wasn't itchy. "Why are you here?"

"Saying hi to an old friend?" She didn't quite meet my eyes, hers skittering away to the recording booth.

"Is that a question?"

She chewed on her bottom lip for a couple of seconds. "I hate Nashville. Or not Nashville, just—" She stopped and ran her hand through her hair, messing up the expensive style someone had given her.

"You hate the music you made there?" I guessed.

She sighed. "Yeah. So much."

I let that sit between us.

"You're not going to tell me I shouldn't?" she asked.

"I have a feeling you're here because you know I wouldn't say that." I knew her too well to think she'd been thrilled with the sound her label had pushed her toward.

"I can't make another record like that. I can't."

I didn't know what to say to that either. If I assured her that she could, that the money would make sure she could, I'd sound snotty. If I said she shouldn't, I'd sound judgmental. And none of this was my business anymore, so I stayed quiet.

"You were right. About signing with the label."

The petty part of me felt a grim sense of satisfaction. "They're hard to work with?"

"Not if you do things exactly the way they want you to," she said with a bleak smile.

"Sorry to hear that."

"Are you?"

"Of course I am. I want the best for you."

She swallowed hard and nodded. "I know." It was very soft.

What was I supposed to do or say? Whatever she needed from me, I didn't have it to give.

"I was wondering," she said. "Or maybe more like hoping? That we could work on another album together."

I couldn't decide if I was surprised to hear this or not, but I was already shaking my head. "I don't think so."

"I know we didn't end on great terms, but what we made together is so much more real than anything I've made in Nashville. I'm losing that. I need to get back to that."

"Even if I wanted to, don't you have a contract binding you to your label?"

She leaned forward, her big, brown eyes earnest and pleading. "Yes, but I could convince them to let me bring you in. And you'd get some major attention that way, get your name in front of the right people."

"But in all the wrong ways, Maggie. I'd get kicked out for 'creative differences' before I even unpacked."

"It's not all bad," she said. "They really do understand how to make a hit."

I shrugged. "I want to make good music. I don't care about hits."

She gave me a sad smile. "I know. That's why my first album was so good."

It was exactly why, but I didn't rub it in with an "I told you so." Instead, I said, "I'm sorry it's been hard."

She leaned back in the chair, her nervous energy gone, like now that I'd said no, she wasn't on edge anymore. "It sounds stupid to say that. I've made more money in a year than my parents will see in their lives. I bought a little farm outside Franklin. I drive a luxury car. And I get to play live to more screaming fans than I would have ever dreamed. But …"

"You wish you were playing something different live?"

Her sigh was her answer.

"Consider it paying dues," I said. "Start putting pressure on your label to rotate in some of your more acoustic stuff in your sets. You'll drive more streaming of your older stuff. It'll slowly build an audience, and you can make your label transition to that sound over time."

"You're being pretty nice about this."

"I want good things for you, Maggie." It was true, in the same way I wanted good things for Big Al or Isaiah or Travell.

"But not enough to produce them for me?"

I let my silence be my answer.

"Fair enough." She glanced around the studio. "I'm glad to hear you're getting back in here. You're too good not to be."

"Thanks." She knew what I could do, and her opinion mattered.

"How's business? Getting many artists?"

"Slow," I admitted. "Enough to keep me busy part-time. Hoping it'll build back up."

"It will," she said. She straightened. "I could help you."

I wrinkled my forehead, not sure where this was going. "But—"

"I mean getting the word out. I have a couple million Instagram followers. How about if I do a selfie with you and post it? It could help the word-of-mouth spread faster."

Bailey had taught me the value of the offer, and I'd seen what Anneke's influence had done for the store. I felt bad again for not appreciating it when she'd done it for me. "That's sweet. That'd be great."

She smiled and turned her chair so the soundboard and recording booth were in the background. "Get in here."

I slid my chair to fit in the frame, and she leaned toward me, pressing her cheek against mine as she smiled at the camera.

"You have to smile too," she said. I slid her a look but managed a half-smile, and she snapped a few pictures. "Okay, I'll post this, and we'll see if it drums up any business for you. I expect it will."

"Thanks, Maggie." I didn't really care about the Instagram post, but it was her olive branch, and I knew it. "If you don't mind, Bailey would probably be thrilled to death if you gave the store a shout-out on social media."

She gave me a doubtful look. "Bailey isn't my biggest fan."

That was true, but I didn't say so. "She's got a big project coming up for graduation, and I think she'd love to have you do an endorsement. She might even forgive you for dumping me."

That made her roll her eyes. "That is *not* how this went down, but I'll check with her before I leave."

She stood and skirted past me to the door. As she was pulling it closed behind her, I said, "Maggie?"

"Yeah?" She paused and turned.

"It was good to see you."

A long beat. "Yeah." Then she disappeared.

I finished in the studio, saving some files and puttering around until I was sure Maggie was gone. Then I helped Bailey in the store the rest of the afternoon and didn't pick up my phone until dinnertime.

There were no messages from Anneke.

Even though avoiding her was exactly why I'd left my phone at home, I didn't realize how much I'd been counting on seeing one until there wasn't one. No missed calls. No DM. Nothing.

I set my phone down and tried not to think about what she was doing right that minute, but like everything else about her, it was already burned into my brain: she'd be on her flight out of Paris, maybe halfway across the Atlantic by now. Which meant that tomorrow, she'd be in New Orleans with me, barely more than two miles away.

Might as well be the Gulf.

I was thankful Uncle Joe would keep me busy, or the temptation to reach out would be too strong. And Sunday, I'd have to find a new and different reason to stay away from her, but like Big Al always said about his sobriety, I was going to have to take this a day at a time. Get through a day without her, then another one, and a few more after that, and then maybe I'd string enough of those days together to believe that I could quit her.

But right now, that felt impossible. All I wanted to do was go camp on Miles's front doorstep, wait as long as it took until she came home, and be the first thing she saw.

I tried to keep busy the rest of the night, but every band worth their salt was gigging, so there was no one to keep me distracted in the studio. Instead, I spent the evening in the store office, looking over the books I'd neglected.

Luckily, Bailey hadn't, quietly taking over the bookkeeping, and my eyebrows rose higher with every line I read. She hadn't been kidding. Business had boomed over the last month. We might even be able to afford another part-timer without my studio money.

I checked my email and had one waiting from the auction site with a note from the buyer, requesting to come in and pick it up Sunday morning before the store opened. Weird request, but fine. Saved me the hassle of shipping and insuring it. And maybe not so weird, really, for someone who wanted to keep their prize unblemished.

It had sat in the safe pretty much since Saul Vandenburg had signed it, but I pulled it out now and listened to it in the quiet of the closed store, wishing Anneke were here to listen with me. This was what I'd wanted: the two of us holed up, sharing music, shutting the world out, just the two of us. The way it had been for months on DM. Before real life happened. Before the reality of the demands on Anneke intruded.

When Maggie had left to chase her dreams, I'd resented it. I'd grown up enough now that I didn't feel that way about Anneke. But my dreams were right here, of weaving myself into the New Orleans music scene, of becoming part of its sound and its story.

I would owe her forever for opening me back up to that. And I would no more get in the way of her dreams than I would try to make a shooting star change course.

But for right now, I would sit alone in the shop, listening to the record that I'd failed to keep for her before I let it—and her—go.

I slept poorly, put on some steel-cut oats to cook for my mom when she woke up around noon, and shuffled over to the store. This was going to be a lonnnnnng day if I didn't find some energy before I showed up to be Uncle Joe's lackey.

But I got a jolt as soon as I rounded the corner to the store and saw Miles standing in front of it, glowering.

"Hey," I said, stopping and trying to remember if I'd forgotten we were meeting.

"What the hell is wrong with you, dude?"

I blinked. "Excuse me?"

"Don't act like you don't know why Anneke is in my kitchen, sobbing to Ellie right now about what an ass you are."

"Whoa. I promise you, I don't."

He whipped out his phone and turned it toward me. "First you ghost her, then this?"

I peered at the phone, desperately trying to catch up. It was the selfie Maggie had taken and finally posted an hour ago. She'd used the first one she'd snapped, the one where I'd slid her a sidelong look when she'd told me to smile. It was meant to say, "You know me better than that." But the angle of the shot made it look like I was into her, looking at her like Bailey looked at bread pudding. Maggie had captioned it, "Getting the band back together? Making beautiful music together with the best-kept secret in New Orleans. Check out producer Jonah C, the genius at Seventh Ward Studio."

"That isn't what it looks like," I said.

He snorted. "Meg isn't your ex?"

"No, I mean it. She is, but this wasn't that kind of visit. Maggie dropped by the studio yesterday out of the blue. Hadn't seen her in two years. Said she'd heard I was getting back into producing and wanted to know if I'd work on an album with her because she hates the label's sound. I told her no."

"Then what's this caption about?"

I shrugged. "That's Maggie's idea of helping. She said she wanted to do me a solid and drum up some more artists for me. This is her trying to make her drop-in seem like a bigger deal to help." It was painfully ironic, given that it only looked like it was about to help me get my ass kicked. "We're not working together. And that look was because she told me to smile, and I hate smiling, and she knows it. That's it."

Miles looked at the picture again, then slid the phone into his pocket. "Doesn't explain why you ghosted Anneke."

"I didn't ghost her," I said. "Not until she ghosted me first. I chose to read the signs and respect her enough to respect her boundaries."

Miles's face squinched up. "The hell you talking about?"

I pulled my beanie down over my eyes, wishing it was the covers on my bed, and I could dive back into them and sleep for three days straight. "It was fine for the first couple of weeks she was gone. But I knew before she left that this probably wasn't going to work. She forgets her real life a little bit when she's here, and being back in that environment, it was going to remind her of all her options."

I pushed the beanie back up and rubbed my eyes, irritated that they were kind of stinging. It had been an intense two days on the lady front. "By Milan, I was hearing from her less. FaceTimes turned into phone calls which turned into texts. Then those got shorter. At first I thought it was no big deal, just a busy week."

"It was," Miles growled.

"Nah. I wish it was." I shook my head. "But that big announcement came out from Lune. She didn't even tell me about that. She's not thinking about gearing down. I'm not dumb, bro. And I like her too well to make her drag this out. She said she wasn't sure she wanted to be tied to one place. That she didn't know how she felt about relationships. That we'd wait and see how the month apart went. So what would *you* think if her communication became sporadic and then she signed a huge endorsement you found out through stalking the fashion news like a creeper?"

Miles blew out a frustrated breath. "She said all that to you?"

I nodded. It stung, but only because I wished life could be different. I didn't really blame her. But I was apparently doomed to be that guy who wasn't quite enough for the women I fell for.

"I can understand how you got this all twisted, but you need to come to the club with me."

"Now?"

"Yes, now."

"I have to open the store."

"You don't have anyone else who can do it?"

I really didn't want to have to call Bailey in early or my mom at all. "Is this an emergency?"

"Yeah," Miles said like he was confirming the death count of a hurricane. "It is."

"Give me a few minutes." I went back to the house and got Bailey up, who was slightly less annoyed when she understood that Miles Crowe was demanding I go to the club.

"Get him on Instagram," she said, as she climbed out of bed and promised to get the store open.

I ignored that and drove over to the Turnaround where Miles waited for me at the back entrance.

"You didn't hear from Anneke as much because Fashion Month is exhausting. Imagine spring training camp for the Saints. They're pushed to their limits all day, then they go back to their hotels and rest. But Anneke is pushed to her limits all day, managing the personalities of panicked creative directors, nervous models, designers who are total wrecks before their shows, then she has to spend the evening at soirees and parties, networking for the agency, making nice with the people who've been making her day hell before the show. It's way worse than when I'm on tour," he said. "She gets *no* downtime for that entire month. Nothing. By week three, she's in self-preservation mode. She ghosts everyone. The fact that she was leaving voicemails and texts at all is impressive. She doesn't even do that for me."

I frowned, trying to process what he was saying. "But ... she signed the contract."

Miles gave an irritated hiss. "She did that for you, you idiot. Follow me."

He unlocked the door, but instead of going into the kitchen, he took the flight of stairs leading up. I remembered Ellie saying that she lived above the club and managed the building. Was I being pulled into a summit? Maybe an intervention?

On the second floor, there were two apartment doors facing each other. He unlocked one and threw it open, revealing a sparsely decorated living room.

"Do you know whose place this is?"

"Ellie's."

"Wrong." He pointed at the door behind us. "*That's* where Ellie and Chloe live. This"—he nodded toward the open door—"is Anneke's. She signed a lease on it a week ago. A one-year lease."

I couldn't process what he was saying. "Why would she do that?"

"For you, you jackhole. Same reason she signed the Lune contract. She wanted to free herself up to explore this thing with you, and you're going around making lover boy eyes at your ex. Which, by the way, is how she found out Erick was cheating on her every time. Instagram."

"I'm not cheating on her. And why isn't she living in a fancier place? Wouldn't she buy a bigger place instead of renting if she was invested in being here?" None of this was making sense. I hadn't misread the situation that badly, had I?

"Do you have any idea who the Prometheus goddess is?"

I truly had no guesses. "No."

"Anneke."

"But she has to have roots here."

"Which are exactly what she's putting down. You want to know why she's not buying a bigger place? Because she saves everything to launch No Beaten Path. But she signed that lease, and if things are going well for you two, she'll sign another one after that. Except maybe you've blown it, and I'll just have to hope she likes hanging out with Ellie and me enough to keep coming back anyway."

I stared into the apartment, its sparseness making more sense now. And another realization was dawning on me. "I think I screwed up."

"Yeah. You're an idiot," Miles said, but he didn't sound as angry as he had up to this point. "Look, I believe you when you say you didn't cheat. But after her experiences with Erick and the way you ghosted her plus your ex's Instagram post, I'm not sure she's going to believe it."

"I need to call Bailey."

"Your sister?"

"Yeah. She might know what to do. I need to …" I trailed off, fighting the wave of acid that washed through my stomach as I realized I was about to lose Anneke if I didn't fix this. "I need to make this right."

"How?" Miles asked. "She's made all the compromises here. Changed her homebase to New Orleans. Signed an exclusive contract to give her more flexibility. Leased a crappy apartment so she can keep investing in herself. What have *you* offered her?"

"I know how it looks, but I really thought I *was* making sacrifices, stepping aside so she could go after what she wanted, pursue her career without making her feel guilty or making it a hard decision. I was trying to do the *un*-selfish thing."

Miles studied me for a long moment. "Do you care about her?"

"Yes." No hesitation there.

"How much?"

I shook my head. "I'm not going to say something to you that I haven't even said to her."

"But you have that in you?" he pressed. "You have the big words in you?"

I hesitated. "All I have is the truth about how I feel, if I'm lucky enough to tell her."

"Can you back those words up? If I get you in front of Anneke, will you be able to show her how invested *you* are in the same way she's shown you?"

My mind had already started whirling, trying to figure out what to say and how to say it in a way that would help her see how invested I really was. "Miles, you don't owe me this at all, but I think I have a plan to make this right."

He gave me another long look and I met it, hoping he could see my sincerity.

"Okay," he said. "Let's hear it."

And I began to talk like the love of my life depended on it. Because I'd suddenly become aware that it very much did.

29
ANNEKE

I pulled at the fabric of my dress, or tried to. It had been fitted for Stormi Branson, and I was a size smaller and two inches taller, so I'd spent the afternoon in a suite at the Grand Duke Hotel with a seamstress doing custom alterations so it fit. She'd done her job almost too well, taking in the bodice and waist so snugly that I felt corseted.

It was a stunning gown, though, and as the two wardrobe assistants helped me into it and settled it around me, even I had to gasp at its magnificence reflected in the floor-to-ceiling mirror. Mardi Gras was about excess and fantasy, and it was all embodied in this ballgown. It was a rich purple satin, embellished with thick gold embroidery and crystals to catch and throw back the light.

It came with an even more breathtaking headpiece, a corona of gold filigree woven around amethyst with a matching necklace and earrings custom designed by Adler's, the most distinguished jeweler in New Orleans, the wardrobe mistress assured me.

"This has been worn by each year's goddess for over eighty years," she said as she settled it around my neck. If it cost less than the jewel-encrusted bra I'd worn for the lingerie show, it wasn't by much. Every single bit of the goddess costume was gorgeous almost beyond comprehension, but somehow, the most magical piece of all was the mask she produced.

It was gold with eyeholes that turned up slightly at the corners, leading to feathered peaks at the edges. Dark purple feathers that were slightly wilder than anything else in the meticulously constructed outfit, and they felt fitting for a goddess.

"This is incredible," I said, gently smoothing the dress. "I'm so honored to wear it."

The wardrobe mistress gave me an approving smile. "That's the right way to think about it. There was skepticism among the committee because you're so new to the city, but that kind of humility shows you understand."

"I think I do," I said.

Ever since Miles had pitched me on the idea of appearing as the goddess, I'd been studying Mardi Gras. At first, I hadn't wanted to do it. It was obvious that the role should go to someone with New Orleans roots. But Jonah's uncle Joe had been in a tight spot, and Miles said when he'd told Joe that I'd signed a lease in New Orleans, he said Joe nearly wept with relief. Then Joe had called at the end of my week in London and convinced me to do it. "We'll just explain you're one of us now," he'd said.

That was when the idea had formed to surprise Jonah. I knew he'd be at the ball. Joe said Jonah was always surprised with everyone else by the king and goddess reveal and promised to keep my identity secret. For almost three more weeks, I'd pushed myself through the grind of shows and photo shoots with the vision of what it would be like to unmask at the Prometheus Ball and show Jonah that I was ready to invest in us.

Not once in any of those daydreams had I been standing in the most stunning gown I'd ever worn while fighting more tears. They'd flooded me this morning when I saw Maggie's post on Instagram. As a fully human woman, I'd started watching her feed out of curiosity to see what the girl who had won his heart first was like.

And I'd gotten a knife straight in mine when I saw their picture this morning in the Lyft over to Miles's house. The warmth in Jonah's face as he looked at her, the unguarded affection … it had made me want to throw up. And her caption …

I'd held it together until the driver dropped me off, but as soon as I'd made it inside, the tears had started, worrying him and Ellie both. The more upset I got, the calmer Miles had grown, telling me that there might be more to the story, that I should listen to Jonah's side first before jumping to conclusions.

But I'd seen this coming after days of no contact. That would have been bad enough, but ...

I shoved the image of him gazing at Maggie adoringly from my mind and tried to focus on my reflection. That was how Ellie had finally gotten me to stop crying this morning: reminding me that I would pay for puffy eyes with unflattering photos all over the internet tomorrow. I knew the tears were excessive, but the jetlag and nonstop schedule for the last month had been building up and finally broken the dam.

He'd texted this afternoon, wondering if we could talk, but I hadn't answered. I'd definitely make sure we had a conversation where he explained himself, but I didn't want to get emotional anymore today, not when I had the ball in an hour.

I would go out there tonight to be presented to the Krewe of Prometheus and their two-thousand guests, knowing that Jonah's eyes would be glued to me from the second my mask lifted. He'd have no reason to think it felt like he'd scraped me empty with a melon baller while I smiled and did my goddess duties.

I tried a trick I'd seen on *Grey's Anatomy* and stared at the ceiling while pressing my tongue to the roof of my mouth. It was supposed to make you stop crying. I wasn't sure if it worked or if I'd just distracted myself long enough to pull back from the edge of tears, but by the time I'd taken a couple of deep breaths, I had myself together. Enough, anyway.

The wardrobe mistress gave me a concerned look, but I returned it with a light smile. "Just feeling the weight of history," I said.

She nodded and made a few more infinitesimal adjustments to the dress.

"All right, you're ready. You won't be able to sit until after you're presented or it will crease the dress, but you can lean on the wet bar. It's a decent height to take the pressure off your back, and you can watch TV besides."

"Can I see Miles? Is his suite up here too?"

"Oh no," she said, gathering up her pins and tape and miscellaneous supplies into her tote. "I have to handle him now. There was a problem with his mask, and we need a solution. I hope I can pull this off in time."

My eyes widened. "Go, go. I don't know how I could help, but if you think of anything, let me know."

She nodded and hurried out, the dressers in her wake.

I turned on the television to the local news, another one of my favorite ways to get the flavor of a city. There was a great deal of parade coverage, including a couple of minor injuries suffered from errant parade throws, and I vowed to aim carefully when we paraded on Tuesday. There was also a great deal of speculation about who the Prometheus king and goddess would be, with "man on the street" interviews asking for guesses. Beyoncé, Ellen DeGeneres, and Sandra Bullock came up. I hoped people weren't too disappointed when they saw me.

But my mind kept wandering to Jonah, and my hand crept toward my phone each time until I caught myself and pulled it back.

He and I were due for a reckoning. I'd make him find time for me tomorrow, and he could tell me why he'd run scared. I wasn't going to try to change his mind. Erick had taught me that I was either going to be enough or I wasn't. Clearly, I wasn't enough for Jonah, but he'd have to man up and say so before he walked away. And then, I could curl up and feel exhausted and sorry for myself for a couple of days until I had to ride on the Prometheus float, but I would let myself feel how crappy it was to once again not be enough for someone.

That was tomorrow, though.

I could *not* think about that until I got through this ball today.

Finally, a knock came on my door, and I opened it to find a pair of young women—high school seniors, probably—standing at my door in sparkly green gowns and Mardi Gras masks.

"We're your royal attendants," one of them said. "We'll walk you down to the ballroom through the service stairs."

I glanced down the hall. "Is Mi—um, the king coming?"

The other one shrugged. "He has his own attendants. I think you meet-up down there before you go onstage."

"We need to attach your mask." She held up a gorgeous, gold half-mask, and I let her tie it on, then stepped into the hallway, the slightly shorter attendant nipping behind me to pick up the train of the ballgown and carry it.

"I'll bustle this after the photos for you," she said. "Then you can dance if you want."

I didn't feel like dancing, but I smiled and thanked her, then allowed the other one to lightly grasp my elbow and lead me the long way around to the end of the hall and the service elevator.

We rode it fifteen floors down, then my guide led us through a labyrinth of service corridors, past custodial closets and storage rooms, until we reached a set of double doors. The muted sound of a live band leaked through.

"Those lead into the ballroom," she said, pointing. "But when you walk through them, you'll come out behind the velvet panels they're using to cover the walls. There will be a set of three steps in front of you. When they announce the presentation of the Prometheus goddess, the attendants on stage will pull back the curtains and you'll climb the stairs and walk through them. An escort up there will walk you to your spot.

"Don't worry," she added as if this was more complicated than the runway shows I had to navigate in total backstage chaos, "Someone will be beside you the whole time until the king joins you."

"Where is he?" I asked, glancing either way down the hall.

"He'll be here," she promised. She pushed open the double doors and led me to the foot of the stairs up to the dais. The other attendant resettled my train. "They can't present the court without him."

The volume of ball-goers on this side of the doors was much louder. The music, too, but it wound down, and then a trumpet flare sounded. I recognized Joe's voice loud and clear over the PA.

"Ladies and gentlemen, this is the moment you've all been waiting for as we reveal the royal court!" He began reading the names of a girl, announcing her as a Prometheus princess, and each of my attendants climbed the stairs.

"We'll see you up there," my guide whispered, and then straightened to perfect posture and stepped through the curtains. Joe called another name as another princess of something, and my train-fixer climbed the stairs and stepped through the curtain.

Where was Miles?!

"Ladies and gentlemen, please welcome our Prometheus goddess!"

I climbed the stairs and stepped through the curtain, a spotlight hitting me as I did, but I had too much experience to flinch. I wondered if it was Jonah running it. He was definitely in the sound booth. Who did he think was behind the mask? Did he recognize me?

A young man in a tux stepped forward and escorted me to a spot near the front of the dais where the audience oohed and aahed over my costume, and my attendant—princess—straightened the train again.

"And now for the King of Prometheus!"

I almost turned back to look at Miles, but experience kicked in again and kept me facing the crowd, smiling.

A moment later, he was standing beside me, extending his gloved hand to take mine. I gave it to him and smiled. His mask was much different than mine. Different than all the Mardi Gras half-masks I'd seen so far. His was longer, more Phantom of the Opera in shape, but far more ornate gold, like mine. His outfit was a white tunic over purple satin pantaloons tucked into boots, and I had to fight a laugh at how much he had to be hating that. The mask matched the gold military-style braiding on the tunic and the clasp of the cape hanging behind him.

Oh, man. He was being a really good sport about this. Harry Styles might love something like this, but Miles's stage wardrobe generally started and ended with jeans and cool—but not flashy gold—jackets.

"Are you ready for the final reveal?" Joe called to the audience. He was standing downstage right as he hyped up the crowd through the mic.

They roared their approval, and Joe held up his hands in a dramatic gesture for silence. "Very well! Allow me to present one of the newest residents of New Orleans who has decided to make our city her home!" He went on with a long list of my accomplishments, and I vaguely noted the rising buzz of the crowd as they began to figure out who I was, but I was still focused on his opening line. Another pang rang in my chest as I thought about how diffcrently that line would have landed if Jonah hadn't decided to bail.

"Presenting Anneke Jansen!" Joe finished, and that was my cue to remove my mask to the crowd's even louder roar. Guess they were okay with me.

He let them holler and applaud for almost a full minute before he called for silence again. "And now for our king, who is a favorite son of New Orleans, a hometown boy who made good and has come home to give back. You'll know him from—"

But his introduction was interrupted by Miles. "Excuse me, Captain Collier, but there's an imposter!"

Miles's voice was not coming from beside me. Miles's voice was coming from *behind* me, and I turned to see him step through the curtains, wearing a different king costume, one that frankly matched my gown better.

"What is the meaning of this?" Joe said, but he was playing it for drama, his voice full of faux outrage. Whatever was going on, he was in on it. The crowd's murmurs grew louder, interspersed with a few gasps.

"You told me *I* was King of Prometheus, Joe. So who is this?"

"I don't know, Miles Crowe," he said, and people cheered as they recognized Miles. "But this is an outrage. Imposter, reveal yourself."

I figured it out just as he was lifting his mask. "Jonah?" I said softly, not believing my eyes.

"Hey," he said softly.

"What's going on here, Jonah?" Miles asked, handing him a mic.

"Ladies and gentlemen, I apologize for the trick, but this was a matter of love."

That settled them right down, but while their mouths closed, mine fell open. Jonah's voice was tight and shook the faintest bit. This was definitely a man who preferred to be behind the scenes, not *be* the scene.

"Anneke," he said, turning to me, his eyes tight with worry but a small smile on his lips. "Bailey, Ellie, and Miles all assure me that this is the point in a movie that requires whoever has been the biggest idiot to make the grand gesture. And that's clearly me. And while you make me laugh all the time, I'm dead serious about the way I feel about you. Which is …" He paused and took a deep breath, and Miles, standing a few steps behind him, narrowed his eyes.

"I love you," Jonah said.

My eyes flew wide. His voice still held a tiny tremor, but his gaze was steady as he reached for my hands. I didn't resist, and the electric spark I only felt with him raced up my arms.

"Jonah, I—"

"Wait," he said, his eyes pleading. "Just let me finish, or I might never have the guts."

"Let him talk, honey," a woman called from the front of the crowd. "The only time a man shouldn't be interrupted during a monologue is when he's apologizing!"

The crowd laughed, and even Jonah gave a slight smile.

"Go ahead, son," a deep voice called it out. "We're invested now!"

He swallowed and continued. "Maybe this seems really fast, because we've only been on a few dates. But I've known you for months now, really. You've been making me laugh and think, and challenging me to dig deep on my opinions this whole time. And since you blew into town, you've been pushing me to be brave, take risks, and be real. I'm sorry you thought I was ghosting you. I told myself I was respecting your boundaries, giving you space when you were in touch less, and then when Lune was announced. But deep down, I was running scared because I knew how much it would hurt."

"And?" Miles said loudly behind him.

"And I've been a total idiot about more than just this." Jonah looked away for a second, out toward the audience. "Bailey?"

"Here!" she called faintly from somewhere in the middle of the crowd.

"I ran the numbers last night. What you've done is incredible. You're so much better at running the store than I am. I care about the music, but I don't love the business. Would you want to take it over full-time, free rein when you're done with school so I can focus on producing?"

Her answer was a whoop that made me smile.

He held up one hand to shield his eyes as he peered out, looking for her, and I immediately wanted it back. "Is that a yes?"

"Yes," she hollered, and he grinned, then turned back to me.

"You don't have to make all the compromises here. Miles says he'll connect me with some LA producers, so I can start working out there, maybe, and Maggie—who I do not love and who I will not be working with—says she'll use her Nashville connections to get me in with some people there. I don't have a lot to offer you right now, Anneke. I know that. Hell, I couldn't even buy you a single lousy record you had your heart set on. But I'll build a roster of artists, Anneke. I'll have to work like a dog, but I'll become the kind of guy you want to be with."

My heart was doing the craziest things inside of my chest. Every bit of me seemed to have forgotten how to function. My eyes wanted to cry, but my mouth wanted to laugh. My stomach was jumping while my feet felt steadier than they'd ever been.

Jonah took a deep, calming breath, and then, I could almost see the moment in his eyes when the rest of the room fell away, and his face relaxed, his breath growing steady. Lacing his fingers through mine, he looked down and smiled into my eyes for several seconds, just seeing *me*.

"Anneke, I'm asking one more time for you to give me another chance. I know you. I know you so well. I know that you are fully who you are, and if fame was going to change you, it already would have. You are what's real and good in this world, and if you'll agree to give me another shot, I promise you will never, ever doubt how I feel, or the place you have in my life."

A loud sniff sounded in the microphone as his uncle watched it all unfold.

"Jonah ..." I said, taking a deep breath as I considered what I wanted to say next, and his hand twitched in mine as he braced himself. "I signed a huge deal with a Paris fashion house because it restricts my options, but it frees up my time, and time with you was worth the trade."

"Told you," Miles said, and a smile spread on Jonah's lips.

"I couldn't have done that if I wasn't sure that I was falling madly in love with you. But I think I was wrong," I said, and the smile that had begun to widen now froze. I leaned forward the tiniest bit to make sure our eyes stayed locked. "I'm not falling in love with you. I'm already there."

A sweet, soft "Awww" rose from the audience, like they didn't want to interrupt but they couldn't help themselves.

"It's still not going to be perfect," I warned. "My schedule will be lighter, but there'll still be demands on my time. There's no way around that. And I still have wild dreams of traveling the world for my secret project."

"I'm here for it," he said. "I'm here for all of it. I only have one request."

"What's that?" I asked, my heart pounding faster.

"Take me with you." His full smile shone down on me, lighting up his face. "I want to be wherever you are." And he swept me into a kiss that gave the Krewe of Prometheus a show worth the price of admission while Bailey whooped and Uncle Joe declared the ball officially open in a tear-clogged voice.

EPILOGUE

JONAH

Jonah: Breakfast before I have to open the store?
Anneke: Can't. Have an errand, but I'll come see you as soon as I'm done. Will bring king cake! Fashion Week over = I'm eating half.
Jonah: You really don't want to come see the dummy that overpaid for this Placemats single by $5K?
Anneke: Wish I could.
Jonah: K. Also, last night was amazing. Love you.
Anneke: Say it again.
Jonah: I. Love. You. Now you.
Anneke: I love YOU. See you in a bit.

Last night had been …
　Nerve-wracking.
　I'd thought I might die of anxiety in that stupid tunic while I waited for Miles to show up and deliver his lines.
　But when Anneke had said she loved me too, every single bit of the

almost-puking and borderline hives while I stood in front of the two thousand people at the Prometheus Ball and waited for my plan to come together had been worth it.

Anneke loved me.

I rattled open the security grate, leaned into the store, and announced, "Anneke Jansen loves ME."

No one answered, of course. It was an hour before opening, and I was only here to meet the buyer of the Placemats record. Even though I was sorry I couldn't give it to Anneke, I was glad it had gone so high at auction. It would buy me a big cushion to do more recording, and while that meant more income, in every other way that mattered, I couldn't put a price on going back to doing what I loved more than anything.

I went to the office and removed the 45 from the safe, getting a cardboard sleeve ready as well as the gloves. And if the buyer wanted to listen to it first before taking off with it, we could do that too. I'd love to hear it one last time before I had to let it go. Maybe I could record it for Anneke? I brought it all to the front counter and eyed the stairs, trying to figure out if I had time to pull it off. Maybe, if the buyer was late …

The door opened and Anneke stepped in.

"Hey, gorgeous." I leaned across the counter and smiled at her. "What brings you in this morning? Me?"

She grinned and leaned across her side of the counter to kiss me. "Always. But today, also the record."

"Decided you needed to see it one last time after all? Don't blame you."

"Actually …" She slid a paper across the counter to me.

No amount of squinting made it make sense. "This looks like the claim ticket for the auction winner."

She said nothing, only looked at me like she was waiting.

I looked from her to it to her again. "Wait. *You* bought this?"

She smiled. "Yeah. I'm the dummy who overpaid by five thousand."

Somehow, it still wasn't sinking in. "But I'd been driving up the bid so that I could keep it."

Her jaw fell open. "That was *you*?"

We stared at each other for several seconds before we started laughing, Anneke so hard that she was crying, and me so hard that my sides hurt.

"Somehow," she said, gasping, "that seems exactly right for the way this has gone between us. You get to keep it, and it only cost me fifteen thousand dollars."

"But I was only trying to keep it to give to you!"

This made her laugh even harder, and I couldn't stop grinning.

"I was buying it for you," she said. "I saw how much you loved it."

I shook my head. "Ditto. But then I realized that Saul wanted it to benefit the store, and it wasn't right for me to keep it, so I gave up on the auction but drove up the price out of bitterness."

"This is amazing," she said. "It may be my favorite thing that's ever happened."

"Don't worry," I told her. "I'll refund the difference so it's fair market value. And if you want to resell it, you'll make your money back in no time."

"No way," she said. "This is a very special present I bought for my boyfriend."

"Your boyfriend, huh?" I said, the laughter settling down. "He must be pretty awesome if you're getting him this record."

She had stopped laughing too, though a smile still played around her lips. "He's pretty special. He's my second favorite human on the planet."

"Only second?"

"Oma gives me cookies."

"Fair. But what if I give you this?" I leaned over far enough to kiss her, letting it say everything I'd been too afraid to say for weeks. *I love you. Thank you for giving me my music back. You're amazing.*

When I leaned back from the kiss, she smiled. "Throw in some cookies, and you definitely get the number one spot."

And I spent the next hour until Bailey came in convincing Anneke she didn't need the cookie bonus after all.

For a bonus scene of Jonah and Anneke a few years in the future, please check the "Bonus Content" on Melanie's website at https://www.melaniejacobson.net

You can also pick up a FREE BOOK while you're there!

You may also enjoy Melanie's delightful small-town Southern romance, *Kiss Me Now*.

ACKNOWLEDGMENTS

This book in particular was helped along by the daily sprints I do on Zoom with my writer friends. In the mix: Brittany Larsen, Clarissa Kae, Esther Hatch, Becky Monson, Tiffany Odekirk, Kaylee Baldwin (extra shout out for the editing), and Raneé Clark (extra shout out for the book formatting). As always, this has the fingerprints of the world's greatest critique group on it: Teri Bailey Black, Aubrey Hartman, Brittany Larsen, Tiffany Odekirk, and Jen White. Thank you to beta readers Nancy Allen, Jen Moore, Camille Maynard. Thank you to Bill at Left of the Dial Records for patiently answering questions for way too long, and the good folks at Rasta Cowboy Records for their input. And thank you to Lefty at Euclid Records in New Orleans for getting the wheels turning for this story. And as always, special thanks to Jenny Proctor for the read, the feedback, and writer therapy.

ABOUT THE AUTHOR

Melanie Bennett Jacobson is an avid reader, amateur cook, and champion shopper. She lives in Southern California with her husband and children, a series of doomed houseplants, and a naughty miniature schnauzer. She substitutes high school English classes for fun and holds a Masters in Writing for Children and Young Adults from the Vermont College of Fine Arts. She is a two-time Whitney Award winner for contemporary romance and a *USA Today* bestseller.

Printed in Great Britain
by Amazon